Select Prais
JEROME CHARYN

"Jerome Charyn, like Nabokov, is that most fiendish sort of writer—so seductive as to beg imitation, so singular as to make imitation impossible." —**Tom Bissell**

"Charyn is a one off: no other living American writer crafts novels with his vibrancy of historical imagination."
—**William Giraldi**

"[Charyn's] sentences are pure vernacular music, his voice unmistakable." —**Jonathan Lethem**

"One of our most rewarding novelists."
—**Larry McMurtry**

"No one writes historical fiction better than Jerome Charyn." —**Brenda Wineapple**

"Charyn has trained his prose and makes it perform tricks. It's a New York prose, street smart, sly and full of lurches, like a series of subway stops on the way to hell."
—**John Leonard,** *New York Times*

"Among Charyn's writerly gifts is a dazzling energy—a highly inflected rapid-fire prose that pulls us along like a pony cart over rough terrain."
—**Joyce Carol Oates,** *New York Review of Books*

Ravage & Son

Ravage & Son

JEROME CHARYN

Bellevue Literary Press
NEW YORK

First published in the United States in 2023
by Bellevue Literary Press, New York

For information, contact:
Bellevue Literary Press
90 Broad Street
Suite 2100
New York, NY 10004
www.blpress.org

Library of Congress Cataloging-in-Publication Data
Names: Charyn, Jerome, author.
Title: Ravage & son / Jerome Charyn.
Other titles: Ravage and son
Description: First Edition. | New York : Bellevue Literary Press, 2023.
Identifiers: LCCN 2022043513 | ISBN 9781954276192 (paperback) |
    ISBN 9781954276208 (ebook)
Subjects: LCGFT: Novels.
Classification: LCC PS3553.H33 R38 2023 | DDC 813/.54--dc23/eng/20220909
LC record available at https://lccn.loc.gov/2022043513

Bellevue Literary Press would like to thank all its generous donors—individuals and
foundations—for their support.

This project is supported in part by an award from
the National Endowment for the Arts.

This publication is made possible by the New York State
Council on the Arts with the support of the Office of the
Governor and the New York State Legislature.

Book design and composition by Mulberry Tree Press, Inc.

Bellevue Literary Press is committed to ecological stewardship in our book production
practices, working to reduce our impact on the natural environment.

∞ This book is printed on acid-free paper.

Manufactured in the United States of America

First Edition

10 9 8 7 6 5 4 3 2 1

paperback ISBN: 978-1-954276-19-2
ebook ISBN: 978-1-954276-20-8

Contents

Ravage & Son

1883

*H*E WAS A SELLER OF METAL PIPES and bones who had accumulated his own dross, a graveyard of fittings and clamps and screws, and had to employ a blond she-cat as big as a church, with paws that could swipe at any intruder, twist a doorknob, or paralyze a monstrous rat that thrived on the lead inside his pipes. Her name was Chlöe, and she answered to no one but the boss himself. She'd hiss at strangers and his employees, but all he had to do was shout "Chlo-o-o-eeee," and she'd abandon the gray rat she was toying with, rise above that graveyard of pipes, and leap right into his lap. Sometimes the whirling force of her would knock him out of his chair, and she clung to him without her claws, while his shop steward muttered under his breath, "Lionel and his lioness."

But he couldn't spend his whole day with a cat. He wandered about and hunted like Chlöe, when he should have gone home to his wife. He'd tired of Henrietta before they were even married at Temple Emanu-El. He slept with her out of some rabbinical rule that had never made sense to him. He preferred Chlöe's musk to Henrietta's. He'd married into a tribe of Bavarian merchant princes, when his own papa was a prince of another sort, a hardware man, like Lionel, a speculator in real estate with husky arms, who collapsed when he was fifty-six and died in the street like a dog, without a soul to offer him a cup of water.

Lionel kept his papa's signboard, *Ravage & Son*, continued to grab up tenements below market price, and went to Allen Street, hunting for female flesh. All he found were rotten sinks—flea-bitten sisters who couldn't amuse him with their practiced steps. And whenever he tore up a brothel and blacked out in a maddening fit, a merchant prince would arrive with a detective from Mulberry Street and bliss was soon restored at the brothel, even if Lionel was covered in blood after all his rampaging.

"Ah, Mr. Ravage, a gentleman like yourself shouldn't be mingling with this kind of trash. These ladies have their cadets, and they might carve you up one fine afternoon. You'd leave us with a stinking mess of paperwork if we found you in the morgue."

So he had a weapon handcrafted for him by a silversmith on Baxter Street. It was much more fashionable than a policeman's billy or a baseball bat. Lionel Ravage had his own pinewood walking stick with a handle in the shape of a wolf's head, burnished in silver. He could crown any cadet with his walking stick, and fend off robbers who wanted to relieve him of his rent bag. He sent more than one of these lowlifes to the Hebrew hospital with a good thwack. Lionel preferred to be his own rent collector. It was his way of meeting a plump housewife who was behind in the rent and whose husband was coughing his lungs out in some charity ward. Lionel was never crude. He wouldn't hammer an eviction notice on her front door, wouldn't call upon the services of the county sheriff. He'd permit three or four months' rent to slide. The housewife would stare into his silver-blue eyes. He'd recite poetry to her. He'd had a semester at Amherst College before his papa pulled him back into their hardware empire, which occupied more and more of Canal Street. Lionel missed the countryside, not the college. His intimate sense of sewers and the arcane world of pipes had made him Amherst's prize plumber. But he'd had to leave. And now, near enough to a bachelor of arts in plumbing, he'd deliver lines from Shakespeare to the housewife in the Yiddish he had picked up from his papa's customers, and Lionel would play all the parts—Prospero one moment, Caliban the next.

> *You taught me language; and my profit on't*
> *Is, I know how to curse. The red plague rid you*
> *For learning me your language!*

The housewife was enthralled. She undressed in front of her lyrical landlord. And if a certain housewife was hard to get, he might offer to marry her on the sly. He plucked a renegade beadle from a Norfolk Street synagogue, produced a wedding band from a variety shop, kissed the bride under a prayer shawl, and drank a cup of kosher wine. Soon Lionel had a dozen mistress-wives, and was sick of every one. He returned to Allen Street with his silver club, like some Caliban of the Lower East Side, master and servant of his own appetites and ambitions, with a crippling anger against his papa's associates, who tried to cheat him out of his patrimony. He ruined them all, bought up their assets, and increased his graveyard of pipes and fittings, with Chlöe as his constant companion. But he couldn't make love to a cat with whiskers and claws, no matter how often she crashed into his lap. Lionel had to troll. . . .

He met her by accident. He was collecting rent on Attorney Street, and she came to the door in a silk robe with loose threads that unraveled all around her. She had the carved cheeks and wild blond hair of a dybbuk. His tenant, Rabinowitz, was a consumptive philosopher from Vilna who sold apples in the street whenever he was lucky enough to locate a pushcart and a consignment of apples. Lionel didn't care about the rent. He could discuss the notion of gravity with Rabinowitz, and the elevator cars that would soon command taller and taller buildings in Manhattan and miles of pipe that only Ravage & Son could furnish.

Lionel didn't believe in dybbuks. He'd been to a college in the middle of Massachusetts. He hadn't come to America in a cattle car—he was an aristocrat with an artisan's grip. Still, he couldn't take his eyes off this blonde in threadbare silk. She'd hooked herself to his own interior plumbing with those high cheeks of hers. She couldn't have been more than eighteen or nineteen.

"Hey," he said, in that rough vocabulary of a rent collector, "are you one of those imported brides, huh? How did the old man pay for the passage? He doesn't have a cent."

She slapped his face. It was a wicked blow, with all the force of Chlöe, but Chlöe wouldn't have been that unkind.

"I'm his daughter," she said, in an accent that couldn't have come from any school in Manhattan. "And he's not *your* old man."

"Yeah, he's an apple polisher who can't pay his rent."

She slapped him again, and those magnificent cheeks throbbed with malice. "I love this crazy girl," he muttered under his breath, and it frightened him. Lionel had never been in love, not with errant housewives, nor uptown princesses like Henrietta, with all their fine breeding, nor brash downtown girls, who would have robbed him blind if they could. All he had was Chlöe. Now he had to deal with this one, and he was at a disadvantage. Rabinowitz's girl with the wild blond hair had much sharper claws than Chlöe.

Her name was Manya, she said. And she'd been raised at her father's feet. Her mother had died giving birth to Manya. She had neither brothers nor sisters. Her father was a maverick in a community of religious Jews. He'd studied the laws of Russian grammar rather than the Talmud. A servant in the castle of a Lithuanian lord, hired to polish silverware, he became, in a matter of months, tutor to the nobleman's son—only Rabinowitz, the Jewish polisher, could instruct the boy how to read and write. Manya lived at the castle with her papa, wearing the discarded silks of the nobleman's daughters. The other servants grew jealous of this self-taught savant, and plotted to kill him and Manya. He couldn't return to the Jewish quarter, where he was considered a pariah.

"So you escaped to the Promised Land," Lionel said. "But I've visited your father many times. Where the hell were you?"

"Hiding in the closet," she said. "Papa says you have an insatiable lust. He didn't want you to feast on my flesh."

"And where did you learn all that pretty talk?"

"From Papa," she said. "He's an alchemist who can breathe languages."

When he's not polishing apples like the silverware he used to polish, Lionel reassured himself. Manya must have had the skills to work as a bookkeeper or a salesclerk, but Rabinowitz wouldn't allow her to descend into the Lower East Side, where some cadet might capture her, and anonymous men with filthy fingernails could ogle her like wild beasts. So the princess would sit in the back room of their tenement palace and recite to her father the Russian and English classics he himself had taught her. And whenever she had to shop on Hester Street, she disguised herself in her father's hat and overcoat.

"Then what made you answer the door? You could have hid in the closet."

"I'm not a child," she said. "And I was curious. I could see you through a crack in the closet door. You have beautiful eyes, you know, when you're not playing the landlord."

Lionel was losing whatever little stature he had left. "But I am the landlord."

"Who allows Papa to live rent-free," she said, and laughed for the first time; her sweet roar was like the rasping jingle of toys he'd had as a child: Manya could have been Lionel's own music box.

"But how many savants do I have on my rent rolls?" he asked. "Our talks enrich me. I don't need to collect from him."

And that's when Rabinowitz returned in fingerless gloves, with a torn blanket as a cloak. He was in a dark mood. He couldn't control the tremors in his jaw. His stoic nature was gone. He'd have butchered Lionel if he'd had a hatchet in his hand.

"Papa," Manya said, "why such a long face? I'm a debutante in America. I've met the landlord. Now wash your hands and invite us both to tea."

That's how it began; Lionel neglected his business, neglected Chlöe, neglected his wife. He had some junior accountant at the office visit the sites and collect whatever rent was due. He did meet with his most important builders, and the pipes moved out of that graveyard. He bought presents for his children only when Manya reminded him. He was always there, at that flat on Attorney Street, with hissing gas jets in the halls and the perennial stink of cabbage. Rabinowitz wouldn't allow Lionel to move him into a front apartment, where he might have had a glimpse of sunlight.

"Ravage, my daughter is not for sale. I am not bartering her, do you hear?"

Lionel remembered the moment he first clutched her hand; Rabinowitz was padding about in his slippers, his memory shot as he was maddened by a jealousy he couldn't quite comprehend. And Lionel seized her hand in his, like a brigand. The two of them were renegades in a rear, sunless apartment that Rabinowitz rented and Lionel owned.

They had to accompany him into the backyard whenever Rabinowitz ran to the privy. Lionel's plumbers had begun to install indoor toilets in some of the newer tenements, but none of these pipes had come to Attorney Street, where the stench was unbearable, even in winter, when the privies froze. Lionel would lick her face like a lunatic while the savant sat on his splintered throne.

"Landlord, we'll lose you once and for all," Rabinowitz cackled from the privy, but he didn't have the courage or the means to move. It was Manya who broke up their little engagement party. Lionel had never once felt her moistness, or fumbled under her clothes.

"Lionel, we're killing him, and he's the last papa I'll ever have."

He returned to his graveyard on Canal with violent dreams. He meant to finish off Rabinowitz, send him to paradise with the silver handle of his cane. But he had some residual fondness for that savant. He didn't hate Rabinowitz. He just wanted him to disappear. Meanwhile, his business seemed to blossom around him. Contractors stood in line to bid for his pipes. He had to install a Teletype machine. Chlöe could sense his moodiness. She bumped him with her head and brought him the carcass of a big brown rat. He was losing inventory. Pirates had come from the Jersey Shore to steal his merchandise, until Chlöe blinded their chieftain with her claws and sent the band back to Hoboken. But not even that victory could heal Lionel's wounds.

A few months later, he heard of Rabinowitz's demise. The savant had dropped dead on the privy. Lionel didn't rush to Attorney Street. He still felt bitter and bruised. Finally he went there without his rent bag and with the wind in his eyes. A gale was blowing. The gas lamps had gone out. Attorney Street had descended into a pit of darkness. The Lower East Side could have been a barren island in a storm. Lionel lost his bearings for a moment. He suffered a kind of vertigo that was near enough to amnesia. But Chlöe came back to him in a flash, the huntress in that graveyard of pipes. He recognized Manya's building in Attorney Street's tenement row. He stood on the crumbling stoop and entered the pitch-black hallway. The banisters were broken. He had to mount the stairs with one hand on a wall of corrugated tin that might collapse and come crashing down on his head. The linoleum on Manya's landing was like a wicked sea of lumps. He knocked on her door, announced himself. "Manya, it's me—the landlord."

The door was unlocked. He entered the apartment while the windows rattled, and the whole tenement seemed to quake. The gas jets hissed a poisonous fire, sputtered, and blew out with a final cough. She wasn't in the front room, a parlor with a ragged settee that Lionel's own men had supplied. They must have found it in a junkyard north of Canal. Lionel's apartments were always fully furnished; that way, he didn't have to endure the crisis of tenants moving in and out. A family came with their linen and left with their linen—and a few additional bedbugs.

He trod into the bedroom, frightened of what he would find.

"Manya," he whispered, "I won't harm you."

She was lying on a rumpled bed in the same threadbare silk robe she'd worn when he first met her. She didn't move, even when he touched her arm. He ran into the kitchen. The shelves were all vacant except for a spiderweb—there wasn't a noodle or a slice of cheese in the house. He returned to the bedroom, wrapped her in his overcoat, and carried her down into the storm. She lay against him like some lanky doll with a bit of breath in her lungs.

The corner lunchroom was closed. Lionel knocked on the door with that silver skull of his cane. The cook appeared with a blanket around his shoulders and shouted through the window, "Are you meshuga, or what? The wind is breaking glass and knocking down trees. I haven't had a customer since last night. Go away!"

Lionel knocked again, and now the cook recognized him as the young prince who owned half of Hester Street. Lionel was his landlord, in fact. He unlocked the door.

"Forgive me, Herr Ravage. The wind was playing tricks. I didn't . . ."

The cook wore a derby and long underwear under his blanket. He had to light a large candlestick—he was lost without his gas jets. Then he saw her wild blond hair and curious pale complexion, like an alabaster idol. Both her eyes were shut.

He went to his stove, almost by instinct. But he couldn't prepare a French omelette or heat a pot of chicken soup on a dead flame. So he leaned into the icebox, with his derby still on, pulled out ingredient after ingredient like a master chef, and was still able to fry an egg on an old fire pit, fix up a cucumber salad and a farmer cheese sandwich, while Lionel fed her little pieces at a time—until she opened her crystal blue eyes, a fixture of the finest Lithuanian Jews. She even managed a slight, trembling smile that was almost like a twitch.

"Landlord, you should have left me in peace."

"What peace?"

"My father's lying in a potter's field. I want to lie there with him."

"He won't lie there very long. We'll bury him again, in my family plot."

"He doesn't belong there," she said, suddenly ravenous. "You have your own children and a wife."

"You're my family. Have you had enough to eat?"

"Yes, Lord Lionel," she said, with a touch of amusement in her voice.

The cook prepared a great bundle of food but wouldn't accept money from his prince. "Please come again, Herr Ravage. You're always welcome in a storm."

And Lionel carried her across the wind in his overcoat, back to her upstairs cave, where the windows rattled through the night. She fell asleep in his arms and woke with the same alabaster look.

"You could work for me, you know. I'll fire my bookkeeper."

"And create a scandal at Ravage & Son. You'll lose the art of collecting rent."

She reached for Lionel, her arms still dug inside his overcoat, and kissed him on the mouth. It was their first kiss. He was trembling now, not Manya. She had the sweetest taste on her tongue. She snapped his suspenders until the pair of them lay curled on the bed. She plucked off his pants and winter underwear like some courtesan in a dream. And he entered her while she was still draped in his long coat. Entwined, they moved together mercifully slow. He did not think of his accounts or his dead father or the cat that waited for him in that endless terminal of pipes. They didn't talk. He listened to her heartbeat, and licked the salt behind her ear.

"I'm embarrassed," she finally said. "Lionel, I haven't bathed in a week."

"That's perfect. You'll live with my smell on you forever, like a Chinaman's tattoo."

He wasn't sure how long he stayed with her. He kept no calendar inside his head. He knew that certain bills had to be paid, but his bookkeeper could worry about that. He should have notified his wife. What could he say? *Henny, I'm on a long voyage. I might never be back.*

They could have gone to Lord & Taylor, or another ladies' shop on Grand Street. But she forbade him to buy her clothes. They never rode the horsecars into another neighborhood, never watched Yiddish jugglers on the Bowery. Lionel ran out of cash. It didn't seem to matter. He signed his name on the grocer's bill, and it was good as gold. The gas jets turned on miraculously a week after the storm, with a lick of blue flame. Lionel carried in pails of water from the leaky faucet near the landing, and he spent hours scrubbing her back. She read to him at night from the leather-bound books her papa had brought from Lithuania, books lent to him by the lord of the castle and never returned, classics of a kind with illustrations. Their favorite was *Barnaby Rudge*; they both reveled in Dickens' greatest outlaw and grotesque, Dennis the hangman, who loved to lead a riot, turn around, and hang the rioters. They were convinced that Dennis could have thrived in America as a police captain on Mulberry Street if he himself hadn't been hanged in the novel.

"What a shame," Manya said. "We might have had Dennis knock on my door."

"*Our* door," he said, and then there was a sudden knock on the front door, as if they were onstage somewhere, thrust into a Yiddish melodrama.

"Come in, please," Manya said.

Lionel's shop steward appeared out of the blue, with a derby in his hands. He wore red suspenders, like Lionel. "There's been a terrible tragedy, boss, or I wouldn't inconvenience you."

"What happened? Was there a fire uptown? Are my children hurt?"

"No, boss, but I think you'd better come with me."

The shop steward had to stand in the corner with his eyes closed while Lionel crept into his pants and overcoat, which had all the dizzying aromas of Manya in every curl of wool.

"Manya," he whispered, "I'll be right back."

The shop steward was silent all the way to Canal Street. Lionel entered that graveyard of pipes in a surly mood. And then he saw her dangling from a hook in the wall, with his best copper wire wound like a necklace under her ears; her blond coat was ripped through with blood, and her paws had been mangled.

Lionel sobbed in front of his own men. "Look at my little girl."

He freed her from the wall with a pair of pliers, held that enormous cat in his arms, and ruffled her bloody coat with one hand. "Idiots, don't we have watchmen around the clock?"

"Boss," said the steward, "it was the same gang from Hoboken. They scared off our watchmen, and didn't steal a thing. It was personal, boss. Them and the cat."

"Shut up," Lionel said. "They couldn't have gotten near Chlöe, not a hundred of them."

"They blinded her, boss, with acid. Look at her eyes."

She didn't have any eyes. She had scorched pits where her eyeballs had been eaten away, and yet he could still feel the luminous green eyes of his dead cat—nothing could diminish her, not that band of louts from Hoboken, all of whom he swore to kill. He'd have to lure members of the harbor patrol to ride across the Hudson with him in a police barge and descend upon those Hoboken rats. He'd pay any price to avenge Chlöe. And while he dreamt of destruction, men in black coats arrived on Canal Street. They were a different kind of pirates, these merchant princes who were Henrietta's uncles, nephews, and brothers, and Lionel himself was the outlaw with a dead cat in his arms.

"Go away," he said. "I'm mourning."

But they didn't cower in front of Lionel like his shop steward. Nor had they come to bargain with him over a glass of schnapps. They ripped off his overcoat, thrashed him with their walking sticks, until he lay in the sawdust, in that world of copper and lead.

Henrietta's favorite uncle loomed over him in his waxed mustache. "Nephew, you haven't been home in a month. Your children are wild animals without their father. You wife is even wilder— with worry. She hasn't slept. She won't eat."

"Uncle," he cried. "I cannot help her. I have another wife."

They thrashed him again and again, until Chlöe dropped beside him, and he saw nothing but the scorched black holes in her head. And then she disappeared, behind the Russian boots of the Bavarians.

"Your father was a bankrupt," said Uncle Rainer. "We pulled him out of ruin. We gave our best flower to you—a bride you didn't deserve. The richest men wanted her, handsome men, brilliant, and she fell in love with a silky blond snake. There are consequences, Lionel. You will lose everything, this shop, your real estate holdings, every plot of land."

"I'll survive," he said.

Uncle Rainer smiled; he was the smartest of the lot.

"The way your cat survived, eh? And what will happen to the

apple peddler's daughter when you've lost your fortune? It won't be a pretty sight. We'll have her arrested as a vagrant. And how will you help? Paupers can't fight the police."

Lionel lunged at Uncle Rainer, whom he'd always admired. Rainer had bailed out Lionel's papa once the wedding contract had been sealed. He and Henny owned half of Ravage & Son.

"I'll kill you," Lionel howled in a ragged voice that signaled his own defeat. Rainer could afford to laugh. The Bavarian princes left him in the sawdust, with his dead cat buried in the pipes somewhere. The blood had gone out of him. He was as blind as Chlöe, but that didn't matter much. He'd grow whiskers, and he'd prowl. He'd make love to Henrietta once in a blue moon, between her menstrual cramps. He'd buy up land, sell his pipes, sit inside the Moorish castle of Temple Emanu-El, pray with the Bavarian princes and plot against them. He'd mangle, he'd maraud, and wear that mask of propriety. Let them all invent their own Lionel Ravage—master plumber, hardware merchant, real estate tycoon. They'd never find the monster or the man. He sat in the sawdust and clucked in front of his shop steward and his pipe fitters, "Chl-o-o-o-eeee." But the cat never came.

One

The Baron of East Broadway

I.

*I*T WAS WELL PAST MIDNIGHT on the Lower East Side, and Cahan had one last article to finish about Congress' latest attempt to shutter Ellis Island and strangle all the life out of the Ghetto. The editor left his falcon's lair at the *Forward* building on East Broadway and decided to prowl the dark, viscous streets near the docks so that he might find some rhythm to write, and that's when a lone rooster crossed his path, a refugee from some cockfighting school run by gamblers in the Ghetto; the rooster had very red eyes, and wattles that had been chewed to pieces. It had only one leg, and hobbled along, hiding from gamblers who resented its lameness, Cahan supposed, and would have chopped off its head with a cleaver. Cahan was tempted to adopt this refugee, but the *Forward*'s secretaries and accountants would have panicked with a one-legged rooster in the building.

And while he considered the rooster's fate, he heard the familiar rumble of a pushcart with damaged wheels. Avram Polski appeared in his winter coat, selling merchandise to an invisible clientele; the peddler should have been locked up. But there was no Yiddish insane asylum, and Avram was better off in the streets with his stock of shoelaces, rubber bands, moldy erasers, splintered pencils, and ink bottles without ink. He was a giant of a man, who had lost his wife and three children in an outbreak of cholera that ravaged his tenement six or seven years ago.

"Shoelaces, a dime a dozen," Avram wailed, like the mourner he was.

Cahan purchased the shoelaces and a clutch of rubber bands, as he always did in his nighttime encounters with Avram, who was still an avid reader of the *Forward*.

"Comrade, why do you advertise White Rose tea? It's poison in a teacup. You'd be better off listing recruits for a pogrom."

Cahan could never win an argument with the peddler, who still knew how to poke him in the ribs, despite his endless voyages through the same dark streets.

"Avram, I'll wait for another brand of tea to come along."

The madman wouldn't listen. He counted his tiny treasure and shrank into the mist, but Cahan couldn't luxuriate in his own solitude. Cadets were still on the prowl with their harems. One such queen of the night solicited the editor. She had a racking cough. Her fingernails were filthy, and her eyebrows looked like faded blue rubber bands. She couldn't have been much older than sixteen. She wore nothing but a cotton dress, and must have been chilled to the bone. She blinked once at Cahan; that was her only mark of seduction.

"Mister," she rasped in a hoarse voice, "would you like to go round the world?"

She belonged in a cot at the Hebrew hospital, not at a whore's station on Cherry Street. Her cheeks were on fire all the while she shivered. Her eyeballs seemed to bulge right out of her head.

"My dear," he whispered as gently as he could, "how much would it take to retire you for the night?"

"A *tenski*," she said between coughs.

Cahan reached into his billfold and handed her a ten-dollar bill. He didn't want to know her name; a name would have hobbled him, added skin and flesh to her skull and given him nightmares. But he hadn't bartered correctly, and he'd complicated the poor girl's life. Her champions arrived, a pair of cadets in identical beaver coats; they must have marched out of some primordial weather, where the crustiest men lived. They had deep scars on their faces that served as souvenirs or medallions of knife fights they had survived. Both of them were carrying firemen's hatchets that looked like tomahawks. Cahan had stumbled upon some secret Wild West near the waterfront. He was furious, even with tomahawks in his face.

"This girl should be in a hospital ward."

The cadets slapped their thighs like Bowery singers, and swatted at him with their hatchets, missing his nose by an inch.

"Mushke, what the hell, let's scalp him. We'll sell him to the tannery, skin and all."

A foghorn bleated in Cahan's ears as another man stepped out of the mist, with the mottled face of some rascal who had been caught in a firestorm. Not even that morass of skin and the wig he wore at a slant to cover the burn marks on his pate could blunt the menace of his blue eyes. He'd once been the handsomest cavalier in the Ghetto. And now he wandered the streets in the middle of the night, wielding a cane with a wolf's silver head. He whacked at the cadets, who went down on their knees as the wolf's teeth bit at them with a silent bark.

"Jesus, Mr. R., we didn't know he was a pal of yours."

"He's not," the man said. "But you shouldn't take such liberties. Get out of here."

And they both ran toward the Bowery.

"Herr Ravage," Cahan said with a note of bitterness, "I'm in your debt." He knew the uptown princes loved to hold on to their Germanic roots. But this one was a rebel, who occupied his own fortress on Canal. He was also an enigma, who financed charity wards, hired Yiddish opera stars from the Metropolitan to sing the chant of the dead at some crumbling synagogue, helped establish a system of monitors at Ellis Island to guide immigrants through the maze of doctors and nurses and petty officials, but he was a ruthless landlord who emptied entire tenements and turned block after block into a sinister shell. He himself had walked out of a burning tenement, with half his face on fire.

"You owe me nothing, Cahan. And you shouldn't be so formal. Lionel is good enough." He tugged at the wig that resembled a lunatic's straw hat. "I could have let them kill you. You've crucified me enough in the *Forward.*"

"How many families have you evicted from your tenement palaces, Lord Lionel?"

The lunatic laughed. "Not without eviction notices. It's strictly legal. And stay off the streets after midnight. This is my nocturne, Cahan, not yours. You grumble all the time about coppers and cadets. Well, one or the other could slap your brains into split-pea soup, and all that eloquence of yours would be lost. Good night."

Suddenly, Cahan had the timbre he needed to scribble his story about Ellis Island, as if that ghost with white hair had awakened him. He returned to East Broadway, knowing he would never understand Herr Lionel Ravage, a man with his own harem, who had spawned a whole tribe of bastards that the editor didn't dare write about, unless he wanted to be sued for libel and plucked off his own masthead without mercy.

2.

He was called "the Pulitzer of Yiddish Land," the Ghetto's William Randolph Hearst. Cahan had a colossus—the *Jewish Daily Forward*. It had more readers than *The Philadelphia Inquirer* and the *St. Louis Post-Dispatch*, and it was published for a population of immigrant Jews. Cahan liked to boast of his million readers, since entire families devoured each issue of the *Forward*, not only on the mean streets surrounding East Broadway but in Buenos Aires and Budapest and all the other world capitals where the paper was sold in 1913. But Cahan could taste the bile on his tongue as he looked into the heart of the Lower East Side from his lair on the tenth floor of the *Forward* building, as his operators next door composed the current issue with the hot-metal slugs of their typesetting machines.

There was a swirl of red dust outside and a din that had nothing to do with his compositors. The dust was no mystery to Abraham Cahan; it was bits of rubble and red chalk that flew off the walls and ragged roof lines of the tenements and other buildings, as if some monstrous sculptor was chipping away at every piece of property in the Ghetto: schools, synagogues, churches, the Ludlow Street jail, the Essex Market Court, the pushcarts, the pylons of the Williamsburg Bridge, the earth that was dug out of Delancey Street for a new subway line, the flanks of dray horses that attracted flies and more dust—the mischievous sculptor was time itself. And time was the great enemy of a Yiddish editor. Cahan could prosper only if new immigrants scrambled off the boat from Ellis Island with their baggage, their children, and their wives. One day soon, this immigration would come to a halt, and the *Forward*'s readers would disappear into the red dust.

And then there was the din, as shattering as the clack of malevolent birds. But East Broadway didn't have an infestation of crows. This sound wasn't the wail of mourners. Cahan would have remembered that. It was more like the rough, irregular purr of a dying animal. Cahan didn't believe in embroidery. Stones didn't weep in the columns of the *Forward*. Men suffered, died of the tailors' disease—tuberculosis. Husbands deserted their wives. Children starved. Still, he wasn't at the Yiddish theater, where whole choruses could cry. It was as if the streets had their own sinister chime, not a death knell, but a sound that mocked him and all his exploits.

He'd been an outlaw long before he was an editor. He'd joined a band of bomb makers in Vilna after a pandemic of pogroms, where Cossacks in white fur caps rampaged across village upon village of Lithuanian Jews, violating old women and young girls, vanishing with their plunder while setting entire streets on fire. Cahan himself had witnessed several of these young girls, who had lost the power of speech and would walk with a limp for the rest of their lives. Other girls had gone mad, and mutilated their own dolls. Cahan had walked through the charred streets, with the burning carcasses of cows, and limbs buried in piles of ash like worthless plunder; he'd never witnessed such fear in his life. Some of the village elders couldn't cease to cry or tremble. That's when Cahan vowed to hunt Cossacks the way Cossacks had hunted Jews, though pistols blew up in his hands and the bombs he assembled sputtered like firecrackers. Another band of bomb makers had tried to blow up the czar's carriage outside the Winter Palace and had succeeded only in maiming themselves.

Cahan arrived in America a wanted man, without a word of English in his skull. There were no night classes for anarchists from Vilna in 1882. He wouldn't despair. He walked into a public school on Hester Street, begged the principal to allow him to sit with thirteen-year-olds in regular day classes; so he sat for two months, absorbed whatever he could, memorizing the teacher's melodies of speech, and within a year or two he was bargaining with editors and writing about life on the Lower East Side for *The Sun*. He attended political rallies, talked of marching up to the capitalists' domain on Fifth Avenue and murdering millionaires in their palaces with an ax. And now he was accepting advertisements from White Rose tea and Maxwell House in the *Forward*, couldn't have survived without them. His enemies called him "a capitalist pawn in a socialist shirt." He'd abandoned the anarchists years ago, couldn't see himself wielding a murderer's ax. He became a police reporter, read Henry James, and began writing stories about the Ghetto—in English—for *Cosmopolitan* and *The Atlantic Monthly*, where James himself had published. Cahan had even written novels in his public school patter and a book of short stories praised in the Anglo-Saxon press.

His wife had pleaded with him not to return to the *Forward*—Cahan had quit three times. Anya, with her pince-nez, saw him as another Tolstoy. He did visit Petersburg once, as a fugitive, and sought out the streets he had memorized from *Anna Karenina*, but he found little solace in the boulevards and canals. Cahan wasn't a cavalier. He was an ex–bomb maker from Vilna, at the *Forward*, probably for life. It was like a death sentence, Anya often parroted, with a hint of almond butter on her tongue.

He'd rescued the paper from bankruptcy and oblivion. He refused to publish moribund socialist tracts that whispered of revolution in the streets and the coming of some proletariat messiah. Cahan preferred Jacob P. Adler in *The Yiddish King Lear* at

the New National. That was enough of a messiah for him. Circulation leapt like a wild storm on the Lower East Side when he
introduced *A Bintel Brief* (A Bundle of Letters), in 1906. He had
to steal from other Yiddish papers and from Hearst. *A Bintel Brief*
was a lonely hearts column, but with Cahan's particular twist.
He would receive letters from his readers—most of them garbled
and illiterate—would revise them with a stroke here and there,
so that the letters sang their tales of woe and grief. And then
Cahan himself would offer his advice, not like some potentate
on the tenth floor, but as a friend, a secular rabbi, like Elijah, the
Gaon of Vilna, transported from the eighteenth century and the
Vilna ghetto to the Ghetto of East Broadway. As a boy of seven,
little Elijah ripped into the learning of every scholar and rabbi at
Vilna's Great Synagogue, and would be a sage for another seventy
years, giving his advice to the poor and the disheartened without
ever asking for a fee. Elijah had no time to sleep. He was always
in demand. No one could inherit Elijah's genius. But Cahan also
had no time to sleep. He was always revising and answering some
Bintel Brief. Men wrote to him as well as women, but Cahan knew
that he had captured every second housewife on the Lower East
Side as a willing slave to his column. Sometimes he had to disguise the writer of a letter, or he would have caused a scandal and
heaped shame upon the heads of his own contributors. So he juggled names, addresses, like a Jewish acrobat. Was Sonya of Sheriff
Street planning to run away with her star boarder and abandon
a pair of little girls and a renegade husband, who was drunk half
the time and beat her black-and-blue? "I love our boarder," she
confessed. "He doesn't have clumsy hands. He never pinches me.
He writes poems while he's at the shop. He loves my daughters.
We'll run to Canada, I swear to God."

Cahan had touched some primitive cord. Adultery was a common-enough theme in the Ghetto, where wives, husbands, and boarders were packed into tenements, rushed half naked in and out of some toilet in a darkened hall. Didn't Cahan publish feuilletons that were fatalistic about love? And hadn't he serialized a condensed version of *Anna Karenina* last year, with Anya translating Tolstoy's electric rhythms into a Yiddish potpourri, filled with every kind of noodle that his readers adored, so that Anna was a fallen heroine who could have walked under the shadows of the Second Avenue El, and landed on the tracks of a trolley car?

His own Anya was a born *littérateure*, and their marriage was as dry and bitter as a decaying bone. He couldn't have had a child, not with such a nun. But Cahan was also barren. He'd fumbled around with a girl from the gymnasium when he was a schoolboy in Vilna, had fondled her in a dark alley, and that had been his only preparation for marriage. He'd separated from Anya six times; somehow, it was just as difficult to live apart. And now they lived uptown, among all the Gentiles and the German Jews. But it had nothing to do with any desire to escape the Ghetto, to swagger on Fifth Avenue in a silk hat. He'd put his Anya in an elegant birdcage, a socialist-anarchist who stuffed herself with charlottes russes, while more often than not, Cahan slept on a table in the composing room.

He could admire the Master, pore over Henry James like a rabbinical scholar, sniff the perfume of every paragraph, but he himself was a creature with crippled wings. His novelist's craft was entombed in the pages of the *Forward*, almost every word of which he wrote or revised. And he seldom had any peace from his subeditors.

While he was glancing out the window, Barush, his managing

editor, marched in, clutching some copy, wound into a scroll, like a satanic Torah in bleeding black ink. Barush wore a pince-nez, the same as Cahan's wife. He'd once been Cahan's boss, on another Yiddish paper. He was a drama critic, a playwright, and a novelist, whose feuilletons appeared in the *Forward*, but no housewife or tailor could have untangled his high-toned Yiddish. Also, his policies were different from Cahan's. He wanted to cooperate with the Kehilla, that conspiracy of uptown Jews, to police and control the Ghetto. Some kind of Kehilla had been around since late medieval times, when rich Jewish merchants spied on their poorer brethren in the ghettos of Eastern Europe, as roving bands of beggar Jews often committed petty crimes—stealing fabrics and half-rotten fruit—to keep from starving and freezing to death.

There were no such Jewish gypsies in Manhattan. But a furor had been created on the Lower East Side several years ago by a former police commissioner, a hothead and a blusterer named Howard Galt. He wrote an article about the Ghetto in *The North American Review*, where Cahan himself had published many times. So he couldn't accuse the magazine of bigotry. Galt claimed that half the crimes in the city were committed by Russian Jews. "They are burglars, firebugs, pickpockets and highway robbers—when they have the courage—but, though all crime is their province, pocket-picking is the one to which they seem to take most naturally."

The German Jews didn't want such a plague to arrive on their doorsteps. Many of them had migrated from Bavaria to the Lower East Side, built their synagogues while making a fortune as dry goods merchants, then moved uptown with their synagogues and department stores and their retinue of uncles, cousins, and wives. These merchants and their allies were anxious to have Cahan and other downtown leaders join the Kehilla, so that they, too, could watch over "Russian recreants" in that cradle of crime on the Lower East Side. But Cahan shunned the Kehilla and its uptown detectives, who were little more than snitches and police lackeys. They would have turned the Ghetto into one vast prison farm.

Barush pleaded with him. "Comrade Cahan, you can't shut out these Allrightniks. They advertise in our pages with their department stores. And what about the Hawthorne School, eh? They've rescued delinquents from a juvenile asylum that was little more than a madhouse and a den of thieves. They had to fight the governor on this, tooth and nail."

"And what do we have, Barush? A Jewish reformatory on the Hudson that's picturesque. Do the boys study Spinoza, Barush? They can become carpenters, bricklayers, plumbers, or printers. That's the complete menu at the Hawthorne School."

"What do you expect, Comrade? Half the boys are brainless. Their souls were beaten out of them at the asylum."

"No, Barush," Cahan insisted. "Not their souls."

He'd gone upstate with the Jewish magnates on a kind of picnic that left from the old Grand Central terminal. He'd shared grapes and wine and cheese with the magnates and their wives in satin slippers and veils that left deep puckers every time they whispered a word. Cahan had even brought Anya, as a kind of peace offering. But she had little to say to these wives. She wouldn't share Tolstoy with them, and her husband had forbidden her to talk politics. So she sat in silence along the route, in her pince-nez, staring at the Hudson, until they arrived at a tiny railroad station with a tin roof, where a flotilla of black mahogany carriages was waiting for them with liveried drivers who could have stepped out of some Russian romance. Cahan had never seen such rehearsed opulence. The carriages drove along a very steep and rocky ravine, then started to climb, and stopped at a little fortress at the top of a mountain.

Cahan was appalled. The Jewish reform school had a baseball diamond, a garden, a synagogue, spacious cottages, and a brick castle, where the machine shops were located and classes were held; it had the antiseptic and chilling air of a penitentiary with a river view. He grew numb as he walked the grounds, and couldn't wait to flee. Barush wasn't wrong. Many of these wild boys had left their souls at some other institution. Yet why should Hawthorne's young bricklayers have distressed him so? Surely the magnates themselves would find jobs for the school's best graduates. But he read nothing in the boys' eyes, not a parcel of emotion or curiosity, as if they dreamt and ate bricks.

"Comrade," Barush said, waving the long rolled-up galley sheet of his article on the Kehilla, half of it scribbled over in the editor's ubiquitous green pencil, "I am not a ventriloquist. You cannot make me swallow my own words. It's for the editorial page, yes or no?"

Cahan knew Barush's little tricks. All his subeditors were novelists and poets. He published their work as often as he could, but they longed for much more than an editorial or a feuilleton in the *Forward*. Barush and the others were hoping that the magnates behind the Kehilla would subsidize the translation of their work into English, and that one of them would become the new sultan of the novel, another Henry James. It was a madness born out of sipping too much tea with raspberry jam.

"I can't praise the Kehilla, Barush, I can't. But we'll run your feuilleton on the Polish riders next week."

Barush was silent for a moment; he had his own wolflike cunning. "Did you like it, Comrade?"

Cahan hadn't read a word of the feuilleton.

"I adored it," he said.

"And on what page will it appear, Comrade Editor?"

"You can have the sixth page all to yourself—with an illustration. Now will you let me do my work, Barush? Go away!"

3.

CAHAN THOUGHT HE WOULD HAVE A MOMENT OF PEACE, but there were problems in the composing room, and he had to admit that all his printers' apprentices had come from the Hawthorne School; these young printers could catch errors in a typeface that fell afoul of his untrained eye. They were wizards of detail, yet none of them could read without reciting every line like choirboys at the synagogue, and he was convinced that little of what these boys recited made any real sense. They learned—and lived—by rote. That was the abiding signature of the Hawthorne School.

He had to meet with his business managers, who didn't want him to contribute to so many strike funds in the *Forward*'s name. But a socialist paper had to support the strikers and their families. And all he had to do was show his managers the *Forward*'s circulation, printed near the banner on the front page: 139,871. They couldn't fire Cahan. His readers would follow him to any paper he decided to run. So he mocked their talk about money and sent his managers away.

Still, he paid a price for the success of *A Bintel Brief*. His devoted readers had to discuss their problems with the editor of the column. They would arrive in droves, stand outside his "official" office, near the newsroom on the seventh floor, while secretaries and assistants fed them nibbles of Russian coffee cake, and had them mount a back staircase, one by one, to his falcon's nest. No other Yiddish paper on the Lower East Side had this mandarin rapport with its readers. He sat, he listened, sometimes prepared a letter and its response while a forlorn housewife was with him. But it was the sixth or seventh visitor who troubled Cahan, a certain Mrs. Samuels. She was a widow in her late thirties, with a seventeen-year-old daughter named Sharon. It was difficult for him to admit how aroused he was by the young widow. He wanted to bite the strands of her raven hair, paw her like a drunken Cossack, crush her nipples until she cried with terror and delight. Yet she had a dreamy presence in her eyes, as if she had just walked out of a nickelodeon. And he kissed her hand like one of Tolstoy's counts to hide his incurable lust. He'd seduced none of these *Bintel Brief* housewives; not a single one had sat on his lap in this falcon's nest of his. He was an old man of fifty-three, with one foot in the grave, and still he lusted, while the aroma of baking powder and bleach on the widow's hand stung his nostrils.

Her daughter had been keeping company with a downtown boy who attended City College and gambled on the side. He wore silk scarves and white buckskin tennis shoes. "A *cadet*," Cahan mumbled to himself, a young sport who probably worked for a gang of white slavers. The college student presented Sharon with an engagement ring, and as Cahan had suspected, she vanished within a month. Then a man came knocking at the widow's door; he wasn't impolite. He took off his derby while he left her with a ransom note. Either Mrs. Samuels collected the five hundred dollars she had in her account at the Jewish bank on Canal or she would never see her daughter again.

The editor of *A Bintel Brief* shook the widow by her shoulders with a kind of desperate fury. "Mrs. Samuels, when did this gangster arrive with his ransom note?"

"Please, Mr. Cahan," the widow said, "why are you so rough?"

"Because we have so little time, my dear reader. When did he knock on your door and what did he look like? Did he have one eye or two?"

"Oh my God," the widow gasped, "you must be a devil. He had a deep black hole where his left eye should have been. And it was three days ago."

The *Forward* had become his own detective bureau. He published articles from *Krokodil*, a half Yiddish, half Russian satirical magazine that flourished in Odessa between 1911 and 1912; several of the articles were about a white slavery ring, imagined or not, run by a mysterious one-eyed pirate, and Cahan always remembered the route of this ring, with its arsenal of cadets; the "fish" they lured into their net traveled between Buenos Aires, lower Manhattan, and the Jewish slums of Odessa in an endless circle, until they lost their looks and were cast out upon some human junk heap.

"Madam, please, it's life or death. What else can you recall about this monster?"

"He carried tea bags in his pocket and pretended to sip from his own glass of tea —yes, and he brushed the dirt from his shoes with a comb. The shoes were made of some yellow bark, not leather. Comrade Cahan, what does this all mean?"

"Everything," he said. He had to reassure her, calm her down. He promised to have her daughter back in a couple of days, when all the time he knew that she might be on a boat to Buenos Aires, and uncollectible. He sent the widow home with a mock smile and a stroke of her cheek, all his lust gone. He had his secretary come up to the tenth floor without alerting the newsroom. She arrived out of breath, wearing a simple white shirtwaist. He would have to assemble all his runners, he said, all his printer's devils, and have them scour the Jewish streets for one of the Kehilla's own detectives.

"Matilda," he whispered, "quick, quick, I need to find our Ben."

She was a large, thick woman, much taller than Cahan, and she barely knew a word of Yiddish. But he could trust her with his life and the *Forward*'s lazy account books; he was always borrowing money to help feed a former contributor who could no longer write. Often he had to borrow against his own salary, but Matilda made sure that the rent was paid on his uptown flat. She ruled his agenda from morning to night; he would never have gone home if Matilda hadn't been there to lock him out of his sanctuary.

"Comrade Boss," she said, mocking him a little. "We don't need your printer's devils. Benjamin's right outside. And he brought with him the Ghetto's greatest ganef."

"Who the hell is that?" he had to ask.

"The jailbird, Monk Eastman."

He couldn't believe that Ben had come to the *Forward* with Eastman, who had once been Tammany Hall's biggest slugger, and had ruled the Ghetto with his thousand thugs. Monk Eastman had a price list for his mayhem. That's how he served his best clients. He or one of his thugs—most of them from the Jewish streets—would chew your enemy's ear off for fifteen dollars, break his arm or leg for nineteen, and do "the big number" on him for a hundred dollars and up, depending on his importance and the bodyguards he had. But Monk was too chaotic in his habits, too whimsical. He might free every canary in a pet shop, or destroy Tammany's favorite saloon because a waiter served him tepid ale.

So after one of his epic battles with another gang, Tammany had the courts grab hold of Monk. He was sent up to Sing Sing, where he sat for five years, and when he returned to the Ghetto in 1909, he was a gangster without a gang. His entire domain was gone. His own thugs had gathered into others gangs and wanted no part of his eccentricities. He wandered the Lower East Side without the protection of Tammany or the police, a lost soul in the land of lost souls. Cahan had forgotten that Monk was still alive.

"Come in, come in," he shouted. "And bring your bodyguard."

They had to squeeze past Matilda on her way out. She blushed at the sight of Benjamin Ravage, a Litvak with blue eyes and blond hair. The tiny scars near his eyes only made him more irresistible. He would have been too beautiful for a man without that little imperfection. Belasco wanted him for one of his theaters uptown, and the Yiddish impresarios wanted him, too; he could have been a matinee idol without uttering a syllable, they said. Benjamin turned them down flat. He was a Harvard man, but you would never know it; he wouldn't even wear his Phi Beta Kappa key, and Cahan had given his own blood to get him that key. He loved the boy, and barren as he was, with bitterness in his loins, he began to think of Benjamin as his family, almost a son.

He babbled to Monk Eastman in gutter Yiddish, like one gangster to another. Cahan couldn't determine the bodyguard's reaction. Monk was essentially a man without a face. He'd been in too many fistfights, and his features were squashed together, so it was hard to tell where his nose ended and his mouth began. And his eyes were hidden in a nest of scars.

Monk remained silent during the whole barrage, and Ben couldn't stop laughing.

"Baron, it's useless. He's not a Hebe."

Cahan sulked. "I'm no baron," he said, though even his ene-mies called him the Baron of East Broadway. "I'm bewildered. The Eastmans were a Jewish gang—in his heyday."

"That's the product of pure chance. His own people are Bap-tists. He happened to inherit the Jewish quarter. So he blended in. Ain't that right, Edward?"

"Yes," said Monk Eastman, one of his pale eyes appearing out of that morass of skin and scar tissue.

"And Monk is your bodyguard, isn't he, Ben?"

"No, Baron. Not at all."

"Then why did you bring him to the tenth floor?" Cahan asked, feeling like some outlier in his own lair. "I'll never figure you, not in my lifetime. Every law firm in Manhattan wanted to hire you, even the anti-Semites, because it's always good for busi-ness to have a Hebe in the house, particularly one with blue eyes. And what's my Benjamin's brainstorm? He decides to become a detective for the Kehilla—a *detective*."

"Baron, I grew up here. I like the grime. I'd die of boredom at a law firm. And I wouldn't be able to help you on the sly."

It was all true. Cahan couldn't have had both hands inside the Kehilla without Ben Ravage. The baron had suddenly become a vigilante. It must have been a secret echo from his days as an anarchist. He still had a bit of the bandit and bomb thrower in his blood. And now he understood why Monk Eastman was here, not as Ben's bodyguard, but as an enforcer. Monk wore the tight jacket and flared trousers of a nineteenth-century hoodlum. His hobnailed boots could tell their own tale. He might erase any cadet on Allen Street with half a dozen kicks. His swagger and a derby that was much too small for his pumpkin-size head were enough to make a den of gamblers and their bodyguards tremble.

And Cahan, with his poor eyesight and woolen vests from Macy's bargain counter, wanted to see the whole Jewish quarter quake. He knew how compromised the coppers were, how detectives took bribes from Tammany chiefs who owned the stuss houses and high-class brothels on Grand Street, where Democratic and Republican bosses liked to gather and have tiny vacations from their wives. So the Kehilla's other detectives were useless with their surveillance tricks. The police commissioner's own men warned gamblers and brothel keepers of every raid a week in advance.

They hadn't counted on Abraham Cahan. He attacked Tammany and the police in editorial after editorial, and vowed to rid Allen Street of its streetwalkers. "It's a Jewish plague," he wrote, "worse than Job had ever seen. They linger right under the El, these Tillies and Sophies, half of whom are unwed mothers belonging to some downtown cadet. They toil in the shadows, bring their clients to a rotting tenement room, and fornicate in front of their own little sisters, who will join this streetwalkers' paradise in the near future. Shame on us all."

But now Cahan had Ben Ravage in his skyscraper that loomed above the Lower East Side, with an elevator that shivered from floor to floor—and a front desk. Ben didn't cavort with the police. He swooped down upon a gambling den before a spy could say, "Nix. The Kehilla is here." He created havoc, destroyed faro tables, padlocked the front door, even if the coppers arrived the next day with their sledgehammers and permits to operate "a penny arcade." Cahan had put a dent in their armor. That's all he could do. There weren't enough Jews on the Lower East Side to elect a socialist mayor, and how many Jews ever bothered to become citizens and cast a ballot? So he had to depend on young Ravage.

"Ben, I have another case for you. It's urgent."

And he told this detective with a Phi Beta Kappa key about the widow, Mrs. Samuels, and the white slavers who had whisked her daughter Sharon away.

"Baron, do you have a photograph of the young lady in question?"

The widow had left him one taken in the Catskills with Sharon's fiancé. The girl had none of her mother's natural beauty. She wore thick lenses, had wiry hair, big feet, and a shrunken chest. But Ben was staring at the fiancé.

"He's a City College boy," Cahan muttered.

Ben laughed. "His City College was the Tombs. He's a very recent graduate. . . . Edward, do you recognize him?"

Monk Eastman squinted at the photograph with his mysterious, hidden eyes. Then he whispered in Ben's ear.

"I thought so," Ben said. "That's Joseph Rein, alias 'Slick Jack.' He could steal the lint out of your pockets. He's had a hundred fiancées, much fancier than this one. He must have been hard up after his recent sit."

"And what about his boss, a white slaver from Odessa with a black hole for an eye?"

Ben laughed again. "That's Moses Brill. He can dream of Odessa all he wants, but he never moves far from Allen Street. And did he offer to return the ugly duckling for a price?"

"Please," Cahan said. "You shouldn't disparage the girl's looks. That's unkind of you."

Ben bowed like a subject at Cahan's court. "I was only trying to make a point. What white slavery ring, wherever its headquarters are, would bother to kidnap a girl who wouldn't bring them a nickel of profit? No, Jack must have bribed someone at the bank and found the widow's worth. And the rest is pure business, Baron."

"I'm not a baron," Cahan said. "You'll give your enforcer a false impression. Call me Abe."

Ben stared at Cahan with rancor in his blue eyes. "No one calls you Abe, not even your Anya. Besides, I have special privileges. You saved my life."

Cahan was trembling now. "I did not. I saw some talent and . . . we're not barbarians; we're Jews."

"You're an atheist," Ben had to remind him. "I was a delinquent, with my mother in the madhouse."

But you had your books, Cahan wanted to shout. Reading had saved his life, not a cross-eyed editor. He'd discovered Ben in one of the machine shops at the Hawthorne School. He'd been invited by the Jewish magnates to talk to some young printers about his newspaper. And the barrenness of the place had disturbed him. There wasn't a single picture on the walls. One of the dullards raised his hand. This boy was blonder than the rest.

"Editor Abraham," he said in that rough reform school idiom, "why do you have stories about a father setting fire to his daughter's hair on your front page, a jealous husband burying his boarder in the basement, when the whole world is on fire?"

The editor was silent for a moment. He hadn't expected a boy at this Jewish jail on the Hudson to bother reading the *Forward*. "That's what readers like."

"But you're not running a circus."

He stole Ben Ravage from the machine shop, took him home to East Seventh Street, where he was living with Anya at the time. She was delighted with her husband's catch. The boy knew Tolstoy and Turgenev. He could have been a violin virtuoso without the

violin. He was sixteen years old, and had shuttled from institution to institution for the past ten years. The boy didn't like to
talk about his past. But Cahan had read his file at the Hawthorne
School. His mother, Manya, had been taken from him when he
was a child of six. She had delusions about a secret marriage to
one of the magnates. Perhaps it wasn't a delusion. The boy had
a startling resemblance to Lionel Ravage, the *old* Lionel, before
he walked out of a burning tenement. That Lionel had a bride on
every block. . . .

Cahan could have marched Ben over to City College on
Twenty-third Street and gotten him admitted to the freshman
class. What dean would have dared question Abraham Cahan?
But he wanted more, as if he'd made his own Faustian pact. He
wrote to the admissions board at Harvard.

> *Esteemed Gentlemen:*
> *This is the smartest boy I have ever met.*
> *(signed) Ab. Cahan*

The admissions board was intrigued. It had never considered
a boy from a reform school, a Jew no less, nor had it ever received
a note from a Yiddish editor, who now had a national reputation. So with its usual reticence, the board invited this prodigy
to Cambridge. Cahan accompanied him to Boston on a Pullman
car. The boy met with a barrage of professors, who questioned
him on literature and philosophy, while Cahan cursed his own
idleness. He'd left the boy naked before these wizards, naked and
alone. He should have devoted more time to Tolstoy and Kant,
should have prepared him better. But Ben Ravage sailed through
the questions, conundrums about Plato's cave that would have

silenced a lesser student. "Kind sirs," he said, "what Plato saw in the reflection of the fire are the shadows we have all become. No matter what we do, or what we accomplish, none of us has any real substance, kind sirs."

Young Ravage was admitted as a special student; he out-flanked his classmates like some raucous kangaroo, leaping from the college to Harvard Law. But Harvard hadn't left a trace on him. He still had the lisp of a reform school addict.

"Baron, we'll find Moses Brill, but who can guarantee that the girl is still alive?"

"Why would they harm her?" he asked, like a child at the Talmud Torah in Vilna, perturbed by his own rabbi.

"Because it's Allen Street. Moses could have kept her in a crib and gotten tired of waiting for ransom money. He's strangled other girls when he's in a drunken stupor."

"Then what are you waiting for? Go there with your golem!"

Benjamin's cheek shivered, as if he'd been slapped. "Edward's been dying to meet you, or I wouldn't have brought him to your inner sanctum."

Cahan clutched his crop of gray hair. "You speak in riddles all the time. I'm not the Vilna Gaon, or an examiner at Harvard. I'm . . ."

"Edward isn't much of a reader. And one of his old gang, a lit-tle Hebe in the next cell at Sing Sing, recited the *Forward* to him, every line, in Yiddish and English, like a song. It kept him sane, and he wanted to thank you."

"Ah, I'm so sorry," Cahan said, while Monk Eastman stood with one scarred paw in his pocket, the other paw cupped over Ben's ear. And Ben had to translate Monk's deep reserve. He'd loved the feuilletons, adventure stories about Jewish swindlers and rogues who outsmarted landlords, merchants, and the czar's men. But these rogues were always bewitched by some merchant's daughter, who liked to sleepwalk through a country village in her nightgown and bare feet, with the painted toenails and throbbing bosoms of a Jezebel. Often these daughters had risen out of the grave, or were under the spell of a demon. The rogues repented, and ran off with a daughter whose limbs might disappear with all the material on her body. Monk Eastman couldn't get enough of these tales, often signed Ab. Cahan, or written under an alias: Max Vilna or Morris Litvak.

Cahan was at his best as the penny author Max Vilna. He preferred these wild children's romances to his East Side tales of plodding immigrants, grocers on the rise, dreaming about the Allrightniks Row of Riverside Drive, or a young garment worker seduced by her boss' favorite son, a ne'er-do-well who would end up as a faro dealer at a Grand Street den. He would write about Cossacks and temptresses who could drain the blood out of a man. This is what Monk Eastman must have admired: the chaos, the violence, and raw love that mirrored his own life, and the phantasmagoria that also drew him into another world.

"Ben, I will dedicate my next tale to Monk, set it at Sing Sing . . . but you must bring the widow's girl back from Allen Street as quickly as you can, or, I promise you, I won't have a moment of peace."

Ben left with his golem, and the editor could feel his empire collapse. The *Forward* covered every step in the macabre dance of the European powers with all their secret and not so secret alliances, but his readers were much more interested in heartbreak and romance in the Jewish quarter. The shifting alliances in Europe had become perilous for the Jews as borders began to close. Fewer boats left from Hamburg. Ellis Island was idle on certain afternoons. And sometimes, when he had business near Battery Park, and he could stare out at that ponderous brick and stone station, it looked like Atlantis in the mist, about to fall right into the sea. That's how fragile the world of Jewish immigration had become in 1913; there were less and less escape routes, more and more pogroms.

Cahan didn't believe in a static universe of skullcaps. Yossele Rosenblatt, the greatest cantor on earth, could sing his heart out at the Roumanian Congregation on Rivington Street, draw merchants and music lovers from uptown, make the sparrows hover over the synagogue, searching for his high notes, as the cantor's business agent loved to boast, but even Yossele couldn't stop the exodus of Jews from the Lower East Side. Cahan himself was partially at fault. The *Forward* preached assimilation. It was a Yiddish paper with a Yankee accent. He advised fathers to send their sons to City College, knowing full well that these sons would forsake their fathers and the Ghetto.

That piercing din of time was against Cahan, like the long whistle from one of the ocean liners in the harbor, an endless, mystifying bleat that could have been a capitalist war cry to every socialist between the Bowery and East Broadway. He couldn't have printed his paper without the revenue from White Rose tea. Yet he breathed a taste of socialism into every article he edited or wrote. He attacked the strikebreakers, hounded the garment manufacturers, many of whom subscribed to the *Forward*. He was the shamas of his own little shul that had grown into a skyscraper, and all he could do was watch after the Ghetto's inhabitants through his secret connection to the Kehilla, while he peered down into the Jewish streets.

It was a boisterous slum, denser than Bombay, with sweat-shops, cafeterias, a "Pig Market" at the corner of Hester and Ludlow, where greenies fresh off the boat would line up in lugubrious silence, waiting until some con man or sweatshop owner would hire them for a few pennies. There were a couple of choice synagogues with jeweled façades, but most of the shuls in the Ghetto were makeshift affairs—a sunken storefront, or the rotting rear room of a tenement. And Cahan could capture his entire domain in a glance—the alleys, the rooftops, the clothes-lines strung across fire escapes, the twin spires of St. Mary's Church on Grand Street, and beyond the spires to the marble arch at Washington Square, half hidden by that infernal red dust of the Jewish streets, so that the arch seemed to float in the wind, like some magical instrument of American power.

No one else had Cahan's privileged view; no one had his fal-con's nest. Half the Ghetto had succumbed to darkness, entire streets without lamps. But Cahan could see the lights of the Yiddish theaters along the Bowery, the glow of the El station at Allen and Grand, the somber yellow lamps of the motorcars along Delancey, the skeletons of cable cars sitting outside the repair shop next to the Williamsburg Bridge.

That bridge had swallowed up Grand Street as Manhattan's great bazaar. A ferry to Brooklyn couldn't compete with the bridge's constant traffic and had to shut down, leaving Grand Street an isolated island of coffeehouses and fabric shops. Once it had been the home of Lord & Taylor and Ridley's, the world's largest retail store, which sat like a magnificent pink elephant five stories high at Allen and Grand, with panoramic windows, a wrought-iron façade, a cupola, and a clock tower. Lord & Taylor shunned the immigrants, but Ridley's was the mecca of Jewish brides looking to build their wedding trousseaus. They could find bargains on every floor—waffle irons, oilcloths, cloaks, lace curtains, corsets, and canaries.

That pink elephant also had a tiny men's department. Cahan himself had shopped there when he first arrived in America, as an anarchist. In truth, he'd come to bomb the store, though he had never manufactured a decent bomb in his life. He went through the large hammered-metal doors at 311½ Grand, expecting to find a capitalist palace of clothing dummies, haughty salesclerks, and pyramids of perfume bottles. But he was disarmed after his first step, as he heard the canaries sing from their cages on the second floor. That soft, sweet hum tantalized Cahan, followed him wherever he went.

The ground floor was swollen with immigrants, girls in their shawls and dresses that looked like burlap sacks, and thick Russian boots that would have served them well in Siberia. These young girls were hypnotized by the brocaded satin slippers that sat on the counters and the shelves, some with buckles and ribbons, others without. They wanted to fondle the slippers but were frightened of the clerks and the enormous cavern of the department store. The salesgirls tried to help. That's what troubled Cahan. These weren't the heartless Yankee witches of Lord & Taylor, who could send you howling into the street with their icy stares. The salesclerks at Ridley's had memorized a few Yiddish sayings, but that wasn't enough to ease the hysteria of the immigrant girls.

So the anarchist stepped in. He'd already had a few classes at the public school on Hester Street. He spoke Russian and Yiddish to the immigrants in their shawls, and English to the clerks. The girls were allowed to fondle the shoes, touch every ribbon and jewel. No one barked at them. The salesclerks were content. One or two of them crumpled a handkerchief to their eyes as they watched the rapture of the immigrant girls, whose roughened hands darted like little wily animals. . . .

A curious thing happened as he stared out his window at the *Forward*. A kind of screen had slipped in front of his eyes, like the outlines of a manuscript that would have enriched a Talmudic scholar, and Cahan could see much deeper into the Ghetto, as if it consisted of multiple layers that he could manipulate with his eyes. And there was Ridley's, rising above the elevated tracks, with its clock tower. And not only that, he could listen to the clop of the horsecar that was bringing Brooklynites to Ridley's from the Grand Street pier. The editor didn't see one immigrant girl on that car. All the women wore bonnets and fur collars; they must have been the hoi polloi of Williamsburg on an excursion to their favorite Manhattan shop.

It was even more curious, because he could hear the canaries sing inside Ridley's; the sound rose above the clock tower with a kind of deafening warble. "Ah," he muttered to himself, "the master of *A Bintel Brief* is losing his mind." And it got worse. He noticed horsemen ride the darkened streets in a perfect line; this wasn't a mounted patrol from the police stables. Not even such an elite squad of horsemen had the radiance of Russian riders. These were Cossacks in their bloodred blouses and white fur caps rumbling toward Seward Park with their sabers. "A pogrom," he whispered, on the Lower East Side, with its own public library and the old Tenth Ward's Republican Party headquarters a few steps from the *Forward* building. It was some sort of havoc from the devil, who could deliver Cossacks across the ocean and destroy this strange Ghetto with its theaters and newspapers and a few synagogues as ornate as Babylon.

Cahan closed his eyes. The Cossacks disappeared. And Ridley's dome was gone, with all the canaries. He gathered up a few manuscripts in his Moroccan leather briefcase and ran like Satan's own accomplice from the tenth floor.

Two

The Downtown Detective

I.

*H*E SAW HIS OWN MOTHER in their pale eyes, in that frantic need to beguile. Manya always painted her lips in the madhouse. She was trying to seduce everyone in sight, looking for that blond Adonis who had married her, though he already had a wife and a couple of brats uptown. She still called herself Mrs. Lionel Ravage. And every time Ben stepped onto Allen Street, with its ghostly streetwalkers, moving in and out of the dark latticework that the El's tracks left on their ravaged bodies, he felt a rage he could hardly control. Not against the girls, but against the medieval customs and laws of the Ghetto that said sons could go to City College or study the Torah until their beards turned white, while daughters had to slave in some foul, dusty shop and treat their brothers like fine princes of the house who couldn't be disturbed. Sometimes the young prince seduced his own sister, commanded her to touch his *schmeckle.* Or else she took a dancing class on her one afternoon off, and a cadet fondled her with his practiced hands, and she ended up on Allen Street. She was always someone's little sister.

They were the only ones on the Lower East Side who were allowed to call him Benny. He couldn't provide for them; their future was sealed: Most of these girls would end up on some ward by the time they were thirty, with sunken cheeks and dust on their lungs from living night and day under the El, where every passing carriage showered them with dust and grime, until their elbows and knees were black by midafternoon. But clients rarely roughed them up or cheated them out of a dollar. The detective always tracked these clients down.

"Ain't you gonna treat a girl to a bottle of ale, Benny?"

"Not right now, Helen. I have work to do for the Kehilla."

He knew most of them by their first and last names, and whatever aliases they used to hide the fact that their father was a rabbi or their brother was a lawyer at a Jewish investment bank. Ben didn't keep index cards like the other detectives of the Kehilla. The only index cards he had were inside his head.

"Benny, that lunatic is back," Helen said.

Allen Street had once had its own ripper, a guy in a cape who cut up Jewish girls. He'd terrorized the district, and then disappeared.

Helen revealed a red mark on her cheek. "That's one of his souvenirs."

Had the ripper hopped out of some time warp and returned to the Lower East Side? It made no sense.

"I'll look into it," he muttered, but he had to find Cahan's missing girl.

He knocked on the icebox doors of the Shilly-Shally Saloon and Social Club, situated right under the El; it had once been the rear entrance of Ridley's, but that retailer's paradise never had icebox doors thick enough to stop an ax and slow down a police raid, or the surprise attack of other ganefs. Someone growled at him through the Judas hole in the double doors.

"Who is it? Friend or foe?"

"Are you blind? It's Benjamin Ravage. I've come to pay for a package. I have Monk Eastman as my intermediary."

There were loud whisperings behind the icebox doors, then bolts began to click, several at a time, and the double doors opened a crack. Ben slipped inside, and Monk Eastman followed right on his heels. Moses Brill ran a school for pickpockets; he fenced stolen goods and also trained cadets. He was protected by Tammany and the police, and when detectives at the Educational Alliance picked him for a raid, he closed the Shilly-Shally for a month and moved uptown.

The long, narrow hall was lit by one ratty red bulb. Moses' thugs patted Ben and all his pockets for concealed weapons. Monk Eastman, they left alone; none of them would dare touch this one-time lord of the Lower East Side. The darkened hall led to a barracks that must have been the ground floor of Ridley's, with cots and a few shelves as its only merchandise. It was much grander, with all its ancient chandeliers, than the temporary shelter that the cops once had for stragglers and waifs in the underground parlors of the Madison Street precinct; Ben had slept there several times with his mother, when Manya would deny the landlord and his son sexual favors; she could rarely pay the rent.

But the tribe of women at the Shilly-Shally wasn't so indigent. And there were no young boys at the school for pickpockets. Moses was a very clever fagin. A clique of young boys always aroused suspicion on a trolley or on board the El. These women in the barracks had all the fineries of uptown—parasols, wide silk hats, satin slippers, and soft scarves. The second they started to chatter, Ben realized they weren't uptown ladies at all. Moses Brill had groomed them like dolls—Ben discovered the clothing barrels at the far end of the dormitory, filled with scarves and slippers and hats. They could smile and comport themselves like ladies of the upper crust, but no one ever bothered to give them elocution lessons. Perhaps it didn't matter. They could steal a wallet, a watch fob, or a purse with nothing more subtle than a smile.

Only Ben had to reconsider what he saw. He had never encountered such a medley of women. What if these pickpockets chose to live in a barracks and weren't waifs at all? They might have abandoned the melodrama of a marriage gone sour, or the loneliness of a tenement room, for a new kind of sisterhood, where they would never starve or have to quarrel. The fagin didn't even have to recruit them. They must have knocked on Moses' double doors, begging to be inducted into his school.

And then he encountered a peculiar cradle near the clothing barrels, covered over with strips of wire mesh, like a madman's chicken coop. Cahan's missing girl, Sharon Samuels, was trapped inside that cradle. Her feet and hands were black, and she wore nothing but a tattered shift. None of the lady pickpockets had bothered about her. Ben could have smashed through the wire mesh, but that would have alerted Moses and he'd have lost whatever bit of surprise he had left. Still, it cost him to look into the cradle and see that frightened girl with her cracked lenses and wiry hair and not be able to comfort her. Somehow he'd failed his benefactor at the *Forward*, but Ben had always been a strategist, or else he'd never have survived watching his own mother unravel.

He said nothing, did nothing, and followed Moses' thugs into another barracks, and it ripped through Ben with an erotic charge he knew would linger for life. He'd been here before. It was the remains of the women's salon at Ridley's, with its spectacular dressing rooms and toilet. He recognized the silver faucets and mirrors that rose to the ceiling; mothers would bring their daughters and little sons into the salon, try the powders and perfumes that the department store left on a marble counter. This was Manya's favorite ritual, even in her ragged winter coat. She would squeeze the bulbs of perfume while she stared at herself in the mirror, and even the matrons were alarmed at her beauty, at the half-mad smile of some beggar princess who must have marched out of a fairy tale. And Ben was this strange princess' little boy. The other women reached under their skirts, and he grew faint from the aroma of their flesh. There was nothing else like it, that dank, forbidden sweetness from the patches of hair under their arms. They never quite closed the curtain of their particular stalls, so he could often see the silk or rough cotton of their undergarments; a few of the women would undress like mermaids and stand in the raw, their buttocks rippling behind the curtain.

The stalls were gone, torn right out of the old dressing rooms, with their outlines on the wall, which Ben might have traced lovingly with a finger if he hadn't been preoccupied with the girl in the wire cradle and Moses Brill, who sat behind one of the mahogany desks that Ridley's matrons had once used. There were no more powders and bulbs of perfume on the marble shelves, just bottles of bourbon and cognac in Moses' private saloon. Ben was startled by the pristine whiteness of his hands. Brill's own thugs had dirt on their knuckles and under their nails. He wore a silk gown, like some impresario. His silver beard seemed to soften the black hole of his eye socket. One of the ladies from the outer barracks was with him. Ben could hardly have imagined that she resided at a school for pickpockets. Her carriage was perfect, like the czar's daughters, who wandered around with books on their heads. And she could open or close her parasol with a flick of her wrist.

"No, no," the fagin muttered, rolling the one eye he still had in his head. "You're calling too much attention to yourself, Sophie. *My* girls have to be invisible."

"I'm all mixed up," said Miss Sophie, the apprentice pickpocket. "I practiced for hours with that umbrella. Ain't I supposed to show off my skills? That's how you draw in the mark. Otherwise, I could be a corpse standing there, Mr. Moses."

"Ah, you amateurs," he said, "you amateurs. You distract them with your parasol, and blind them to everything else. Now disappear, please. I have important business with this young rascal, Mr. Benjamin Ravage, Esquire, the nosy detective who makes guest appearances at night court."

Miss Sophie didn't move. She must have been starved for the company of men. The fagin had to rise up from behind his desk and tap her on the forehead. Then she returned to the outer barracks while Moses stared at her elegant carriage.

"It takes six months to train a girl, to wash the wrinkles out, give her a pair of clever hands, and her longevity comes without a guarantee. Sometimes she gets religious, or she loses her touch. And I'm stuck with her. I can't relinquish her bed. I don't have the heart."

Ben knew that this master fagin kept all the girl's fineries and tossed her into the cold, but he hadn't come here to contradict Moses Brill. A school for pickpockets had to have its casualties, and none of these girls belonged to a burial society. They would end up unclaimed, at a potter's field. It wasn't villainy on Moses' part. He abided by the Ghetto's rules. You found your family, or you fell into the dark.

"My dear boys," Moses said, caressing his eyehole, "can I offer you a drink? We serve nothing but the best at the Shilly-Shally." He turned to Eastman. "You'll have to pardon me, Monk, if I never visited you at Sing Sing. But I did send you an occasional salami. I wrapped it myself in silver paper. Did the salami arrive?"

Monk removed a yellow canary from his pocket and perched it on top of his hat. He tickled its beak once, and the canary began to sing. He removed another yellow bird from a different pocket. Moses and all his thugs weren't blind to the ritual. They hadn't forgotten Monk's folklore, even if Tammany had deserted him and also tried to have him killed; he survived Sing Sing, with a few short stays in the hospital ward. He didn't miss the camaraderie of his gang or the company of women; he missed his birds. And one bird on his shoulder and one on his hat meant that Monk Eastman was open for business. Once upon a time he'd put rival fagins out of commission for Moses Brill, chased other "Talmud Torahs" out of the Ghetto, always with a yellow bird on his hat.

"Moses, I never got your salami. . . ."

They couldn't see his eyes; that's what troubled them most. They still had their guns and knives and truncheons, which they had to keep concealed inside the club, because of the Sullivan Act; they could no longer descend into the streets with their handguns, no longer prowl unless they had a special "license" from the police.

"Benjamin," Moses said with a slight squeal in his voice, "did you come here with some cash?"

"No," Ben said.

"Then why should I give you the package?"

"Because there's a complication. The widow, Mrs. Samuels, recognized the black hole in your head."

"I never laid a finger on her, swear to God."

"But she went to Cahan, and he could drive you out of the district with two or three editorials in the *Forward*."

Moses thumped his chest. "What do I care about Cahan? Is that cockeyed editor gonna put me in *A Bintel Brief*?"

"Brill, do you know what Captain Kittleberger does the first thing in the morning, before he settles in? He has one of the crime reporters read *A Bintel Brief* to him. He doesn't want to see himself or any of his coppers mentioned in Cahan's column."

It was only a rumor, of course. But rumors had very reliable wings in the Ghetto. And Kittleberger was frightened of Cahan's wrath. The Madison Street station sat like a squalid brick cupcake near East Broadway, and Captain Kitt couldn't have an editor like Cahan scream that a white slavery racket was operating a few blocks from his precinct, within the skeletal remains of Ridley's department store. Kittleberger ruled the Lower East Side. Police headquarters, a Beaux-Arts limestone palace on Centre Street, seldom interfered with Captain Kitt.

"Moses, you'll have to give up the Samuels girl."

"Not for free. I pay Kitt and his men good coin. They wouldn't desert me in a pinch."

Ben had one last trump card. "Would you like me to write up this little visit, Moses? The readers of the *Forward* would love to hear about your clothing barrels and female dips. I have a good eye for detail. Trust me. I'm sure I can describe that cradle."

Moses cackled at him like a clever lunatic. "What if you had an accident, Ben? What if you fell down, and I strangled all of Monk's canaries? Then there would be no one left to sing."

He shouldn't have mentioned the canaries. Monk pulled Moses out from behind his desk and dangled him by his collar with one hand while his thugs stood half hypnotized and the canaries chirped like children and flew from chandelier to chandelier. As a boy, Ben had seen Monk battle several times on Sheriff Street, where the gang leader kept his canaries in a milk can on the stoop of an abandoned building. Monk's rivals from the Five Points Gang had tried to steal the can with all the canaries. There must have been a dozen hoodlums with oily guns and lead pipes. Monk was wearing suspenders, without a shirt. He had to dodge the bullets and protect his cache of canaries. Ben had never met such a battler. Eastman hurled his rivals to the ground, while some of the canaries clung to his hat. It was like being at the nickelodeon, with its magic storm of light and dark—that's how fast Monk moved. Ben's eyes couldn't catch him in flight. All he could do was watch the Five Pointers groan and crawl away from battle.

Moses was still dangling in the air while his thugs watched the canaries circle over their heads. "Mr. Monk, don't kill us."

Monk sat Moses down behind his desk again like a doll. The doll began to shiver in his silk gown. Ben grabbed his telephone, clicked once, and had the operator connect him to Cahan's private line at the *Forward*. He was very brief. "Yes, Baron, I have the girl. Don't move. I'll bring her myself."

He left Moses sitting there with all his guns and ammunition. In his own mind he blamed Moses for the vanished dressing rooms, for Ridley's disappearance and the death of the women's salon. His whole erotic life was contained behind a curtain where some anonymous housewife or mistress of a Russian Jewish doctor revealed her buttocks to a six-year-old boy.

He poked through the wire mesh of the cradle with a nail clipper and freed the girl. Her eyes went round and round, as if she were in a state of delirium. He had one of the female pickpockets find him a jar of fresh water and he wet the girl's lips with his own sleeve. He had Monk reach into a clothing barrel and pull out a turban, a long cape, and patent-leather walking boots with crisp new heels.

"Miss Samuels, do you know where you are?" he asked in his gentlest voice as he sat her down on a lopsided bench near the cradle, furled the cape around her shoulders, and buckled her into the boots. She was silent, and Ben wondered if the fagin had fed her some bad candy to keep her comatose.

"Monk," he whispered, "we need to fatten her up, get her some food, or she could die on us."

Eastman stole a piece of strudel and a blackened fork from one of the apprentice pickpockets. He sat on his haunches and fed the girl while the canaries hovered around his hat.

Sharon blinked. "Birds," she said in between bites of strudel.

"Sharon, do you know where you are?" the detective asked her again.

"Honeymoon," she said. "Aren't we aboard the *British Lion*? Where's my Joseph?"

They had doped her up and kept her here in a permanent fog until the widow came through with her bank account. Sharon would have died of dehydration in a couple of days, and all these apprentice pickpockets wouldn't have even noticed. They were oblivious to everything but the touch of a wallet in their own smooth hands. Ben had run out of strategies. And now he felt a rage against Ridley's, where his mother ran in midwinter to get out of the cold, while the male clerks would dream of that velvet body under her ragged coat, and he raged against the pickpockets and Moses' pretentious Talmud Torah; Monk could see the blind fury in Ben's blue eyes. The detective had his mother's mad streak.

"Mr. Ben, calm down. You'll frighten the girl."

"I can't help it, Monk."

He smashed the cradle with his fists, overturned the barrels, and the apprentice pickpockets huddled into one corner of that cavern, shrieking, covering their eyes with silk scarves, but he didn't frighten Sharon Samuels at all. She giggled at all the mayhem, and then her brows knit, and she looked at Ben with a kind of longing.

"Where's my fiancé? Are you my Joseph?"

"Yes," he whispered to calm her nerves.

"Then you'll have to carry me over the altar."

He was used to madwomen all his life. He picked up Sharon Samuels in her cape and turban and carried her through the icebox doors of the Shilly-Shally Club and into the darkness under the El; and with the ribbons of light from the tracks on her lenses and wild face, Sharon almost looked serene. But Ben was startled as the editor of the *Forward* rushed from under the tracks in the wool suit he wore summer and winter in the Ghetto.

"Baron, how did you know where to find me?"

Cahan had that puckish smile he sometimes reserved for Ben. "Do you think you're the only one with a detective bureau? But you haven't finished your job, Benjamin. Where's that lousy cadet and the bank clerk who sold the widow's account to the one-eyed bandit?"

The Baron of East Broadway would never grasp the real ingredients of a detective's life. Ben couldn't march into the Jewish bank on Canal and round up all the clerks. He'd have caused a scandal and put the Kehilla out of business in a week. Anyway, it might have been one of the bank's managers who compromised Mrs. Samuel's account, and not a clerk. The detective kept away from banks, uptown or downtown.

"Baron," he whispered in Cahan's ear, "the girl's delusional. She thinks *I'm* the cadet. But you haven't said hello to her."

Cahan bowed like an aristocrat and shook the girl's hand. She was staring into the darkness like a jilted bride.

Ben had an appointment with the Kehilla's Jewish kings, and he didn't want to be late. So he left Sharon with Cahan and Monk Eastman. It was futile business. She was still in love with the cadet. Even if he threatened extinction to Joseph Rein, her Slick Jack, and made him move to Vilna or Odessa or New Orleans, she'd have found another cadet; that sort of subterranean romance was in her blood, and he wouldn't have been surprised if she ended up back on Allen Street, under the El. He kissed her good-bye and ran to Kehilla headquarters with a sense of disaster in his soul. Some ghost could have been chasing Ben. That ghost, he realized, was himself.

2.

THE KEHILLA'S MAGNATES HAD COME DOWN to the Educational Alliance on East Broadway to celebrate their most controversial and heralded creation, the Bureau of Social Morals, a Jewish secret service in the heart of the Ghetto. Ben avoided the Alliance whenever he could. It was a poor man's stone palazzo on East Broadway that the German Jews had built as a monument to themselves— the Alliance was meant to transform the barbarous Oriental Jews of the Lower East Side into stout American souls. Ben knew it was an uptown fairy tale, but he was summoned to the Alliance by the Bureau's chief investigator and spy, Marcus Mendelssohn, a malignant fop who also served as Jacob Schiff's bodyguard.

Marcus wore a cutaway and spats, like his master, unless he

was on a police raid. He was in charge of Schiff's private state-room on board the ferryboat *Asbury Park* that carted his master between the Jersey Shore and Manhattan's Jewish investment houses during the summer months. He growled like a bulldog if some stranger tried to approach Schiff, the lord of Kuhn, Loeb. And in a classroom at the Alliance, where the magnates had assembled like arrogant children, he boasted about his accomplishments at the Kehilla.

He had packs of index cards, where he listed every known Jewish criminal on the Lower East Side, along with their establishments and their particular crafts. The cards had been supplied to him by the coppers, who fed Marcus a convenient list of horse poisoners, pickpockets, gamblers, and petty thieves; all were loners who wouldn't contribute to the department's own protection racket. So Marcus put them out of business, slapping at a harebrained thief with his kid gloves, or knocking the wind out of some poor pickpocket in the dusty cellars of police head-quarters. Ben had to watch the mad pleasure in Marcus' eyes as he changed kid gloves in the middle of a beating. It had become a ritual, that slow unpeeling of a glove.

"Gentlemen, Jewish crime will disappear from the streets by the end of 1913. You have my guarantee."

And that's when Meyer Bristol, the real estate mogul, stood up and shouted, "Marcus, enough. I want to hear from the down-town detective."

Ben was a bit bewildered that a board member would have heard of him. He'd been careful to cover his tracks, giving credit to the chief investigator whenever he nabbed a thief, so that he was like some skeleton rattling in the closet.

"This boy's a wonder, isn't he, Lionel?" Meyer Bristol asked.

Lionel Ravage was half hidden in the shadows. Ben could see his head of straw hair, like some aristocratic mannequin—and the raw flesh where the fire must have bit; his still handsome face looked like a wound that had never healed.

Lionel had once been Meyer's mentor. The two of them owned entire blocks on the Lower East Side. Lionel was also the hardware king of Canal, and Meyer suffered on account of that. He couldn't build his empire without the copper pipes of Ravage & Son.

"Yes, a wonder," Lionel said, and Ben had to suck on his lip as thoughts rippled through his brain. *I could leap right over the desks and mangle that son of a bitch in front of his uptown brothers. One good squeeze is all I want.* "This is for Manya," *I'll say as I spit into his eyes.* "Do you remember her?" But these Allrightniks would only have considered Ben a candidate for the lunatic asylum.

Meyer Bristol was shrewd enough to catch a glimmer of Ben's masked rage.

"What's your own assessment of the situation, Herr Downtown Detective? Do you agree that crime will vanish from the Ghetto this year?"

"Crime," he said, "will get worse and worse while the Ghetto remains poor."

And suddenly the patriarch himself, Jacob Schiff, rose from his seat, with his grand mustache and goatee, his blue eyes burning right into Ben.

"Young man, are you another socialist, like Cahan, who blames all our miseries on the bankers?"

"No, sir," Ben said. "But we can't rely on the police. They are even more corrupt than the criminals."

"And still," said Jacob Schiff, almost taunting Ben, "you've had your successes. You capture thieves on your own. You put horse poisoners out of business. . . ."

"But there's still a madman on the prowl," Ben said. "He appears and disappears, attacks Jewish girls on Allen Street."

"Not refined girls," said Schiff. "Prostitutes—they should be sent to Siberia!"

The patriarch's mind had wandered off somewhere. He adjourned the meeting and insisted that one and all go up to the roof garden and have some schnapps. Marcus tagged along behind his master like a pet monkey. There was venom in his eyes, but he wouldn't have dared get rid of the downtown detective, not after the magnates had heard about his exploits in the Ghetto. Ben despised these halls. Most of the settlements had started as delousing stations, even if the Alliance had a much grander mission. The ceiling was chipped, the walls were painted an institutional green, and Ben nearly tripped over a mousetrap. But the rooftop garden had been revamped by the magnates. That's where they congregated on their trips to the Ghetto. The garden had winter flowers and dwarf trees that grew in gigantic pots. It overlooked Seward Park and the water fountain that was almost as big as the Russian bathhouse on Eldridge Street; the Allrightniks had donated the fountain in honor of Jacob Schiff.

Ben must have been a curio to them; they knew he'd gone to Harvard *and* the Hawthorne School, their own private sanctuary for imbecilic boys. He was a "love baby," one more bastard Lionel had never acknowledged. Lionel could have swept him right off the Kehilla, but he took scant notice of this boy. And now they stood face-to-face on the roof garden, both of them with silver-blue eyes, Lionel Ravage and his invisible son.

"A madman on the prowl, and you intend to catch him, Herr Detective? What does he look like?"

Lionel was baiting him, but Ben didn't care. He invented his own portrait of the ripper.

"Some say he's dark. Others say he has straw hair—like you."

The roof garden turned silent. Marcus began to twitch. He snarled at Ben.

"You can't make such accusations. You must apologize to the esteemed president of our board."

"Shut up," Lionel said. "We're all suspects. Would you care to question me, Herr Detective?"

Ben bowed to Lionel Ravage. "Not today, Herr President. I do not have the resources to mount an investigation."

"But the Kehilla has all the resources in the world," Lionel said. "Shall I write you a check?"

"Not today."

And it was while they were all having schnapps on the roof that Meyer Bristol's daughter was mentioned—Bad Babette, who went away to Smith College and had had a love affair with another woman. Marcus had to threaten the life of this Smithie, Leila Montague, and bribe her with cash and stock certificates, before she vanished. But that didn't cure Bad Babette. She dressed in a man's dinner jacket and toured the clubs of Satan's Circus, in the Tenderloin above Twenty-third Street, until Meyer paid the police to arrest the club owners. Babs sat in the Women's House of Detention for a week, and now none of the magnates could find a suitor for her, even among the minor Jewish nobles.

Meyer waved a picture of Babs in front of Ben's eyes, and his spine began to tingle. The girl was as blond as his mother, with the same sad, half-wild expression.

"I told Babs about you," Meyer said. "And she wants to meet the Kehilla's downtown detective. Who knows what's inside her head? I have to warn you. She's a witch."

That's what the hospital attendants and the landlords and shopkeepers had shouted at Manya—"Witch, witch, witch."

"Herr Bristol, I have a weakness for witches."

THREE

On the Prowl

I.

*M*EYER BRISTOL LIVED in a limestone apartment-palace at Seventy-seventh and Riverside that was like a mausoleum twelve stories high, with a mansard roof. There were doormen in dinner jackets, elevator operators with tulips in their lapels, and a harpist in the lobby who sat in a gilded chair. It wasn't the opulence that confused Ben. It was the willful perversity of it all, so unlike the other German Jewish patriarchs. They built their summer cottages in the Adirondacks or on the Jersey Shore, away from the inquisitive eyes of the Gentiles. They had their private charity balls, established the Jewish Four Hundred, bankrolled the Kehilla, but none of them, except Meyer Bristol, would have welcomed a downtown detective into his home. . . .

Ben couldn't recall how many mirrored doors he went through with the butler until he found his way to Babs. Her bedroom faced a brick wall. *Who could live in such an asylum?* But he felt a strange comfort here, amid all the confusion—pillows and books and a hard-boiled egg with bite marks, and Babs wearing a nightgown in the afternoon. She was nearly as tall as Ben. She had blond hair and high cheekbones, like a Tartar princess. He could see the swirls of her navel through the silk gown as she growled at him.

"I won't sleep with you—*ever.*"

He laughed. "I thought you wanted a detective, not a stud."

"You're my father's detective. That means you are a stud. You can have one wish. I'll do anything, anything you ask, but you can't touch the simplest part of me with your paws. What does Poppa's sweet detective desire? Remember, I'm Bad Babette."

He wondered if she was out of her mind. He never should have gone to the Shilly-Shally Club. Now he'd be back at Ridley's for the rest of his days, dreaming of some Russian housewife who would only bare her buttocks to a little boy from behind the curtain of a dressing closet.

"Bad Babette, I'd like you to stand in your closet with the door half open, bend over, and raise the nightgown to your hips."

She had him in her talons. She'd turn her father's detective into a slave.

"You've been to Satan's Circus, haven't you? You're one of those naughty boys who get their thrills fondling themselves in a corner. How long shall I stand with my bummy in the air?"

"Not long," he said, and watched her unravel like some uptown Cinderella, raising the skirts of her nightgown with all the aplomb of a front-line chorus girl, her buttocks ripening in front of his eyes as both cheeks protruded from the closet. He shouldn't have revealed his own secrets to a stranger. The wound in him left by that woman's salon years and years ago could still evoke Manya with such clarity that he lost all sense of who he was.

Babs emerged from the closet with her skirts intact and her confidence in disarray. She was trying to arouse the detective, reassure herself that he was like any client of Satan's Circus, interested in her flesh. The dark rings under his blue eyes disturbed Babs, who had never once had the slightest desire to comfort a man. They smelled funny, the whole lot of them, like hairy creatures who bumbled along on broken legs.

"Darling," she whispered, stroking the little scars near his eyes, feeling the bumpy texture of his skin, "Poppa doesn't take my flings at Satan's Circus seriously. He wants me for himself, but he doesn't have the courage to grab his own daughter. He'd be banned from that country club of illustrious Jews."

The gentle way Babs touched his scars had soothed Ben, but he was still the downtown detective.

"If Meyer's not interested in your flings, why did he nearly have one of your classmates killed?"

"Oh, you men," she hissed. "Leila Montague was different. I *loved* Leila. That made her a threat. Poppa and his cohorts had the college throw her out. They're chummy with the president of Smith."

"And where is Leila now?"

"Hiding. She must be frightened out of her wits, Poppa and Jacob Schiff behaving like frontier marshals on their own frontier. But she's in Manhattan. I know that."

Babette plucked a postcard from between her bosoms and handed it to Ben.

"The maids and the butler are all Poppa's spies. I had to *wear* the damn card or one of the maids would find it."

The card was all wrinkled and "wrapped" in Babette's perfume. It was a picture postcard of a woman standing in front of a fake montage of Coney Island. The woman's face was superimposed upon the scenery. She had dark hair and plucked eyebrows and a defiant smile. Her cheeks were deeply chiseled, as if she suffered from the tailor's disease. That sunken face of hers sat on the voluptuous body of a bathing queen. Leila Montague must have posed for that picture at one of the rotogravure shops on Grand Street. Ben had seen her face before, but he couldn't remember where. Was she listed in some rogue's gallery at the Kehilla?

There was a note scribbled on the back in Leila's hand.

> *Puss, I miss our languid afternoons.*
> *Your affectionate satyr, LM*

"Kehilla boy," Babs said with a certain swagger, "I'll give you a hundred dollars out of my own purse to find Leila."

"I'll find your sweetheart . . . if she's still alive."

He must have startled Babs. She pulled away from him. "Leila is alive. Now get the hell out of here. . . ."

2.

BEN ARRIVED AT NIGHT COURT IN THE NICK OF TIME. The Essex Market Court, a grim gray monolith connected to the old jailhouse next door, had been a travesty of justice for as long as he could remember. It was where everyone—judges, clerks, politicians' runners, bail bondsmen, cops, doormen, attendants, shoeshine boys, and candy peddlers—flailed the hides of those poor souls who were arraigned while they fattened their own pocketbooks. These unlucky ones who were corralled into court by capricious, lying cops had to walk across that "bridge of sighs," a winding path to the judge with banister rails on both sides, where whatever friends or families they had bunched together in confusion and were fleeced by an array of crooked lawyers and their accomplices.

Ben often had to meander in other parts of the Ghetto, and he missed many arraignments. He couldn't save every soul. These lawyers and bondsmen at the Essex Market Court despised the downtown detective and would have had him bushwhacked long ago if he didn't have Monk Eastman at his side. They were frightened to death of Monk and his canaries and wanted to keep those birds as far away from court as they could. So they tolerated Ben's quixotic appearances and factored them into running a courthouse swindle. Ben Ravage was their one indulgence, the shame these scavengers had to bear.

They groaned as soon as they saw Ben, and signaled to their runners and the judge, a hack who belonged to the pirates of Tammany Hall. The Honorable Clarence Strong had a pronounced nasal drip. He coughed constantly and dredged up phlegm. His pockets were swollen with dollar bills that the runners would bring to him, crawling behind his bench and whispering in his ear. He tried to have Ben flung out of court, but he worried about his own superiors, since the detective did have a license to practice law. So he shut his eyes, gargled his throat, spat into the narrow wooden well near his feet, yawned, and muttered, "Who's next on the docket?"

"Call Silas Lipinsky, janitor, who resides at 317 Attorney Street," shouted the bailiff.

And this man, Lipinsky, who squinted at the blinding oval lights on the judge's bench, was the perfect pigeon. His wife and children, and a coterie of relatives clutching ragged hats and scarves, clawed at him as he trudged across the bridge of sighs. The bondsmen could have made a fortune on Silas if Ben hadn't been around. The lawyers and runners would have whispered about the direct avenue they had to the judge; all these relatives had to do was sell their furniture and come with their shekels to Ned Silver, also known as "Silver Dollars," a bail bondsman who was the ultimate boss of the Lower East Side. His headquarters was right across the street from the jailhouse and the court.

Ned was descended from a family of rabbis and rabbinical scholars. But he'd been a runner at the Essex Market Court when he was a boy, and he rose through the ranks, breaking the heads of those who wouldn't clear a wide-enough path for him. His own titular boss was Big Tim Sullivan, Tammany's chief of the old Tenth Ward, but Tim had contracted Venus' curse and was in and out of insane asylums, so Ned ruled in Big Tim's absence, ruled from his enormous desk behind a medieval screen of twisted wires. It had become his personal coffin. Ned had a family somewhere, but he always trod between those wires and the court. He was a fat man made of solid flesh. No one interfered with Silver Dollars, neither the police nor the magistrates. And when he heard that Ben was in the house, he barreled into court with his ruthless red face. He might have had the best tailor in Manhattan, but nothing he wore ever fit. He looked like a balding child who was breaking out of his clothes. He leaned against the rear wall, surrounded by acolytes, while the judge went through his rigmarole.

"Does the prisoner have counsel?"

And Ben had to shout, "Yes, Your Honor, he does—Benjamin Ravage, attorney-at-law."

One of Silver Dollars' henchmen shouted back, "This man doesn't have the right to be here. He has no legitimate office."

Ben grabbed a derby away from Lipinsky's brother, bowed to the judge, and said, "My office, Your Honor, is in my hat."

Ben wasn't given a moment to learn the particulars of the case, so he had to whisper in Silas' ear while the arresting officer was summoned to a little altar near the bench. He'd met this officer many times, a sergeant from the Madison Street station who liked to pluck pigeons off the street and invent some fairy tale about them. He usually had his way at night court. No one half sane would dare question the word of Sgt. Patrick Simms, who strode the Jewish quarter on behalf of Silver Dollars.

An underling from the district attorney's office should have been at night court, but that underling also belonged to Ned and was seldom there. Ned liked to be the purveyor of his own chaos.

"The little Jew was reeling when I caught up with him," Sgt. Patrick Simms said to the judge in a courtroom full of Gentile and Jewish souls. "He knocked a lady on the head. He turned a wagon over. He must have had mayhem in his bones. The Jew would have committed highway robbery at the butcher shop if I hadn't prevailed, Your Honor."

"Thank you, Sergeant Pat," said the judge, with a mouth full of phlegm. "That's a worthy rendering of the law."

Ben stood near the bridge of sighs with one arm on the rail and shouted above the constant roar of the room. "And what time did this mayhem occur, Sergeant Pat?"

"After dark, Counselor. At a quarter to ten precisely."

"And were there any witnesses?" Ben asked in a much lower voice.

"The wind was howling. It nearly blew the wagons along the length of Attorney Street. There were no reliable witnesses, except a little girl, and her testimony wouldn't hold up in a court of law."

"Understood," said Ben. "But how could my client have considered robbing a butcher shop at a quarter to ten?"

"The sheenies like to keep late hours," said the sergeant with a malicious smile.

Ben had memorized the contours of every street in the Ghetto—the cellar groceries and storefront synagogues, the ritual bathhouses for women, the cafés and lunchrooms, the rag shops, the ground-floor brothels, the moneylenders' stalls, the wholesalers' paradise along Canal. . . . "Sergeant Pat, there are no butcher shops along Attorney Street, neither at one end nor the other."

The sergeant rose up from behind his altar. "Are you calling me a liar, Counselor?"

Ben had been to the Yiddish theater, had seen Clara Karp as Lady Hamlet a dozen times, and knew the power of silence and song. He let Sergeant Pat dangle a little.

"Your Honor, shall the court reconvene outside this hypothetical butcher shop on Attorney Street? We can empty the whole house and have a look."

The judge panicked on his bench, his eyes darting everywhere until they settled on Ned Silver, who turned one thick thumb down, like Nero signaling the death of a gladiator.

"Case dismissed," the judge said, pounding the bench with his gavel and clearing his throat as the lamps shivered on both sides of him. He was perturbed because Ned's thumb was still down. "The whole docket is cleared. . . . Bailiff, empty the court."

The court attendants herded people out of that vile, gaseous courtroom with its cracked windows and broken chandeliers; the janitor and his family couldn't even clasp Ben's hand. They disappeared into the darkness, while Ben remained in court with Ned Silver and his lackeys.

"Counselor," the bondsman said, "sit with me awhile."

Ned's bulk couldn't fit into a chair; he lay on a couch that had come from his headquarters. Ben sat beside him on a camp chair. The bondsman took very loud breaths.

"What are we going to do, Ben? We can't have you interrupt our sessions. And you won't accept any hush money from us. I could put you on retainer for the rest of your life, and include Monk Eastman in the package. I know you're taking gelt from the stablemen. Are you as naïve as Cahan, eh? The reformers may come in one day. But none of them lasts. There's a difference, Ben, between grand ideas and governing a metropolis. Will you cooperate?"

"No."

"Then you should buy life insurance as quickly as you can and leave a couple of heirs. You'll be buried in an unmarked grave on Hart Island, with Eastman in the same hole. That's not a threat. It's a fact of life. No cantor will sing a death song for you; no candles will be lit. You'll be forgotten before you ever touch the ground. I beg you, Benny boy."

"Don't call me that. I'll rip out your tongue, Ned, before your lieutenants have a chance to interfere."

The bondsman's belly rumbled on his couch. "Boys, look how brash the little bastard is. He'd murder us in a minute."

Ben knew how adroit Silver Dollars could be, even from his languid position on the couch. He'd watched Ned pluck out an alderman's eye, hurl a runner across the room and smash his head.

"A thousand pardons, Ben. I wouldn't insult Jacob Schiff's favorite detective. But if you ruffle *my* court another time, it will be the last interruption of your life. Now get the hell out of here."

The fat man seemed a little too sanguine, a little too sleek. Ned had already made up his mind to have Ben killed. The Lower East Side was one great checkerboard to the fat man, with every single square covered in case of an emergency. But as Ben strode out of night court, he wasn't thinking of Silver Dollars' assassins. He remembered now where he had seen Leila Montague. It wasn't inside the morgue at Bellevue. He hadn't seen Leila in the cooler. He seldom went to the city morgue, though he had the right to look at the cadavers as a Kehilla detective. He'd seen Leila, or her double, in Marcus Mendelssohn's own "morgue" at the Alliance. Marcus had a photo or a sketch of half the murder victims in the Jewish quarter over the past twenty-five years. Leila—name and address unknown—had been dredged out of the East River like a broken mermaid a month ago. Her mouth was bruised, but she had the same plucked eyebrows and sunken cheeks. . . .

Ben wandered into the dark. The lampposts had all been smashed. But Ben could see Silver Dollars' bodyguards in the light that came off the tenement windows; there were six or seven roughnecks, former Monk Eastmans who had graduated to Silver Dollars' squad; they were all smiling in that dim light, their cropped heads lunging like gruesome, twisted Halloween masks.

"Counselor, you shouldn't have come here."

Their shadows seemed to multiply as they moved toward Ben. They had no weapons other than the rings they wore and the nails on their boots. They surrounded Ben, their bodies forming some kind of noose that could tighten at will. They meant to toy with Ben before they punched and kicked him to pieces. They'd lost the old chivalry of Monk's lads. These were hooligans for hire.

Then they heard a faint warble in the wind that grew into a familiar tweet. They stopped in their tracks as the canaries they dreaded circled one of the lampposts their runners had dismantled. Monk's derby rose out of the dark. But they couldn't afford to run, not while they worked for Silver Dollars. Their shoulders rocked with their dilemma.

A pair of hands clapped, mimicking the crisp report of a gun. Silver Dollars' corpulent shadow suddenly emerged from the courthouse. He was dancing on his toes like a much lighter man.

"Bravo, Edward, you arrived with your cavalry," he warbled, pointing to the yellow birds.

"Those birds were once *your* cavalry, Mr. Silver. How many skulls did I dent for you?"

"I wouldn't even dare to count. That was a different time, almost the Middle Ages. But I'd never have come into power had it not been for you, Edward. You were the most able lieutenant of all time."

"More like a general," Monk said, "who let you share a little of my command."

He walked right through that knot of hooligans, as if such men were as porous as gunpowder, while the canaries descended from the lamppost and climbed onto Monk Eastman's hat. And the downtown detective walked a pace behind this former general of the Jewish streets.

FOUR

The Master

I.

*I*T MUST HAVE BEEN IN 1904 when Cahan rode out to Ellis
Island with the Master, who wore a bow tie and a wing collar,
and looked like an elegant penguin with striped trousers and a
double chin. The Master had read a story of his in *The Atlantic*
and wanted some company on the Isle of Tears. After all, Cahan
spoke Russian and Yiddish, and would be an excellent guide and
interpreter should the Master need one. But Cahan shivered with
every splash of the ferry. It wasn't the subject matter of the Master's novels that intimidated him. As a former anarchist, he might
have murdered every one of the Master's American heiresses and
impoverished European aristocrats. But he felt like a provincial
with his Ghetto tales, because he had no aristocracy of style. The
Master could bend language to his own will, enter the minds of
his heiresses and gallivanting American girls with the crisp, heartless stroke of a scalpel, while whatever instruments Cahan used
would always be blunt. He was a fine juggler, who could shape and
reinvent *A Bintel Brief,* while the Master's most recent tale, *The
Beast in the Jungle,* had chilled Cahan to the bone.

The Master's hero, John Marcher, had prowled through
life like a man on a tiger hunt, only to discover that he was his

own morbid prey; the creature had sprung without him and left Marcher in an abyss. The companion he might have had, May Bartram, was imprisoned in silver powder from head to toe, silver he could not touch. Cahan was another John Marcher. His jungle was the Lower East Side. He had little passion for his wife uptown. Cahan himself was a cross-eyed creature in some unwritten tale who showered women in silver and made them all untouchable. And that's why the Master had such a hold on him.

Henry James had abandoned the New World. He was a great wanderer, who had devoured the capitals of Europe, one by one, and currently lived near London, in the tiny medieval town of Rye, a modest country gentleman who managed to survive on the income his writing produced. Yet there was a paradox to this tale of the independent novelist. Cahan had heard that it was Edith Wharton who really supported the Master with the royalties from her own novels, and he would have been enfeebled without that extra income. Still, his collars were clean. There was no stubble on the Master's chin. He'd come back to the New World on a long voyage as some forlorn pilgrim blinded by America's material gloss. America had become a series of crude gold mountains, and he didn't like such mountains at all. He arrived in the metropolis after a trip to the cloistered world of Harvard Square; he'd been a law student at Harvard once upon a time, and felt more comfortable in the magnificent red ruins of College Yard than in this "terrible town," with its skyscrapers that were like pins in an over-planted cushion, he said. The Master was in a sour mood.

Cahan expected him to be equally irascible once they landed on Ellis Island. Yet the Master's cheeks began to contort and his lips trembled and turned ashen while both of them stood on the bridge overlooking the Great Hall and watched a new horde of immigrants climb the stairs of the station, with inspectors plucking at their coats, shouting at them in a babel of tongues, with that inevitable question, in Yiddish or English, in Russian or Greek—"Are you an anarchist?"—while doctors poked at them once they arrived on the second floor, and chalked the coat of some pathetic boy with a congenital disease, had him put inside a wire cage. The whole relentless panorama was visible to the Master and Cahan: women standing naked and trembling behind a curtain, boys waiting in a line with their private parts exposed, a maze of metal railings everywhere; men and women were lost in that maze, with nowhere to wander, nowhere to flee, and Cahan heard one almost inaudible sob as the Master stood with a crumpled silk handkerchief in his chubby fist.

"I cannot bear it, Cahan, all this misery. We have to go."

Cahan didn't tell him about the corrupt inspectors, the doctors who never even bothered to wash or change their rubber gloves, the nurses who robbed wholesale and retail. They got off the island, took the elevated cars to Rivington Street, and went into the Pinnacle Café, where the Master wasn't even recognized. This was Cahan country, a world away from College Yard. The editor sat at his own table, under a somber image of Karl Marx, looking like an uncombed maniac rather than a prophet. But Cahan was the prophet here. Yiddish poets, philosophers, playwrights, artists, actors, and actresses, even jugglers and acrobats, swarmed to the Pinnacle, clogged the café to catch a glimpse of Cahan. A mention in the *Forward*, just a few words, could advance or destroy someone's career. He had the power to bite or caress, and not a living soul could determine the mood of his pen. Often he praised and damned in the same sentence. He could have slept with ingenues at the Thalia, if he hadn't been so shy and incorruptible. But on that afternoon, in 1904, he invited several Yiddish poets and novelists to sit with him and Henry James. They were all startled to see how modest the Master was, ingrown, almost walleyed. He talked of Turgenev and Maupassant in a musical tone, as if he were delivering an aria at the table.

He told everyone who would listen that he had learned more about the art of the novel from Turgenev than from any other writer, living or dead. The Yiddish poets were appalled. Not one of them took Turgenev seriously.

"Master, more than Tolstoy and that one with the walrus mustache—Flaubert?"

"Indeed," James insisted between sips of bloodred tea. "Tolstoy and Flaubert are magnificent conjurers who can create—and untangle—a whole forest of words, but Turgenev was a huntsman in a much different forest. Dear Ivan Sergeyevich was never cruel. He killed with a much more gentle stroke. That's the mark of the finest craftsman."

John Marcher, Cahan thought to himself. The Pinnacle was a dreary little café, with clouded mirrors, low ceilings, and a toilet that always leaked. There was hardly enough room to piss in that humpbacked little closet. The Pinnacle couldn't compete with the Royale, where Jacob P. Adler presided with all his followers amid the grandiose lights and gilded mirrors, and aristocratic water closets with perfumed tissue paper. Adler often copulated with his female admirers in one of the Royale's stalls while his current wife and mistress spat at each other near the front window. But the Royale didn't have a poet's corner. Poets came to the Pinnacle, which had once been the premier anarchists' café of the Jewish quarter. The conversation was just as lively, even after the anarchists were kicked out and had to find a less conspicuous café.

The Master wolfed down half a dozen pastries, then wiped the powdered sugar from his lips. He talked about Maupassant's mental decline, about Turgenev's sunlit rooms in Montmartre, about the Parisian literary salon where he first met Flaubert, as he spun stories like a man on a treadle, with his own silken web. And he departed from the café with such gusto, touching every poet's sleeve as he climbed into his hansom cab, that Cahan thought he had a friend for life.

The bombshell would come three years later when James published *The American Scene.* The Master had captured the deep sadness and distress of "terrible little Ellis Island," where immigrants were sifted and searched like human cattle. And James would be haunted by the dislocation he had seen and felt. But his sympathies didn't extend to the Jewish quarter. Cahan had been utterly wrong about the Master's visit to the Pinnacle Café. James felt as if he had landed "at the bottom of some vast sallow aquarium in which innumerable fish, of over-developed proboscis, were to bump together, for ever, amid heaped spoils of the sea."

Tales of Turgenev and bloodred tea had been discarded and forgotten. And the cafés he'd gone to, with or without Cahan, were revealed "beneath their bedizenment, as torture-rooms of the living idiom." James sensed an apocalyptic future, fueled by "the Hebrew conquest of New York," where English itself would disappear from the streets in this babel land.

Ah, how promiscuous the Master had been about the Jewish quarter. There was no Ellis Island for Americans abroad, no doctors with probing fingers, or inspectors with swollen eyes and satanic grins. Henry James' leap from the New World to the Old had come from the same recognizable quilt. He could deal with whatever cultivated savagery he found in the sinking palaces of Venice. But the Jews of the Pale, running from poverty, pogroms, and the conscription of ten-year-old boys, had come to this babel land equipped with nothing but superstition and stale myths to match the chicanery of the New World. Hundreds would commit suicide in the Great Hall and leave the Isle of Tears in a simple pine box. Thousands would go mad within a year. The bewilderment the Master saw in "the flaring streets" was a defiant, rattling song of the Ghetto that said the greenies had to swagger and move about or sink into their own graves. There would be no Hebrew conquest of Manhattan. Ports would shut down. Soon steamships would arrive with ghosts rather than passengers. And the Ghetto would also be riddled with ghosts. It always was. But Henry hadn't bothered to look.

So Cahan scribbled a letter to his god.

> *Master:*
>
> *I was so disheartened by your attack on the Jewish quarter, in your capacity as an incurable man of letters, worried that we might despoil the English language. I, too, am an incurable man of letters, and I see no signs that the living idiom is disappearing on our streets. On the contrary, it is Yiddish that will soon disappear. If you had listened hard, you would have sensed all the rhythm of a dying tongue.*
>
> *I only wish I had taken you to see Clara Karp perform Hamlet—in your accents, sir—better than any uptown actress. She is our jewel, Master. Yes, Polonius speaks in Yiddish. But that is a small matter. I await your next visit to babel land.*
>
> *Your Devoted Reader,*
> *Ab. Cahan*

Of course, the letter was never sent. He could imagine the Master reading it in Rye, and he was immediately ashamed. He dug his scribbles under a pile of manuscripts in his falcon's lair. He thought of composing an editorial about *The American Scene*, or writing a critique of the book. But he could not excoriate the Master. It would have been like an act of self-immolation. He had dared write fiction only after reading Henry James. And if he had turned to feuilletons and *A Bintel Brief* it was because he did not have the power to do his own *Portrait of a Lady*.

2.

CAHAN NEVER SAW THE MASTER AGAIN, though he had some secret desire that James might reappear one afternoon at the Pinnacle, that "torture-room of the living idiom." And so he trod to the café almost every evening, while he dreamt of the Master . . . and Clara Karp. It was Cahan who had made her career, who had spotted her when she first arrived, a refugee from the Ukraine, after the czar had shut down every Yiddish theater in his empire. She was tall, with fleshy arms and a full bosom, as if she had strolled out of a painting by Rubens. Clara had dark hair and dark eyes. She could play a man or a woman with equal agility. She'd started as an acrobat in a troupe of wandering minstrels from Odessa. Men usually played women's roles in the troupe's productions, since no Jewish father would ever allow his daughter to appear with minstrels and clowns. But Clara ran away from home by the time she was fourteen. She was as husky as all the other acrobats, and none of the minstrels dared take advantage of her. She chose her bedmates and discarded them.

Clara was a few years younger than Cahan, a woman well

into her forties, sensual and sultry in spite of her broad shoulders and muscular calves. She'd come to America with her troupe of clowns, passed through Ellis Island—Cahan could imagine the inspectors leering at her while she undressed. But she didn't want to work with jugglers and acrobats on the Bowery. So she started all over again as an extra on the Yiddish stage, traveling from company to company, until she ended up at the Thalia. He watched her flourish in the tiniest parts, and began mentioning Clara in his columns, like little ink blots. He never once visited her backstage, never asked her for tea at the Pinnacle. He was faithful to Clara as he had been to no other actress. Cahan hinted to the Thalia's producers that she play Hamlet. He did more than hint. He lined up backers, invested money from the *Forward*'s accounts, without telling his business manager or his wife.

Clara Karp delivered her lines in Yiddish and English on opening night. Her voice never wavered—it was like a magnificent chanting drum as Hamlet hopped across the Thalia's stage, her calves bulging in black tights, the audience in a kind of constant delirium. Clara never overplayed. She was a soft, cunning murderess. The whole house wept while Hamlet dies. The audience made Clara repeat half her lines. They stopped chewing on peanuts and devouring pies when Clara was onstage. They wouldn't release Clara, wouldn't give her back. And after the ninth or tenth curtain call, they tossed their hats at her like feathery flowers and screamed, "Author, author, author." That growling might have lasted all night. The play's backers pleaded with Cahan to rescue them. He had to climb the boards.

They all recognized the editor of the *Forward*, with his sad grimace and shock of gray hair.

"Ladies and gentlemen, this theater piece is in the public

domain. It was written long ago by an obscure actor named Will. But that doesn't matter. Clara Karp is the real authoress of *Hamlet*. . . ."

Still, he wouldn't visit her backstage. She had her own dressing room now right under the boards. He would read about her lovers in uptown gossip columns, rage with jealousy, and do nothing. And more often than not he would bump into Clara at the Pinnacle, where she sat with her toadies at the next table. She did nothing more volatile than offer to buy him a piece of sponge cake and a glass of bloodred tea. He would nod his head in acknowledgment. "Good evening, Madame Clara."

No one dared call her "Miss." She was a mature "maiden" who romped around as Hamlet or Don Quixote or Medea night after night; Clara Karp was much too regal for the Thalia's usual repertoire of tales about devoted daughters and spurned Ghetto brides. Her face seemed like a burning mask in the Pinnacle's mediocre light. And Cahan sat like an amputee while he ached for the actress. He was John Marcher, after all. And she was his May Bartram, mysterious, constant, and aloof. He couldn't get the Master out of his blood after all these years. He composed other letters to Rye, full of vitriol and slavish respect, and these letters were all unsent. The Master had visited Manhattan at least once in the last nine years. Cahan could have found him at some jolly corner, such as the Century Association or the Salmagundi Club. But he never sought out Henry James. He clung to his territories, basked in the bits of glory he had at the café.

There was an odd subterranean code between the actress and Cahan, as if they were conspirators of some sort. She never sat with her lovers, never kissed a man while at the café. Clara was chaste in his presence, as if she belonged to the editor who had woven her career with a basket of words. And while he imagined her kicking off her boots at some Bowery hotel, his spectacles on the nightstand, as he sank into her flesh, his nose buried in her bosoms, Clara winked at him like a Jewish nun. She pretended to flirt.

"Your lavish praise frightens all the other critics, Monsieur Cahan, but they're the ones who come to my dressing room at the Thalia and wait in line to kiss my hand, and you, you're the ghost who's never there."

"That's my weakness, madame," he said, his heart contracting like some wild gourd. "I would have to stop writing about you if I ever kissed your hand. It might compromise whatever judgment I have left."

She smiled at him, her chest heaving under a silk blouse. "But I'm a gambler. You know that. You've written about my folly. *Clara Karp always takes risks.* Well, I'll risk your silence, monsieur, even your wrath."

She laughed out loud, and her whole body quivered.

Cahan didn't have the Master's lashing rhythms or ability to probe like a conjurer with a sharp stick. But he did understand the art of Clara Karp. She had refused the ordinary dross of Yiddish theater, the *shund* of acrobats and gaping clowns. Clara was merciless with an audience. The lightning of her moves, the terrifyingly sharp gestures and screams—the Yiddish Hamlet shouted her soliloquies into the rafters—shook the tired bones of men and women who'd come to the Thalia to laugh and sleep a little. Clara always left the audience in a state of unrest.

Flo Ziegfeld had wanted to meet the downtown diva and tempt her to join the *Follies*. She wouldn't audition for him at the Jardin de Paris, wouldn't ride uptown, even in his chauffeured car; so he came to the Bowery two years ago, his chauffeur wearing goggles, and the impresario arriving in a sable coat, with a scowling band of critics and acrobats. He watched one of her leaps, stared at her sultry form in Hamlet's black tights, her magnificent shoulders marking a perfect line, and offered her a contract with the *Follies* for its 1911 run. "Madame Clara," he said, "the Bowery is wonderful, but you aren't blind. You're an artiste. You can tell the difference between a Ziegfeld girl and a downtown diva."

She quit her dressing room at the Thalia and went uptown with her boxes of ribbons, all her boots, and the daggers she wore onstage. Cahan mourned her in his columns, wrote a mock obituary: "Our theater has suffered one more dead soul." He vowed never to write about the Yiddish Hamlet again. But his curiosity overwhelmed him. He had to see her perform with all the fanfare of the *Follies*. So he took the subway to Forty-second Street, stole into the Olympia Theatre like a common thief, walked upstairs to the Jardin de Paris, stood behind a curtain of Ziegfeld's rented roof garden with its silvery wisps of air from an immense barreled skylight, and watched a constant array of jugglers, dancers, singers, comedians, and clowns, plus a squadron of tall, ethereal girls who drifted across the stage in floppy hats, their nipples rising under their gossamer gowns.

Cahan wasn't aroused at all. He felt a fury in him as Clara pranced onto the boards; she was much more Byzantine than Ziegfeld's uptown goddesses in gossamer gowns. She wore her usual black tights and a sheer fabric over her midriff that accented every fold of flesh; she recited her soliloquies in Yiddish as the jugglers juggled behind her and the clowns did barrel rolls and stood on their heads. Her dark eyes didn't focus, with all the bedlam around her; she could have been a giant at some rooftop circus with hanging gardens and spangled pools of light.

He left the Jardin de Paris while Clara ranted in a language that must have been like that "torture-room" of tongues Henry James had heard in the babel land of the Lower East Side. Cahan couldn't comprehend a syllable of what she said.

He returned to the *Forward*, wrote a critique of the *Follies*, praising the relentless, madcap energy of its human décor. "Flo Ziegfeld doesn't rely on props. The Ziegfeld girl stitches the action together like a marvelous, statuesque seamstress with every sort of juggler in her wake. One of those jugglers disappointed this writer. She doesn't belong in a hanging garden. She's not uptown material, even if she doesn't know it. Hamlet is also a juggler, a creature of clowns. But *our* Hamlet cannot perform in a perpetual fugue state while everyone around her twists and turns with the brutal energy of a cannonball. Still, we wish her well with her new family and friends."

Clara was back on the Bowery by the end of the week, without the patina of a Ziegfeld girl. She was Medea again, where her crazed eye meant something, where her medley of Yiddish and English clung to the audience's skin. But she never forgave Cahan for that slight. And that's why she was often waspish with him at the café, even after two years, sitting like a sultry goddess in her Russian boots, laughing and smoldering at the same time, while impresarios and their mistresses begged Clara for her autograph.

"Go away," she muttered, "before I spill tea on your head." Cahan could feel the demon in her, daggers in her dark eyes.

"Madame Clara," he said from his table, "I do not like to bring up old wounds, but I was wrong to criticize your career at the *Follies*. It was selfish of me. I'm a vain, heartless man, who missed you every moment. And in your absence, the Thalia was another haunted house."

"Illustrious editor," she said, intoning as if she were onstage, "I happen to like haunted houses. And shame on you, monsieur. I could have invited you to meet Flo if you wanted to travel that far uptown. Critics are supposed to announce themselves at the box office, not sneak around in the back rows. I might have enunciated better if I had known you were there."

Cahan was blushing now; he took great delight watching the diva slump in her chair, as if he could suck at her like some cannibal, swallow her fingers one by one. He had all the lurid romance of a schoolboy.

Slap me, step on me with your boots, he cried to himself. *I don't care.* Would she ever offer him a glass of bloodred tea again? But she was tied to Cahan, or she wouldn't have come to the Pinnacle and sat one table away. She grew jovial with all her admirers, sang Russian songs. She must have had the grip of a stevedore in bed. Cahan would have gladly perished in her arms. Kaput!

She drank slivovitz that the café owner offered up from a private bottle kept behind the counter. Not even Cahan could drink from Clara's bottle. She slurped and slurped, her face a merry mask, until her eyes suddenly popped out of the holes in that mask, and the diva nearly spilled the brandy in her shot glass. Cahan had never seen her tremble, as if Hamlet had fallen deep inside his own soliloquies.

He turned around. Benjamin Ravage had entered the café with all his startling blondness. Ben strode across the Pinnacle's pocked floor, his blue eyes like pinpricks as he sat down next to Cahan.

"Baron, I need your help."

Cahan wasn't listening. He was the last one at the Pinnacle to learn that *his* Clara adored the downtown detective. Silent now, she swatted at all her admirers, who fled from the table. Clara sat alone, shivering so hard that the owner had to put a shawl around her great sweeping shoulders.

"Ben," she cooed in front of the café, with the same recklessness she had on the boards, "are you still upset with your sweetie pie?"

The detective jumped up, tightened the shawl around her throat, as if he were strangling and caressing Clara at the same time, and whispered in her ear. She rose from the table, took one last slurp of slivovitz, and walked out of the Pinnacle like a somnambulist. It wasn't the exit of any artiste.

Cahan had never been jealous of Ben before, not of his youth, nor his blinding blond looks, and that ability to prowl. Ben was the beast in the jungle that had ripped Cahan to ribbons in his wild dreams. Yet he still loved the boy, even with his jealous rage. He wouldn't mention Clara.

"What's wrong?" he asked in his gloom.

"Baron, when you worked at *The Sun* as a crime reporter, was there an epidemic of missing girls in the Jewish quarter?"

"That was years and years ago," Cahan said, recalling the reporters' shack on Mulberry Street, near the old police headquarters. It was helter-skelter, harum-scarum, with reporters collecting whatever they could on the fly.

"A missing girl, Leila Montague, from Smith College, was dredged out of the East River with bruise marks all over her body. And I'm wondering if there's some pattern."

"You mean if the Ghetto once had its own Jack the Ripper or Jekyll and Hyde?"

"Exactly," Ben said. "Our Mr. Hyde."

Cahan had to summon up whatever ancient notes he still had

in his skull, all the scatterings of a crime reporter who was fed whatever the police wanted to feed him.

"Not a pattern, exactly. Several streetwalkers, as I recall. They might have been suicides. And the marks on their bodies could have come from the trawler and the river itself."

"But there must have been a coroner's report," Ben insisted.

"The coroners were all alcoholics in those days, sipping on their own formaldehyde." Then Cahan shivered as he summoned up one particular note. "Ah, we had a corpse, not from Allen Street. A young bride was dragged out of the river, her face ripped beyond recognition. But the coroner was able to identify certain moles. And there was actually a Dr. Jekyll involved—a Grand Street abortionist who had bungled the job. We called him 'Hyde.' He was arrested with the husband. And she was the last girl found in the river on my watch. . . ."

The boy wouldn't let go. "And while you were on the *Forward*, no missing daughters in *A Bintel Brief*?"

"They were always found, Benjamin, sooner or later."

Cahan was a dreamer who delved into his own folly and tore at the very wound he had desperately tried to heal. "Have you been visiting Clara?"

The boy was silent for a moment, his blue eyes clutching at Cahan like some mysterious trawler.

"I'm one of her ardent admirers," he finally said.

Cahan pictured the two of them in her private closet at the Thalia, coupling like a pair of savages, her powerful calves crushing the wind out of Ben. The Baron of East Broadway grew bitter, and wished he had left Ben to flounder in the printing shop at the Hawthorne School. The boy was also Anya's protégé; Anya had groomed him for Harvard, had fed him buckwheat groats, sent him through the minefields of literature. Yet he couldn't disown the boy. Ben was as near a son as he'd ever have.

He had to take his mind off Clara. "Have you read Henry James?"

Ben blinked at him and started to laugh. "I have a little culture, Baron, even if I work for the Kehilla. . . . I had lunch with Henry several years ago, at the Salmagundi Club."

"I don't understand. How did you meet Henry James?"

"His brother first introduced us," Benjamin said. "Did you forget? I went to Harvard on your account. I studied with Santayana and William James. William wanted me to stay on, become a tutor in philosophy. But I'd been in enough asylums. I was sick of College Yard."

Cahan was stupefied. The boy had kept Henry James a secret all these years.

"How did the Master get in touch? You're like the wind. You don't seem to have an address. I can never find you without some abracadabra."

The Master had written Ben at the Educational Alliance, in care of the Kehilla, and invited him to lunch. Salmagundi was an artists' club, but James had the privilege of dining there, as America's most prominent "transatlantic exile."

Ben wasn't sure about the menu, but he could recollect champagne and lobster cakes in the club's cramped dining room a little north of the Ghetto.

"Does the Master still fear that some Hebrew horde will overtake Manhattan?"

"Baron, I chastised him about that chapter in his book, asked him to measure my own proboscis. He was beyond mortification."

"And what did he do?"

The Master had stood up like a bashful boy, bent over, kissed the downtown detective on the ear, and returned to his seat.

"In front of the Salmagundi Club?" Cahan muttered. "That's ridiculous."

"It was his way of apologizing."

They talked of Venice, where Ben had never been; they talked of College Yard and the burnt red colors of Cambridge; they talked of the Master's peripatetic childhood, and of Ben's travels from orphanage to orphanage; then the Master covered his steel gray eyes with both hands and peered through the peepholes his fingers had made.

"Dear boy, did you ever have to kill a man?"

"Yes."

The Master smiled. "I thought so. Violence seems to hover over you like a willful angel. I admire that. It's a quality I lack." He seemed a bit disheveled to Ben, like someone who had wandered into the Salmagundi Club off the street. He'd fallen into a deep depression. The Master had stopped writing novels. He suffered from palpitations and some kind of distress of the bowels. He reminded Ben of a senescent child, with his fat hands and a bald pate. His steel gray eyes wandered from object to object, from the chandeliers to the crystal decanter and the paintings on the walls, as if he were caught in his own panic. Ben had never seen a man so emptied, so distraught; he could have had a snake in his bowels that was eating him alive. He talked of other projects, of biographies he meant to write, of travel books, and Ben realized that all the demonic music had gone out of him. Ben was sitting with a husk: Henry James.

"I dare not believe it," Cahan said to the boy.

"Baron, it's true. He was stumbling when I left him at the door of his hotel."

Cahan was aggrieved; he forgave the Master his remarks about the Israelites of Manhattan, and shuddered over his diminished state. Shoddy, Ben had told him, with a lose thread here and there, as if the Master's own fictional mirrors had abandoned him. And perhaps that's what the Master had meant in his portrait of John Marcher—Marcher might have been Henry James' conscious or unconscious double, and the beast that finally leapt was the waning of his own powers.

"And what if I need you, Ben? Where can I find you?"

"With the wind," Ben told him, reached across the table, gulped down Clara Karp's last drop of slivovitz, and left the Pinnacle with that blond aura of his. The Master had guessed Ben's little secret. An angel of death. How many men had his protégé killed? Was he Mr. Hyde looking for another, earlier Hyde? Would he march from the café to Clara's boudoir under the boards? Cahan had to blot out the image of Ben and Clara behind some intimate screen at the Thalia, or he would collapse at the table. Perhaps he, too, had become a husk. To calm himself, he began composing a letter to Henry James. The entire café could hear each scratch of his pencil stub on the tablecloth, like the claws of a relentlessly tired tiger.

FIVE

Montefiore

I.

THE DOWNTOWN DETECTIVE had to sail across the wind, melt into the darkness like a wax doll, or never make it across Rivington Street alive. He ducked as far as he could from the lights of the café. It was like an elaborate game of hide-and-seek, a game with one goal—to spill Ben's blood. He couldn't have a permanent residence, any residence at all. Wherever he went, Ned Silver's hirelings would wait for him with hammers, knives, and claws.

These jackals crept out of every corner, and Ben had to lurch from lamppost to lamppost, warbling like a canary, to hurl these jackals off his scent, make them pause and wonder if Monk Eastman was half a step behind them. That's how Ben had survived. He used all his cunning and all his wits when he was a lone bird at some orphanage where guards and other boys brutalized him and demanded sexual favors. He endured beating after beating. The scars near his eyes had come from one sadistic guard, who dug at Ben with a sharpened stick and nearly blinded him. The other orphans laughed and dubbed Ben their little "choirboy." He found rat poison in a gardener's trough at the Hebrew asylum, hoarded it like a pharmacist, and meant to sprinkle the guard's soup and watch him run howling into the infirmary. But he couldn't use the rat poison. He kept it under his pillow and dodged the blows. He feigned a mad fit, pretended to bite a boy's ear off, and now they feared him. Even the guards left Crazy Ben alone. He used his isolation as a shield.

He did the same with Silver's men, never giving them a chance to track his moves. He sank into one of the cellars on Rivington, raced through the yards where privies had once stood like slanted sentinels and were now toolsheds and carpenters' shacks, and arrived at the rear door of a millinery shop on Stanton Street; Ben sprang the lock with an old key and entered one of his roosts— it was the home and headquarters of Sarah "Marm" Mandel, an ancient Allen Street pawnbroker and procuress who had outwitted local hoodlums and cadets and was now one of the richest landladies on the Lower East Side. Sarah was no saint. She had properties all along Allen Street, and when her fellow landlords, fierce in their desire to get rid of Sarah, tried to burn her out of existence, Ben had Monk toss his canaries into the sky and cool their ardor. The landlords capitulated after a ten-minute talk with Ben and promised never to interfere with Sarah Mandel.

So she looked after Ben, let him keep some clothes in a closet at her shop and in apartments that tenants had abandoned and she hadn't bothered to rerent. She was in her seventies and still had dozens of suitors—poets, dentists, bankers—but she preferred her solitude. A husband would only have been like another cadet.

She hadn't lost her coquetry, even with her bald spots and gnarled hands. She was always dressed for a rendezvous, with painted eyes and pearls around her neck. "Have you come to romance me, Benjamin?"

"Not today, Marm. I'm a little too tired."

"That's a relief," she said, and now Ben didn't have to play her lovesick suitor. "I wish I had been kinder to your mother. She was so blond and so beautiful. But when I sold the property, I couldn't protect her. . . ."

"Marm, you were the best landlord we ever had. You never gouged us, and you left her groceries."

The skin seemed to float right off the stark leather mask of Sarah's face. "How could you recollect all that? You were a *pisher* in short pants."

"Marm, I need other recollections right now."

"Ah," she muttered, pretending to be annoyed. "You're wearing your Kehilla hat."

The downtown detective never wore a hat, even when he was escorting some uptown lady to the opera, or had to attend a masked ball in Satan's Circus.

"I'm looking for a certain character, Marm, a son of a bitch who may have been rough with the girls on the street."

"I didn't cater to any rough customers," she said, growing a little surly with Ben.

"Not you, Marm, never you. But there must have been *accidents* while you were there."

"Girls were always cut and beaten. You can't run a place without a casualty list," she said, running a crooked finger along her lip. "And we made sure these nudniks never came back. Sometimes we knocked the sand out of their pants. I had all the hired muscle I could ever want in those days."

"You were the queen of Jewtown," he said.

"Don't flatter me, Benjamin. . . . When we did have a repeater, I branded him. We tattooed his forehead with a red star, and he was outlawed everywhere in Manhattan, even in the black-and-tan dives. But there was an exception, someone we couldn't touch."

Hyde, Ben muttered to himself, *Mr. Hyde*. And Marm told him about the man in a tall hat and a coachman's cape who rampaged through Allen Street with police protection. There was always a copper downstairs wherever he went. He ruined several girls, split their faces, and then he would return with flowers and boxes of candy. He would rock a damaged girl in his arms, sit with her for hours, read to her some tale—a touch of Tolstoy. No one could determine his moods or his flights of fancy. Sarah was frightened of him and his whimsical nature. The hooligans she had on her payroll kept out of sight when Mr. Hyde was around.

"What did he look like, Marm?"

She turned away from Ben. "He had long white hair . . ."

And fire scars astride his cheek.

"He belongs to your fraternity of landlords, doesn't he, Marm? He owns half of Canal Street. And I'm his accidental progeny, the bastard he left behind. Why did you keep this a secret from me for so long?"

"To protect your life," she spat at him, like a warm-blooded viper.

"But I'm the detective, and he's the hardware man—"

"Who burns down buildings and has his own army of thugs, miles from his Fifth Avenue mansion. He's still untouchable, and he always was." And she started to cry, this procuress who had branded more than one wicked client. "My poor Ben. You won't last very long. The closer you get to Lionel, the less chance you have to survive."

"I don't care," Ben told her. "Was there a cover-up, Marm? Did he ever kill a girl? The coppers could have carted her away, tossed her in the river, and said good-bye."

"Benjamin," she said, "your father was never out of control.

It was like a melody—no, a magic faucet he could turn on and off, on and off. He would inflict pain, and then apply a balm. Some of the girls could retire on his gifts. But he wasn't in the homicide business, not on Allen Street."

The detective stripped off his clothes in front of Sarah, stepped into the bathtub she had at the back of her shop. Sarah was still a fence. The hats and lace in her window were just a front. She had no stock inside the store, nothing but piles of empty hatboxes. He didn't linger in the tub. He changed his underwear while she pretended to caress the little scars all over his body—old knife wounds from the different asylums.

"Such a beautiful boy," she said. "It's a shame. I'll have to hire someone to sing Kaddish for you."

"Marm, I'd rather you did all the singing. That could really rouse the dead."

He plucked a blue serge suit from the closet, one that a Hungarian tailor had cut and sewn for him on Hester Street. He wouldn't wear the vest. He had a Sulka shirt and tie that Monk Eastman had pilfered from a storeroom near the docks. His white buckskin oxfords came from another storeroom. He looked like downtown royalty after he combed his hair. Sarah handed him a pistol she kept under her skirts.

"Benjamin, you'll need it more than I do if you're going after that maniac."

"And give the coppers an excuse to put me away? Besides, I'm an officer of the courts. I've sworn to uphold the law."

"Yes, darling, in a stolen shirt and shoes," she said with a pout. "And I hear that Silver Dollars already has a price on your head."

He kissed her on the mouth. "I'll manage, Marm. Not to worry."

And he walked out the front door of the shop with its wealth of hats in the window. Marm Mandel kept a tidy façade. She'd survived because she was never greedy and understood the chaotic, irrational laws of local politics, where Mr. Hyde had beaten up girl after girl and could still prosper as the hardware king of Canal. Ben didn't have the same resilience or powerful connections. He could only slip through the cracks.

2.

MARCUS MENDELSSOHN, HIS OWN BOSS AT THE KEHILLA, was waiting for him outside Marm's in a chauffeur's puttees and Jacob Schiff's Pierce-Arrow, with its sleek fuselage, ruby red frame, and silver arrow over the grille. All of Ben's wanderings had been futile. The Kehilla simply sidestepped Silver's jackals and found him in a blink.

"The Old Man wants to see you," Marcus said. "Master Jacob is doing his charity work. He's expecting us up at Montefiore."

Jacob Schiff could have built the Montefiore Home for Chronic Invalids with his fat little fingers. He'd raised all the money for that mansion with its two jutting wings that overlooked the Hudson. He wasn't like the other Allrightniks. He'd come from a line of rabbinical scholars. This lord of the Jewish Four Hundred had created a kind of bridge between uptown and downtown. He was the only one of the uptown aristocrats respected on the Lower East Side, and would have been welcomed by all the truculent poets at the Pinnacle. Even the Baron of East Broadway tolerated him at times. Schiff could have made a fortune bankrolling the czar during the Russo-Japanese War of 1904–1905, but he wouldn't support an empire that tolerated and endorsed pogroms. Instead, he bankrolled the Japanese, and made an even bigger fortune. . . .

Ben had never been to the hills of Hamilton Heights at West 138th Street. The mansion had several gables and a little forest of roofs. Chimney pots stared down at him like monumental dwarfs. He'd arrived with Marcus around midnight, but the mansion wasn't entombed in darkness; the lights in every window were still on, reminding Ben of some celestial pattern, as if he were preparing to enter God's own house of blazing stars. Perhaps he had it all wrong, and the devil lived behind those lights.

There were four barren trees in front of the home, with branches that twisted in every shape and direction. Marcus left the Pierce-Arrow under one of the trees and they entered the stone labyrinth that Master Jacob had reserved for Jewish invalids of the Lower East Side. The German Jews had some private palace in the Adirondacks for their own enfeebled grandmothers and grandfathers. None of them would end up in a charity ward. Still, Ben was startled by the opulence of Montefiore. It didn't smell of charity, at least not in the vestibule, with its marble pillars and chandeliers. Marcus accompanied Ben into the central ward, wearing a holster and a Colt .45 strapped to his vest; the chief investigator was the only one at the Bureau of Social Morals who had a license to carry a firearm, but Ben wondered why he would need a gun at a home for chronic invalids. Was Schiff in any danger inside the primitive landscape of Hamilton Heights?

The central ward didn't have the same majesty as the vestibule. The cots resembled cribs—or prison carts—with their high metal rails. The flatulence and odor of carbolic acid were unbearable. Ben had to lean against the wall for a moment. He couldn't fathom what was wrong with half the invalids in the male ward;

he discovered children and young men as well as grandfathers, who wore their homburgs in bed; their faces seemed dull and feckless until a company of doctors arrived with Jacob Schiff.

Suddenly, they were all alert as Schiff walked along the row of cribs and clutched each invalid's hand. Ben was surprised how well the Old Man bantered in Yiddish; he could have been a Russian Jew. His Yiddish didn't have an uptown flavor—it was as fluid and melodious as the constant carping at the Pinnacle Café.

"How are you, Mendel?" he asked a solemn patriarch in a skullcap.

"Constipated," said the patriarch.

"Did you forget your prunes? I can't hound you every single day. And I'm much too old to spank you, Mendele. . . ."

He knew the names of everyone in that crooked line of cribs. He wasn't the master of his tribe at Montefiore. He was a confidant, an ally, a friend. He remembered birthdays and bar mitzvahs and the anniversary of a loved one's death. He spent most of his time with the young boys, who were crippled for life or ravaged by some incurable disease. He would stroke their hands, or sing them a lullaby his grandmother had made him memorize in Yiddish. He wasn't like those Bavarian banker princes. He'd come to this country in steerage, right after the Civil War. He'd suffered that endless rocking in the bowels of a steamer, even though he'd had hard cash in his pocket, a sponsor, and a potent English vocabulary.

"Uncle Jacob," said one boy with black circles around his eyes, "my father calls you a rotten capitalist and swears you only come here to do penance for your sins."

Jacob plucked his beard. "Henry, he could be right. But I still enjoy your company."

The boy was in great turmoil. "I cannot accept your gifts any longer. No more halvah from Essex Street."

"Ah," said Jacob, "that saddens me. . . . It was one of my greatest treasures—to watch you eat and share a few crumbs."

He was like a magnificent tumbler as he passed from crib to crib. He wouldn't acknowledge the downtown detective until he came to the end of the line.

"Ravage, come with me. I'm starving. I haven't had a bite."

Marcus led the way to an anteroom behind the ward, where a simple meal was set on a card table—blue cheese and black bread, with half-sour pickles, a cucumber salad, and a decanter of red wine. The china, cutlery, damask napkins, and crystal came from Jacob's Fifth Avenue mansion. The three men sat on folding chairs.

"To your health," the Old Man said—he was sixty-six, and seemed as vigorous as Ben, who had to navigate with a fork that weighed two pounds. "A Kehilla detective shouldn't be poking around in Leila Montague's affairs. She has nothing to do with crime in the Ghetto."

A rage began to loom inside Ben. *Midnight suppers in a closet, with silverware as heavy as Indian clubs.* "Are you trying to muzzle me, sir? I can always quit the Kehilla."

"Eat your salad and listen. Marcus, tell him about that cutie from Smith."

The chief investigator called her an "adventuress" who came from a family of con artists. That was their particular ticket, he said. The family preyed on the daughters of millionaires.

"That's hard to swallow," Ben said. "They send their own predator to a women's college in Northampton, have her seduce Meyer Bristol's little girl, and then what? It sounds like Sodom and Gomorrah."

"Ravage," said the Old Man, "it was much worse. Her real name wasn't Leila—it was Lily Pringle, and Lily had the nerve to blackmail us. Marcus, show this young man the letters *and* the pictures."

The chief investigator put down his knife and fork and removed a crumpled envelope from his pocket; he had a sliver of blue cheese on his lip.

"Wipe your mouth, for God's sake," the Old Man said. "We're at Montefiore, not a brothel. Show a little respect."

The Old Man reached across the card table and swiped at the sliver of cheese with his napkin while Ben looked at picture postcards of Babette and Leila with their long, sleek bodies entwined; they weren't posing for a pornographer—they were in the throes of some irreverent and joyful romp. He wouldn't read the letters.

"What happened to Leila? How did she end up in the East River with all the other mermaids?"

Jacob ripped a piece of black bread like some muzhik and stuffed it into his mouth. "Marcus, leave us for a moment. I have to educate this young man. He considers himself an expert on the Lower East Side."

"But Master Jacob," Marcus whined. "I ought to be here. Leila's fate concerns me."

Jacob tossed his napkin at the chief investigator. "Go!"

Marcus left the anteroom with a few morsels on his plate. And Jacob started to choreograph Leila Montague's death. Lily/Leila wouldn't leave Babs alone even after the Old Man paid her a handsome sum. It was impossible to buy her off. She had blackmail in her blood. So Marcus kidnapped her with the help of the Kehilla—and the cops.

"I thought they would keep her at some cottage in Poughkeepsie. But Marcus had a brainstorm. He dragged her to Montefiore without my permission, put her in the attic. And the little fool tried to escape. She fell five flights. Marcus panicked. He's a good boy, devoted to me, but sometimes he's also a dolt. He wrapped her in a hospital blanket and had her dropped into the river."

Ben peered at the Old Man across the narrow table. "Sir, why are you telling me all this?"

"So we can establish some rapport and you'll know in the future that Jacob Schiff doesn't lie."

"But Marcus might have pushed her out the attic window."

"He's not that big a dumbbell," the Old Man said. "He wouldn't have used Montefiore as the scene for such mischief. No, it was an unfortunate accident. I can't have that dead girl bring scandal to our doorstep. And how would you profit from it?"

"I promised Meyer Bristol's daughter that I would find her missing sweetheart."

"*Sweetheart*," Jacob said with a sour smile. "I'd call her a conniving whore who dug into Babs' intestines and wouldn't let go. Marcus can corroborate everything. I told Babs the truth about Lily Pringle, how she came up with a counterfeit high school diploma, entered Smith under false pretenses, with a manufactured name."

Ben's temples pounded with raw, murderous blood. "Master Jacob, did you also investigate Mr. Hyde?"

All the warmth went out of the Old Man's blue eyes. He could have been inside an icebox, not a home for chronic invalids with the allure of a country estate. "Please, Ravage, no riddles. Not after midnight."

"My loving, devoted father, Lionel Ravage, was as much of a flimflam artist as the late Leila Montague. He married my mother while he still had a wife. He produced a rabbi, who must have been another flimflammer, and then the two of them floated somewhere into infinity. How many other abandoned brides were there, Master Jacob, and little blond bastards who were neatly tucked away in some asylum?"

The Old Man fumbled with his fork. "I didn't even know you were alive until . . ."

"You rescued me from oblivion."

He'd lived in a ramshackle rooming house on Brattle Street while he was a law student. Cambridge felt like one more land of exile, with its high red walls and crooked lanes. He missed the Lower East Side, where he had crept from address to address with his mother, from landlord to landlord. He could recall every rotting gate, every cellar, every single stoop of Attorney Street. He'd become friends with a retarded boy who lived in the same rooming house and loved to sweep the stones of Brattle Street with an ancient broom. But three members of the varsity crew, emboldened by the worth of their crimson sweaters, swiped the boy's broom and kept taunting him. Ben could hear the boy wail from his own closet of a room. He ran into the street and pounced on the crew members like a maddened wolf, ripping the red wool off their backs. They filed a complaint. He was summoned before a disciplinary board. He would have been expelled for striking three Harvard upperclassmen, but Ben's savior, the Baron of East Broadway, swallowed his pride, went uptown to Jacob Schiff, and begged him to intervene. Schiff scribbled a note to Harvard's president, Charles Eliot, who was his hiking companion and longtime confidant, and the charges were dropped.

Ben recapitulated the entire tale, and the Old Man smiled. "That wasn't my first note to President Eliot about you. It was my third. Do you think you could have crept into Harvard from the Hawthorne School, even with a recommendation from Cahan?"

Ben was even more bewildered by Harvard's mandarin ways. "But I took an entrance exam. I sat with professors, talked of Plato."

"Plato didn't get you into Harvard. That exam was like dressing windows at Lord & Taylor. I concocted it . . . after I saw your name in Cahan's letter to Harvard. And I realized you were one of ours."

"So I was your good deed for the day."

Jacob sat with his little empire of cucumber salad and cutlery on a card table. "You're the detective, and not even you could locate all of Lionel's brides."

"I'm not talking about his brides, Master Jacob. I'm talking about the women he assaulted on Allen Street. And no one arrested our Mr. Hyde. Lionel doesn't even have a yellow sheet."

"Yellow sheet," the Old Man muttered. "Cahan was a crime reporter, and you were a delinquent from the age of six or seven, and both of you believe in yellow sheets."

And Master Jacob told him about his thirty-year encounter with the Manhattan police. Arrest records could appear and disappear with the will of any precinct captain. Headquarters didn't have a clue what was happening within the arcane world of a station house. Nothing was centralized; nothing came from the top. The chief of detectives sat in his office at headquarters and went through his rogue's gallery, looking for some grand scheme of crime. The master jewel thieves and bank robbers he sought were either crippled with arthritis or foraging through another town where no police chief could find them. The local precinct captain on Madison Street and his little band of detectives were rulers of the roost and they milked the Lower East Side with the help of corrupt magistrates, bondsmen like Ned Silver, and Tammany Hall.

The current precinct captain, Kittleberger, was as rotten as the last. He could have become police commissioner, but he said it would have pauperized him. Kittleberger was the one who created the brilliant strategy of the "dead line." He'd been a detective on the bunko squad. And he declared every area just north, south, east, and west of the Ghetto off-limits to pickpockets and bunko artists; they'd be arrested on sight if they ever crossed over this line. The Lower East Side became a kind of Byzantium for pickpockets, and Kittleberger collected tribute from them all.

This was the Manhattan that Jacob Schiff inherited when he arrived in the New World. He found the Ghetto crawling with every sort of vermin, pickpockets and robber bands. Twice his own pockets were picked. A gang crushed his straw hat on Hester Street. And the minute he acquired some wealth, he established his own small squad of "clerks," a decade before the other Jewish aristocrats ever dreamt of a Manhattan Kehilla. He had to make peace with Captain Kittleberger, or his clerks couldn't have roamed the Jewish quarter, settling whatever scores they had to settle.

"And what about Hyde?" Ben asked this chronicler of the Ghetto.

And still the Old Man resisted; he'd blanked out the details of Lionel's rampage as he sat in his little chair. "Lionel Ravage clubbed no one to death. He was a bit wild on Allen Street years and years ago."

"Ah, but it seems he's back in business, *still* marking up girls.

He was spotted with that silver cane of his. I guess old habits die hard."

"You have no proof of this," said Jacob Schiff. "It could be some madman imitating his moves. Allen Street is full of mayhem."

"Then and now," Ben said. "Then and now. . . . And if Lionel had attacked uptown girls, daughters of the Jewish Four Hundred, would you feel the same way, Master Jacob? I've read about your daily habits. You march from your mansion to lower Fifth Avenue, and then you have your chauffeur drive you right across the Ghetto and down to Wall Street. Are you worried we would contaminate you with our dirt?"

"How dare you!" the Old Man said. "I wandered the Ghetto before you were born. And you owe me your life, young man. I got you into Harvard and kept you there."

Ben wondered if he might have been better off as a printer's devil, without Santayana and Henry James boiling inside his head. He was like a zebra in camel land, belonging somewhere between Harvard and hell. The bullies and guards at his first asylum had made him walk around with rouge on his face, clucked at him, "Benjam*ina*, Benjam*ina*," until he couldn't bear to look in a mirror. Even now he was frightened of his own reflection.

"Master Jacob, you still haven't answered me. Couldn't you have kept Lionel from harming those poor girls?"

A crimson patch appeared on Jacob's cheek. "You shouldn't talk to me in that tone. I could have you crushed in a minute."

Ben smiled. He had the patriarch in the palm of his hand, this builder of castles for impoverished Jews, who had re-created paradise in the northlands of Hamilton Heights.

"And you, Master Jacob, shouldn't talk so cavalierly about violence when I'm the killer at this table."

Ben made the Old Man sit while he talked about the Ludlow Street annex of the Hebrew orphan asylum and the guard who had forced him to wear rouge and parade in front of the other boys. Ben plotted his revenge while he wore the rouge. He waited ten years. The guard was still on Ludlow Street, brutalizing boys while he painted their cheeks. Ben followed him home to a tidy little house on Cherry Street, near the river. His name was Rosenberg, and he wore the rank of captain now. The captain had his own garden in back of the house. Ben could hear the tugboats on the river. He stood in the dark until Rosenberg went out to his garden with a watering can. Ben was clutching a strip of wire he had braided with his own hands. The captain was completely absorbed in his little patch as Ben crept behind him and pounced. He climbed onto the captain's back, dug the strip of wire around his neck like a silver bracelet with barbs, leaned as hard as he could, and the captain strangled on the weight of his own body. Ben didn't bother to bury him in his garden. It would have been a fitting touch, but he didn't have the time.

"Master Jacob, do you still want me inside the Kehilla?"

"Indeed," the Old Man said, all the brilliance back in his blue eyes. "I'm sorry that so many Jewish orphans had to suffer. . . . Marcus will take you wherever you want to go."

3.

THE PIERCE-ARROW WAS GONE. The chief investigator must have hidden it somewhere in one of the mansion's sheds. Ben stood alone in the moonlight, near the barren trees. The wind purled in his ears like a temptress' song. The mansion was unlit now save for an eerie glow from the attic. Ben wondered what other prisoners that attic still held. He should have realized that the Kehilla had always been Jacob Schiff's private police force. Ben was the aberration—the lone detective who worked in the dark. He heard a soft growl as the Pierce-Arrow sped toward him. He had to leap out of the way, or he might have been bumped right into the river.

The chief investigator laughed and opened the car's ruby red door. "Get in, you clown."

They rode along Riverside Drive, went under the aqueduct, without another motorcar in sight. "Ravage, if you mock me in front of the Old Man, you'll regret it."

He caressed his Colt and continued to laugh. Ben clutched Marcus' ear, and the Pierce-Arrow swerved and nearly crashed into the greensward of Riverside Park.

"Maniac, you'll wreck the car, and the Old Man will murder me."

Marcus drove in silence after that, beyond the stone palaces that the richest Russian Jews—landlords and shop owners—had built out of their hunger to escape the foul air of the Ghetto; these mansions had minarets and balconies with Roman columns that seemed concocted from some nightmare of poverty that would linger until they died. Ben wouldn't have wanted to live among those minarets.

"I'll take you to the El," Marcus rasped, "and then you're on your own, pretty boy."

Ben climbed up the enormous gallery of stairs to the El station on Fifty-ninth, purchased his five-cent ticket at the tollbooth—there'd been rumors of raising the fare to a dime—and thrust his ticket into the chopping box. The guard saluted Ben as he went through the iron grille and stepped onto the platform with its buckled planks. It was like living out on a troublesome sea; the whole platform shivered as the train arrived. The car was littered with candy wrappers and crushed bits of newspaper. The only occupants were night watchmen coming off their shift and coal stokers who worked for the railroad company. They were silent, brooding men. And then the jackals arrived, one by one, wearing derbies that were much too small, a habit they had picked up from Monk Eastman. Ben could catch a glimmer of the iron claws in their sleeves. Most of the watchmen disembarked at the Thirty-fourth Street Ferry Station. Not a single new passenger climbed aboard except for the jackals themselves. And by Ninth Street, he was left all alone with them. They were loyal Giant fans, devotees of Fred Merkle, Christy Mathewson, and John McGraw. McGraw himself had appeared in the *Follies* with his bulbous red nose. His fiefdom extended well beyond the Polo Grounds—he was partners with Ned Silver in several saloons and gambling houses. The jackals plucked baseballs out of their pockets and tossed them at one another with a kind of delirium in their eyes, like madcap pitchers before the most important game of their lives; even from a distance, Ben could see that McGraw or Mathewson had signed the balls. The jackals wouldn't have risked hurling these trophies at Ben. They smiled and hummed the tune that had become the craze of 1913, about Beryl the Yiddish batsman.

> *Beryl, Beryl, where are you,*
> *With your leather glove and Louisville Slugger?*
> *Will you play at the Polo Grounds, with Muggsy McGraw*
> *Or sit out the pennant run in the peanut leagues?*

The jackals tipped their derbies and climbed off the train with Ben. There were seven of these derby hats with their baseballs and their claws. They kept humming about Beryl and his leather mitt as Ben marched along the Bowery. He didn't intend to outrun them. He would have to pick them off one or two at a time until he found a haven. Many of the saloons were closed. The luncheon dives were all gated and locked. Half the lanterns were unlit. He would have climbed aboard a trolley and battled it out, but there were no trolley cars with their steel skirts on any of the tracks. There wasn't even a motorcar, just a band of wild dogs that had no interest in the menacing gait of human beings.

Ben slowed his pace, and as one of the jackals approached, he grabbed the baseball out of his hand and hurled him down the well of a tailor shop under the street. That jackal lost his derby and ripped his coat on the wicked cellar steps. Ben wound up like Christy Mathewson with his long, fluid pump, his left foot dangling in the air, tossed the baseball with a wide arc, and beaned the second jackal, knocking him and his hat into the gutter. But he'd paid too much attention to his own artistry. It could have been fatal, as he felt a rip that went from his right shoulder down to his spine. He saw a splatter of red dots and was about to swoon until he began to sing, "Beryl, Beryl . . ."

A third jackal had crept behind him with one of Ned Silver's claws, which was shaped like a human hand and had its own knuckled grip. Ben blinked, and the red dots melted into the night air. He swirled around, swallowing his own blood, and caught the jackal between the eyes with his bare knuckles. But the wind had gone out of him. He stumbled along until he arrived at the Thalia. The entire front of the theater, above the box office and the night watchman's shed, was covered with a billboard of Clara Karp, in full silhouette, with her shoulders, her bosom, and her ample thighs in the signature black tights she wore onstage. There wasn't much need to advertise her name. No actor, male or female, would have dared usurp her role as Hamlet while Clara was still on the boards. Even while he winced with pain, Ben was struck by the beauty of that silhouette, how it shimmered in the dark and seemed to come alive. That was the power of her performance. No one could resist it. He fell in love with Clara the first time he saw her onstage. He wasn't much older than a boy, during his first year at Harvard, and she was like a glorious ghost in black, a hallucination that was carnal and ethereal in the same breath, mad and calculating, and perfectly sane, as he imagined her ampleness in his own hands, her legs like dancing trees, her mouth a steaming wound. . . .

He had to reconnoiter, and stop dreaming about the Yiddish Hamlet, or he'd have another claw in his back. He walked around the watchman's shed, rubbed the theater's side wall like a blind man, and found the stage door. It was locked. But he knew the Thalia's foibles and idiosyncrasies. He'd slept at the theater many times, long after the lights were dark and Clara had gone to Luchow's with one of her admirers. He had to juggle with the door until it clicked open, but he didn't have a burglar's freedom to roam. There were jackals right behind him, humming to themselves how *this* Beryl would soon become their prey.

Ben squeezed the knob twice, and the stage door sprang open. He entered the blackened house, but he couldn't lock the door from the inside—the latch was broken. He crept into the bowels of the theater, under the boards, while he heard the remaining jackals whisper, "Where are you, sweetheart? Come to Papa." They weren't more than a few paces behind him. The downtown detective didn't have much of a chance. His right arm was useless, and his shoulder blade was on fire. He tripped against some stage prop, landed on his ass, against the shaft of an ancient fire ax, while the jackals fumbled around him for a lightbulb.

"Jesus," one of the jackals said. "I don't trust that monkey. He could bite off my balls."

"Hush, Mordecai," said another. "He won't live long enough to do us any harm."

Ben clutched the fire ax with his left hand, but the rusty blade spilled right into his lap. The jackals couldn't seem to find the bulb. And then a light appeared in the distance, like a blinking star that drew closer and closer. The jackals were hypnotized by that light. They forgot the claws they held; they even forgot Ben. Suddenly, a wraith was upon them in a robe that clung to her skin. She clutched a lantern lit with gas in one hand and a broomstick in the other. A stage cap like an enormous rubber yarmulke hid her scalp. She had charcoal around her eyes, and the rest of her was painted a very pale gray—it wasn't a ghost's complexion. It was the Yiddish Hamlet sans her black tights. The lantern sputtered and hissed as she grabbed the broomstick like a lance and poked at the jackals with a furious persuasion.

"I'll squeeze the blood and shit out of you," she said.

They growled back at her and tumbled all over themselves.

"Hey, lads," their leader moaned. "Silver Dollars didn't pay us for this." And the jackals limped out of the Thalia with their precious baseballs and their arsenal of claws.

Clara tossed the broomstick into the darkness, helped the detective to his feet, and dragged him into her dressing room. She had her own apartment uptown, but she was seldom there—she couldn't thrive without the rumble of the theater, dinner at Delmonico's, and the merchant princes who wanted to marry her. She flirted with every one and refused them all. She'd fall into the grave without this roughneck who would visit her in the middle of the night and break her bones with his sweet movements on her divan.

"You don't have to work for the Kehilla," she said. "I have enough shekels to take care of us, Ben."

His tongue was swollen with blood, and he could barely utter a sound. "But neither of us are . . . in the same league . . . with Jacob Schiff."

"I know all his partners. They sneak into the Thalia and call me 'that Russian Jewess in Hamlet's underwear.' I could show up at Schiff's banking house anytime I want."

She put a hand over his mouth when he started to groan. She couldn't undress him; every lurch cost him a swallow of blood. She removed the scissors from her sewing kit, cut him out of his jacket and his fancy white shirt, and shucked off his trousers with one long pull. Clara turned him on his side and could see the claw marks on his back, with the welling of blood. She would have summoned the Thalia's doctor, but she looked into the desolation of Ben's blue eyes.

"No doctors, Clara. You'll have to stop the bleeding on your own."

"And if you have an infection?"

"Then I'll die in your arms."

Clara wasn't a nurse; she was a comedienne who had once toured the tiny Yiddish capitals of the Russian Empire with a troupe of jugglers and acrobats. She'd watched the acrobats battle over a lost object and bathe their deepest cuts in some bubbly solution. She found the same dark bottle of hydrogen peroxide in the cabinet above her sink, and she swabbed Ben's wounds with that solution while he cursed and screamed and scratched at her elbow. She tore a pillowcase into shreds and rinsed the rags in boiling water from her teakettle. Then she staunched the blood welling out of his wounds with the hot rags, pressing down hard, so that her hands themselves served as a dike. She wouldn't allow her detective to fall asleep. She recalled the wounded acrobat who once fell into a coma and never woke up again.

She shucked off her robe and lay down beside Ben on the divan. Even with his raw back, Ben was aroused. Her body was like a marvelous circus of pleasures. He never tired of looking at her. Her breasts bobbed above his mouth. He chewed on her left nipple. He could feel her silken bush near his groin and was about to enter her.

"Don't you dare," she growled at him, her eyes fluttering with her own insane desire. "Your wounds will open, and I'll become a murderess."

"Clara," he whispered, since he barely had the strength to talk, "you destroy men and women by the dozen every night in that play of yours. It's the most murderous *Hamlet* I've ever seen. That's why the critics adore you. You don't need a rapier. You kill with a glance."

"Is that why you fell in love with me, darling?"

He'd been to productions of *Hamlet* inside Harvard Square, with student players and amateurs from the local houses. The bombast and the sword fights had cozened him, and obscured the poetry of the play. And then he returned to Manhattan during the winter break, went to see the Yiddish Hamlet, almost by accident. The spectators were a travesty. They'd come out of the cold to warm their feet. They whistled and swallowed mouthfuls of halvah, chomping like horses. Then Clara appeared in her black tights, and all the chomping stopped. She was as nimble as a butterfly, with a roundness that delighted them. And her Yiddish broke from her in deep, guttural sounds, as if each accent, each syllable, was like a slap in the face. No one slept in the balcony. No one snored. And Ben understood the menace. Clara had turned *Hamlet* into a revenge play, not against a calculating king, a court that had coddled the young prince, and a mother who hadn't really mourned, but against that imperial uptown language and customs that had squeezed the heart out of the Ghetto. Hamlet's cry was a woman's cry, a woman dressed as a man, breaking whatever grip these outsiders had. Her English was far more aristocratic than that of the student players of Harvard Square. But this Hamlet would only pounce within the Ghetto walls.

She must have stopped the bleeding with her rags. She fed him Russian coffee cake while she pranced without her clothes, her breasts quivering like musical instruments that would tantalize him until he died. He wanted to clutch at Clara and never stir from her divan. She was the wounded one, with invisible claw marks, as she plunged into his arms.

Six

Feathers of Blood

I.

ANYA LOVED THE BOY—perhaps more than she had ever loved Cahan—loved him as much as she loved Tolstoy, yet nothing could stir her to enter a mansion on Fifth Avenue to discuss the boy's fate. Cahan had to bargain with her.

"Anya, the banker wants the both of us. He knows how much influence you have on Ben."

"Fool," she said, staring at him through her thick lenses, even thicker than his. She was the real revolutionary, not Cahan. She considered him a straw socialist, a merchant of palatable ideas. They hadn't kissed in years.

"That capitalist is playing with you," she said. "He has no interest in Ben. He's your enemy, Abraham. He hires strikebreakers. So why do you run to him at his first invitation?"

What answer could he give? "It's better to talk than not to talk."

"Go," she said. "Run into Jacob Schiff's arms. Have your honeymoon."

There had always been strife between them, from the beginning. They would separate, and come back together, without a moment of marital bliss. He couldn't dream of biting Anya's flesh.

She didn't have the magical aromas of Clara Karp. She was an anarchist in a high collar. And he, Abraham Cahan, was a hypocrite. A straw socialist, she said.

"Anya, for the last time, will you come with me?"

"No."

And Cahan walked alone from his uptown "estate," a cramped apartment where Anya piled her books in every corner, until his nostrils were filled with the perfume of musty, rotting pages. He wore a wing collar like Henry James and a dark waistcoat. The air was crisp and clean, without the red dust that mottled the windows of his falcon's nest at the *Forward*. He had to chase after his own fedora in the March wind. And suddenly he lurched as he recaptured the pinched crown of his hat. Soon he would have to mark the second anniversary of the Triangle fire. And he realized where the red dust had come from.

He recalled that time in 1911 when he heard the deafening clank of fire trucks that had crossed over from Brooklyn with their teams of horses and ladders that tilted in the sky. And he raced uptown with members of his staff to that burning loft on Greene Street. He couldn't have saved a soul. The bosses themselves had bolted the doors of the women's shirtwaist factory on the eighth, ninth, and tenth floors. They didn't want girls, some as young as fourteen, to loiter in the halls and steal worthless scraps of cloth. The fire had started with a cigarette butt in a scrap bin—and it raged in a matter of minutes, fed by a universe of dry material. The fire escapes crumpled in the heat, closing off whatever escape route the girls had, while the bosses climbed to the roof with the managers of the shop and their own children who had come to visit them on that unfortunate afternoon. The ladders of the fire trucks reached only to the sixth floor, their hoses to the seventh—they reminded Cahan of linen and leather snakes that zigzagged out of control. The girls who jumped from the windows tore through the safety nets that the firemen had prepared, almost like sinister clowns at a circus fire, and had their skulls crushed. But Cahan didn't blame the firemen. They were relics of an earlier age, when no ladder had to reach above five flights. . . .

He crucified the shop owners in the *Forward*. But neither of them went to jail. No one could prove they'd been negligent. Still, they had to pay seventy-five dollars for every girl who died in the fire. And Cahan brooded over the sum of that indemnity. The red dust that seemed to devour East Broadway, and only blew downtown, was the residue of blood and brick from the Triangle fire. In his dreams, the girls continued to plummet like weighted feathers of blood and flesh. There was no resolution, and there would never be—not in dollars or new legislation and unbolted doors.

He arrived on Fifth Avenue in a state of deep distress. A footman met him under the white marble pillars of the patriarch's mansion. *Editor Abraham Cahan* had to be checked off a list of invited guests; Cahan hadn't realized he was coming to some kind of afternoon affair.

He handed the footman his gray fedora and went into the vestibule. The walls were lined with red and green damask, the mirrors scalloped in gold, the tables topped with pink marble, and at his back, Cahan could feel a ghostly wind, as if he were about to levitate on Fifth Avenue. He would go mad among the Allrightniks. In his mind's eye he watched creatures descend from the air like bombs that burst into blood and bone.

Butlers led him into the grand salon. He was an interloper here among the uptown elite, men with silken mustaches and paunches, their wives with plucked eyebrows and waxed flesh, appraising the humpbacked sofas and the chandeliers like the shrewdest of livery drivers.

He recognized the mayor of New York, Judge Gaynor, who had almost been assassinated three years ago by a disgruntled civil servant while they were on board the *Kaiser Wilhelm*, in Hoboken. The bullet couldn't be dislodged; it was still stuck in the mayor's larynx, and he had to speak in a hoarse whisper. He was a machine Democrat who had tried to declare his independence from Tammany Hall. But the city had grown even more chaotic and corrupt under his rule. He'd surrounded himself with undersecretaries, and everyone, including Cahan, had to wait in line for an appointment to see the judge.

Gaynor was talking to Lionel Ravage. Cahan never questioned Ben about his mother and Lionel; he shied away from the subject—a bastard boy with a father who wouldn't acknowledge his existence yet had identical blue eyes. And the boy was much better off. Lionel had a sinister streak. He wasn't satisfied with chewing up the Ghetto. He had an air of endless want about him. His wife, Henrietta, was at his side in a sack dress; she had the darting eyes of a frightened mouse. She fidgeted, as if she were about to scream. Their worthless son was with them, Waldo, who had grown fat and would inherit his father's properties. He had mean little eyes and liked to suck on his lip. He bordered on being an idiot. And still he was Lionel's heir.

Waldo had come with his younger sister, Becky, who wore a white gown and looked like a demented bridesmaid. Her eyes were slightly crossed. She was brazen at this affair, flirted with men as old as her father, even flirted with Cahan, dug her hand deep into his pocket and called him "Daddy," until Lionel reined her in. She seemed forlorn and drugged to the editor, tottering in and out of control.

Lionel dragged her into a corner, stroked her hair as he might have done with a damaged colt, then returned to the mayor, and summoned Cahan.

"Baron," he said, "you'll have to excuse my daughter. She has grand illusions. Becky thinks she's at a carnival and can play with any man in sight. I'll have to cure her of that habit. . . . Ah, I don't believe you've met His Honor."

"I haven't had that privilege," Cahan said, still a bit perturbed by that cross-eyed girl, who was as wanton as Lionel. "Mr. Mayor, you're a hard man to pin down."

"Can you blame me?" Judge Gaynor said, his voice sounding like an echo out of a crumbling well. "You've covered my administration in a crown of thorns."

"I might have been more charitable, sir, if your police department didn't prey on the Lower East Side."

The mayor coughed into a clotted handkerchief and sucked on a hard candy. "You've been to the station houses. The captains are like little kings. And however I rotate them, the new captain is worse than the last."

Cahan had heard this argument time and again from past mayors and police chiefs—the corruption that spread like a fatal disease, from rookie to roundsman, from the morals squad to the detective bureau and to their handpicked aides; they all had deeper pockets than their pensions, bankbooks under an assumed name, houses hidden somewhere in Westchester or Canarsie, prostitutes with a precinct's own stamp on their rumps, like common cattle. Cahan preferred the lawlessness of the old gangs, who kept the coppers out of their territories upon the pain of death. Monk

Eastman ruled with his own magnanimity. Housewives were never carted off to the station house and charged with soliciting on the streets. Pickpockets couldn't molest shoppers inside Lord & Taylor; Monk wouldn't give them a license. He policed the Ghetto far too well until Tammany sent him to rot in Sing Sing, and the roundsmen returned to all their tricks.

"Mr. Mayor, I'd hire Monk Eastman as one of your captains, and the stealing might stop."

Judge Gaynor guffawed until his yellow teeth jiggled in his mouth. He was entombed by his civil servants, who owed their jobs to Tammany Hall, could outlast most mayors and mark time until their retirement. "Now that's a novel idea," the mayor said. "Monk Eastman with a badge. I didn't know he was still alive."

"Oh, he's alive," Cahan said.

Schiff suddenly appeared out of a hall of mirrors. "Baron," he said, "come with me," and Cahan had a flash of those poor Triangle girls falling like crippled canaries through the firemen's nets.

2.

CAHAN WANTED TO SCREAM OUT; he was the viceroy of the Yiddish press, who had met Karl Marx's daughter in London, and was astonished to learn that Marx himself had once been able to read and write Yiddish; Cahan was fêted everywhere he went, could interview ministers in Prague and sit with Captain Dreyfus in Paris. But he was hopeless on Fifth Avenue, an obedient little boy who followed Schiff through a doorway in the grand salon that had been cut into the red damask. He climbed up a stairway at the rear of the mansion, passing a flurry of maids; they were all blond and uncorseted, with flesh that seemed to liquefy under their white uniforms, these Brunhildes with a taste of sweat that terrified the editor and made him fly toward their blondness like a magnet.

Schiff shouted at the maids in German, and they scurried down the hall, leaving Cahan with the insatiable lust of a man who would have preferred to ride their rumps all afternoon, with their clothes on, rather than meet with the master of the house. He, Cahan, was an incurable satyr who should have been locked up.

He sat down with Jacob in an office that was very wide and could have belonged on the *Kaiser Wilhelm*. There were photographs on the walls of the patriarch with presidents of the United States, past and present: Schiff smoking a cigar with Teddy Roosevelt when he was police commissioner; Schiff with Taft, looking like a pair of high-class tricksters or bon vivants in their top hats; Schiff at Woodrow Wilson's inauguration earlier this month. But the photograph that seemed to etch right into his soul was of Schiff standing beside a very gaunt Ulysses S. Grant, who had a blanket around his shoulders, like an Indian chief. Grant was a bit of an anti-Semite, who had tried to keep Jewish peddlers away from his military camp, but Cahan had still published scraps of Grant's memoirs in the *Forward*, in Anya's stark translation. The book was written in a dreamlike, telegraphic prose. Grant never puffed himself up as a general, never talked about his accomplishments in battle. Cahan couldn't have understood America's Civil War, all the bloodbaths and the matter-of-fact slaughter, without Ulysses Grant. And he wondered if some of that slaughter would be visited upon the Ghetto, with Yankee Cossacks riding through the narrow streets and creating pogrom after pogrom, as he had dreamt so many times.

"Jacob," he said, "it's not safe."

"What are you talking about?" Schiff asked from behind his mahogany desk.

"I know," he said, "you wish we would all go away, disappear into the dust."

"That's preposterous. Don't I spend almost every night at Montefiore?"

"Yes, yes, you have your charities, Jacob, but you still wish we would all go away, so that your uptown friends wouldn't be reminded of the lice and dirt of steerage, of Jews coughing their lungs out in closets without a window. . . . It's not safe."

"Have you lost your mind?" the patriarch asked, pounding his maritime desk that had once belonged to Admiral Dewey at Manila Bay. He'd discovered it lying under a great wrapper at an auction house and had to remind the auctioneers how valuable it was. He liked his treasures to come at an exorbitant price.

"Congress," Cahan said. "It will start installing quotas, with a little nudge from you, and soon Ellis Island will become a house of ghosts."

"Why do you malign us? I don't have to deal with Congress. Taft and Teddy Roosevelt vetoed every anti-immigration measure that got through the House. And Woodrow will do the same. I've met with him and Mrs. Wilson at the White House. I want to work with you, Abraham. I know our differences. . . . Where's your wife?"

"She wouldn't come here, Jacob. She's not so fond of Fifth Avenue."

"And not so fond of me," Schiff said with an owlish smile. "But she's like a second mother to Ben. He might listen to her . . . and leave Lionel Ravage alone."

Cahan could only imagine more and more conspiracies, the

gates of the Ghetto flung open to whatever Cossacks were for hire—Pinkertons, rogue politicians and cops, strikebreakers, hooligans from Satan's Circus; then he realized that the Ghetto had no gates. And his mind drifted back to Jacob.

"You're mistaken," he said. "My Anya is even less fond of Lionel."

"We have to settle this, or we'll find ourselves in a catastrophe."

Cahan kept looking at the photograph of Grant, whose gaunt face revealed a man suffering from throat cancer—his cigars had turned into a death sentence. But why would he pose with Jacob and other Jewish bankers while he was so sick? Jacob told him the story. Grant had been a ruinous president, in a time of great plunder, and he'd ruined himself after his second term in office. That clarity he'd had in battle had deserted him. He was bilked out of his own small fortune. And Jewish bankers, like the Seligman brothers and Schiff, financed Ulysses Grant so that he could work in peace while he finished his memoirs.

Cahan was bewildered by the world of Wall Street. "But you must have lost a good deal of money."

Jacob sat smoking a cigar, like some bearded Buddha. "Ulys had always been kind to us," he said. Jacob would visit Grant's modest little house on East Sixty-sixth Street, right off Fifth Avenue. Grant worked at his desk on the second floor, near the window. He wore a bandage around his neck, like a wounded officer. The ulcer in his throat would have maddened him without cocaine. His eyes were glazed, Schiff recalled. He finished his memoirs just days before he died. The first Jewish magnates owed everything to Grant. They'd established their fortunes selling blankets to Union generals.

"But Grant despised Jewish peddlers," Cahan had to insist.

"He still bought the blankets," Jacob said. "And our families prospered. That's why I'm in a position to help you. Never mind our differences. I've read your editorials, Abraham. You condemn us as a bunch of ogres who squeezed the blood out of every garment worker in Manhattan."

Cahan looked into the blue eyes of that bearded Buddha. "And would the owners of the Triangle Shirtwaist Company have bolted girls inside that firetrap if they hadn't had your fidelity and support?"

"Silence!" Jacob said. "I won't be called a murderer by a man who spent his boyhood making bombs. The owners of that wretched company had nothing to do with us. I did not finance their callousness. I grieved in my own way. I worked all night at the temporary morgue on the piers. I saw the charred bodies, Abraham. I helped mothers identify the remains of their own children. We opened up a pavilion for them at Montefiore where they could rest for a month."

And after that month? Cahan wanted to ask. But who was he to judge? Another juggler of lost souls.

He couldn't concentrate on Jacob Schiff. He pictured Ulysses Grant coughing and spitting up blood as he crafted those sentences like a war correspondent rather than a general recapturing his career. Grant did not write about his presidency or his wanderings around the world, when he sailed up the Nile or sat with Victoria at the queen's table. Memory for him resided in battle, and everything else was a damaged dream. It touched Cahan to read about a war that was foreign and yet familiar, as if those battlefields had mutated into the rubble of the Lower East Side, without the dead soldiers, of course, or a rumpled Samson, like "Ulys."

"It's not safe," he said.

"Stop that!"

"I don't want Ben to be swallowed alive."

"Abraham, he's done most of the swallowing. He marches into courthouses and disrupts the proceedings."

"Yes," Cahan said, "he's *our* detective. But his father's a maniac. Why do you protect him?"

The patriarch sat there with an ancient Haggadah on his desk that must have been rescued from some ransacked synagogue. The pages were tattered and burnt at their edges, and should have been couched behind a glass wall like any relic, but he kept fingering them, even as they crumbled. Cahan couldn't fathom this son of banker-scholars from Frankfurt-am-Main.

"Baron, you have the answer. We're a closed colony, and Lionel is one of ours. We've had to cover up his blemishes. But we cannot rend the fabric, or we'll never survive."

"Yes," Cahan said, "one false stitch, and the fabric will disappear."

This was the man who had bested Pierpont Morgan in the biggest railroad deal of all time—control of the Northern Pacific and all its ancillaries. He was the one person on Wall Street whom the House of Morgan feared. Yet he could do nothing about an avaricious merchant who attacked strangers with his wolf's-head walking stick and set fire to entire blocks on the Lower East Side.

"If Lionel attacks Benjamin with that silver cane of his, one of them will kill the other. . . . What can we do to stop this carnage?" the editor asked.

"Work together."

Cahan laughed bitterly under his breath. He held no cards at this table. The German Jews could build and destroy railroads, decide a war between Japan and the czar, and Cahan couldn't even get to see the mayor.

"Jacob, you've been generous to us, but I'm sorry, uptown and downtown don't mix."

He left the patriarch with his torn Haggadah, rushed out of the room, and ran downstairs, worried that he might be way-laid by one of the Brunehildes and lose whatever little he had of his self-respect. But none of the blond maids were around in their white uniforms to tantalize him with bits of uncorseted flesh. He passed through a doorway and into the red damask of the grand salon. All the guests were gone. Waiters from Sherry's in bright duck coats were cleaning up all the debris—empty splits of champagne, unwashed cutlery, slabs of whipped cream from a cake that Cahan had never seen. His gray hat was on a taboret near the front door. But he couldn't escape from Schiff, even with his own hat. The front door was locked. And he heard strange noises; the sound of fire trucks wailed in his ears; no matter where he went, uptown or downtown, bodies would continue to fly like feathers of bone and flesh.

Fourteen-year-old girls in that temporary morgue on the East River, with blood seeping through the canvas covers. Bands had played on the same pier during the nightly promenades. . . .

One of the Brunehildes appeared with a gigantic key, her blond hair all braided. She must have crossed over recently on the *Kaiser Wilhelm.* She babbled in German while she blushed, telling him how sorry she was. She hadn't realized that he was in the house. Cahan answered her in his own mongrel mix of German and that musical Yiddish Clara Karp had perfected at the Thalia whenever she appeared as Hamlet or Medea.

"My child," he said, "you mustn't be afraid. I'm not an ogre."

He guided her hand as she unlocked the door with that gigantic key, his fingers curled around her swanlike wrist. The garters that held up his stockings nearly collapsed. He shivered under his waistcoat, and with an impulsiveness that shocked him, he pecked her on the mouth. It wasn't a passionate kiss, but more like the movement of a fossilized bird. Still, he was deeply troubled that he had abused his privileges as a gentleman and sullied the virtue of Schiff's blond maid. She giggled and stroked his arm.

He had little solace on the street. Lionel's mansion was right next door. It was a Gothic castle with gargoyles of winged birds crouching near the roof. Cahan was startled for a moment as he imagined those birds taking on flesh; they could alight from the stones, pursue him down Fifth Avenue, and peck out his eyes. Then the wonderment was gone and all his rational powers came back. Gargoyles couldn't fly, not even from Lionel Ravage's rooftop. And he raced from this avenue of mansions, his fedora blinding him as it slipped down his forehead with its own perverse power.

SEVEN

Satan's Circus

I.

*B*AD BABETTE HAD RUN OFF to Satan's Circus, and Ben was elected to bring her back. His wounds still hadn't healed, and he had a bracelet of gauze clapped around his chest, but he'd been summoned by the Kehilla *and* Meyer Bristol. So he and Monk sailed up to the Circus with its panorama of human flesh.

He was heading for the Haymarket, the most notorious dance hall in the district. It had lost much of its luster, and was now a pickpocket's paradise, where lonely sailors and other rubes were fleeced. The Haymarket had once been the meeting ground of Manhattan's roughest gangs, from the Baxter Street Dudes to the Hudson Dusters. The old gangs were gone, replaced by little packets of hoodlums that worked for the Wigwam—Tammany Hall—or thieving bondsmen like Ned Silver, or the shop owners who wanted to rip the heart out of a potential strike. The Haymarket was too old-fashioned for them. They frequented the Burnt Rag or another sporting house. But there were remnants of the Baxter Street Dudes outside the Haymarket's mustard yellow front wall, with its familiar sign hanging at a terrific tilt from a rusty old hook:

INTRUDERS BEWARE

THIS IS THE HAYMARKET

GRANDE SOIREE DANSANTE

And now these last members of the Baxter Street Dudes watched Monk with legend's own raw disbelief. They genuflected, grabbing his battered knuckles.

"Edward, we haven't come to make trouble, honest to God."

They couldn't have read his face, even if he had smiled or frowned at them. The glare of the lights was brutal. Every window on that mustard yellow wall seemed to have its own blinding color. The doorman tipped his hat to monk. "Edward, it's a fine season when you're here. How was Sing Sing?"

Monk ignored him and escorted Ben into the Haymarket. The roar nearly buckled Ben's knees. There was a constant chanting and crowing in a cavern that went all the way to the roof, with galleries that curled above the stage like a horseshoe that had lost its velvet veneer. Ben had to keep close to Monk, or he might have been lost in the jostle. That's how much traffic there was at the Haymarket, a milling about that never seemed to end. But he didn't meet one of the Vanderbilt boys in a carnival mask, or an uptown lady curious about the latest dance steps. He met only dips and cadets of the worst kind, with rotten teeth and bulging eyes. The Haymarket had become their home and headquarters of last resort. There was little money to be made in this cavern. Ben knew it would close down. The chandeliers clung over his head on flimsy wires. The balconies swayed above all the din. It reminded Ben of a vast insane asylum, where men and women moved in a mindless circle. It could have been the house of bedlam on Blackwell's Island, where his mother had been sent in absolute exile, and where Ben was never allowed to visit, since he was a ward of the state and a delinquent without any rights. Yet he imagined a cavern like this on Blackwell's Island, had seen pictures of its main pavilion in a book he had borrowed from an antiquarian's shop in Harvard Square, with all the mad milling about in nightshirts, above a caption: *The Hopeless on Display.*

And perhaps that's why Ben didn't want to leave a permanent trace of himself; he was at war with the whole caste that had incarcerated his mother, from the judge who had condemned her to the captain who had ferried her to Blackwell's Island in a gown buckled up with leather straps—did she howl or whisper his name? He couldn't get his mind clear of it. The more he remembered, the more he seemed to go mad. He was much better off without an address, or an office with his name inscribed in glass: *Benjamin Ravage, Esq.* There was no such creature. He was the howling in his mother's head.

2.

MONK STEERED HIM THROUGH A NARROW DOOR under one of the balconies and into a self-enclosed universe of velvet and silk without a single pickpocket or cadet. Ben recognized a superior court judge, a Wall Street trader, a few uptown merchants, a fellow graduate of Harvard Law, and a whole slew of socialite princesses in this secret annex of a dying dance hall. He realized soon enough that it was a club for *lesbiankes*, or at least a dive where a woman might dance with other women and kiss without having a detective on her tail. But that wasn't the club's main attraction. He'd come to a velvet hole in the wall where a person's sexual tastes could spin on a dime. And it frightened Ben a little. The judge was dancing with a muscular boy embalmed in lipstick and mascara. And Ben couldn't help but think of that time at the orphans' home when his face was daubed with rouge and he had to wear a dress for some phantom sin he had committed. The other boys masturbated in front of his eyes, and the guards tried to fondle him in their own closet. He kicked at their groins, but he couldn't escape without a bloody eye and a boot in his ass. He was Crazy Ben, after all, with a crazy mom.

This dive had its own circus master, a mulatto from Paris named Franz. He'd performed at the Black Box and other cabarets, a female man who wouldn't hop around like a little girl, or paint his lips. Franz had amber eyes in the weak glow of the lights. He had a limber look, with high cheekbones, black hair, and a narrow, delicate nose; he would have had his own majesty if his teeth hadn't been stained with tobacco and his mouth hadn't curled into a slight sneer.

He wore pointy boots, striped trousers, and a black coat with tails; he was at the zinc bar with Bad Babette, who stood defiantly in a simple white sack that could have served as a bridal gown in Satan's Circus.

"Ah, Poppa's pigeon," she spat at Ben, and moved closer to the circus master. "Darling, let's dance before I go insane."

There was a black trumpeter behind them who could mute the sound of his own horn with the cup of his hand, and Babs danced with the circus master to that staccato wail. It wasn't like the helter-skelter racket of the Baxter Street Dudes; they danced a slow two-step that Ben had never seen in a Manhattan cabaret. She put her head on Franz's shoulder and began to cry. He comforted Babs, whispered in her ear.

Ben's mind began to drift. Bad Babette must have come here

with Leila Montague. Was this their secret palace? While Babs danced with Franz, it seemed as if she mourned Leila too little or a little too much.

"Come, come, sweethearts," Franz said to Ben and Monk in the musical baritone of a cantor at a Stanton Street shul, beckoning them with those lithe hands of his. Neither Monk nor Ben moved toward the dancers.

"This is my cabaret," Babs said. "I get to call the shots."

Ben still wouldn't move. And then he recalled that mermaid who was fished out of the water with bruises on her cheek—Leila the *lesbianke*. He signaled to Monk, and both of them embraced Babs and the circus master, and trod along to the staccato music of the horn without entangling themselves or stepping on someone's toe.

"You lied to me," Babs said. "I gave you one simple task—to find Leila. And you failed."

"Babs," Franz whispered, "it's not his fault that Leila is dead."

"He's a shamas," Babs said. "He could have kept her alive."

"And you're a spoiled brat," the mulatto said, his amber eyes smoldering in the dark as another figure stumbled into the cabaret in a top hat with a crooked crown. It was Waldo Ravage, Lionel's fat heir, who was as violent and boisterous as his father but didn't have the skills to be a salesclerk in one of Lionel's hardware stores. Still, he knew how to ferret with both fists inside a cash register.

"What is this fucking place?" he said, flashing hundred-dollar bills. "Is it fairyland, huh? Doesn't my dad come here a lot? Well, I'll dance with a fairy. And I'll pay for the privilege."

The circus master broke from Babs and confronted Waldo, whose eyes wandered about the décor like those of some besotted imp who was used to destroying whatever he wanted and having his father sweep away the debris.

"This is a private club," Franz said in a neutral tone; he could have been talking to an infant who had stumbled through the wrong door.

"But it isn't locked," Waldo said. "And I like fairyland."

"You'll have to leave."

Waldo was carrying a stick like his father's, with a wolf's head embossed in silver, and now Ben understood the sudden resurrection of Mr. Hyde. It was Waldo who visited the prostitutes of Allen Street in his father's wake, Waldo who slashed at them out of meanness and spite, or some sullen desire. He brandished that wolf's head near Franz's eyes. "Hey, Mr. Fairyland, I could really do some damage."

The mulatto plucked the stick out of Waldo's hand and beat him along his back, as if he were thrashing a brutish animal.

Good, Ben thought. *I won't have to kill him myself.* But he didn't have much pleasure watching the blows rain down on Waldo. He grew melancholy. This wasn't the way he wanted to attack Lionel, through some back portal, with his son as a wounded trophy.

"Mr. Franz," he said, "you'll have to stop."

But the mulatto didn't stop as Waldo shrieked and begged in a girlish voice and spilled to the floor. "Please, please . . . I'll give you every penny I have. You can ransom me. My father's rich. . . . Oh my God."

"You'll have to stop," Ben said. "This sack of shit is my half brother, believe it or not."

"But it's my parlor," the mulatto said. "And you'll have to play by my rules. Fat Boy's not so innocent. He's been here before. And he's hurt people. He has to pay the price."

"Not tonight," Ben said, grabbing at the stick. And then he must have fallen into a rapid-fire dream, like some flash of light out of the flickers where bodies went flying, because he landed on his rump in this secretive cabaret with sawdust under his soles. He'd been utterly blind to the maneuvering of the circus master. Franz hadn't lost a beat. He'd lashed out at Ben with the toe of his buckskin boot while he continued to thrash Waldo with the silver-headed cane. Ben sat on his ass for a moment and signaled to Monk. He didn't want Eastman to interrupt his "dialogue" with Franz.

Waldo kept crying as each blow landed with the staccato rhythm of the trumpeter's horn. Meanwhile, Ben clambered to his feet. His temples were pounding, and he saw two wolf's heads rather than one. "You'll have to cease and desist, Mr. Franz."

The circus master laughed with his tobacco teeth. "Spoken like a barrister," he said, flicking at Ben with the same boot. And the detective found himself in the sawdust again. This time, he rose with a bit more clarity. He could catch Franz's opaque form and that wolf's head in the somber light of the cabaret. And when the boot lashed out, he slapped at Franz's knee with the blade of his hand and sent him tumbling into the zinc bar. The circus master sat there, all crumpled up and laughing with a great roar.

"Congratulations, Mr. Ben. I got a little lazy. I should have recognized that you had an orphan's will."

"Don't hit him," Babs said with a sudden urgency in her voice.

"Then say good-bye to Franz like a good little girl."

"I'm not your little girl," she whimpered.

3.

Ben had to scrub Waldo in the subterranean toilets at the Haymarket, where pensioned-off roundsmen served as armed guards, or no one would have left the toilets with their wallets intact. The old, decaying dance hall had clubbers and pickpockets in every damn corner. Ben had to fight the crazed desire in him to duck Waldo's head in one of the toilet bowls while Waldo was still blubbering. "I don't welcome you as my brother. You're just a bastard from the orphans' barn who was fucked by wild boys."

Ben reached under Waldo's trousers and squeezed his testicles. "How does that feel, brother? If you ever go near Allen Street again, and scar another girl with that cane of yours, you'll have to eat a mouthful of your own silver."

"Oh, please, please," Waldo whispered with fat tears in his eyes. "I'll be good."

It was Monk who had to become Waldo's babysitter and escort him to Fifth Avenue while Ben sat in total silence with Babs on the soft cushions of a Packard cab with a grille that was shaped like the metallic teeth of a shark. The Packard had to steer around policemen on bicycles, a flurry of rats, piles of manure, and promenaders under the El; Ben didn't bring Bad Babette home to her father's palace above the Hudson until well after midnight.

Babs blinked as he helped her out of the cab. She had none of Clara Karp's plump lines. She was much too angular for him.

"Aren't you coming up with me?" she asked, all her petulance gone.

He followed her into the building, with its harpist's chair in the lobby, and rode up to her bedroom that faced a brick wall.

Ben had to unclasp the cape of this *lesbianke* Little Red Riding Hood trapped in some mysterious forest he couldn't hope to penetrate. He sat her down on the same bed she'd occupied since she was a child.

"Babs, it's my fault. I'm no better than a burglar. I do your father's bidding to help me crack a special safe—Lionel Ravage."

Suddenly, she looked at him with liquid eyes; her nostrils flared. "I like burglars," she said. "But I can't bring you closer to Lionel. No one can. . . . Do you really care that Lionel hasn't anointed you? He's raised a family of idiots."

"But he took my family from me," Ben muttered while Babs reached out, called him onto her bed, as if they were conspirators.

"Christ, we all knew about Lionel's collection of brides. Schiff and the others have tracked them all down. Lionel used the same shamas from the same shul. I can't even tell you about the fund Schiff had to establish for Lionel's supposed progeny—sons and daughters keep popping out of the woodwork. Most of them are liars and lunatics, with their rehearsed tales of the marriages he wrecked and the mamas he ruined. If you believe such *heirs*, he must have seduced half the Lower East Side."

"My mother was different," Ben protested. "She adored him until the day she died. She was always Mrs. Lionel Ravage. Even in the madhouse, she waited for Lionel's knock on the door. Somebody has to pay."

"Darling, it won't be Lionel."

He left her there on the bed in that white sack of a dress that must have been composed in patches of pure silk by seamstresses at B. Altman's, one stitch at a time.

EIGHT

The Thirteenth Store

I.

*T*HE SMOKING ROOM AT THE HARDWARE CLUB reminded Cahan of a military barracks; the walls had begun to peel, and the windows faced an air shaft on Murray Street. But Frank Woolworth seemed comfortable in this room; it's where he spent his time when he first landed in Manhattan, a retailer who hadn't made his fortune yet and was still welcomed by these hardware men, most of whom worked for him now.

The room had one large table, and on it Cahan recognized the crayoned sketch of a new five-and-ten with its signature white awning and signboard of fire engine red. He also recognized the location—311½ Grand Street, where Ridley's department store once stood.

The president of the Jewish bank sat around the table with members of the Kehilla, toy manufacturers, several landlords, and Lionel Ravage, who must have met Woolworth years ago at the Hardware Club, and supplied the pipes, toilets, and sinks for Woolworth's Manhattan stores.

"Gentlemen," Woolworth said as his lieutenants hovered around him, "I can't sit still. That's my weakness. My competitors call it 'Mr. Frank's disease.' "

"Sir, you have no competitors," shouted his chief lieutenant, with a crayon in his fist. "Most of 'em have climbed aboard our wagon. And the others are dead."

"Don't flatter me, Paul. Not in front of these men. They'll think I've hired you as a carnival shill."

There was a moment of raucous laughter around the table, but Cahan didn't laugh. He sat like a mummy while Woolworth's chief lieutenant shuffled about with his crayon and drew stick figures to populate a phantom five-and-ten. Cahan understood the real casualty of that equation: the Lower East Side. Woolworth was dreaming of another Ladies' Mile.

"Now I know there's been trouble in that neighborhood," Woolworth said. "Every kind of vermin seems to operate around Grand—whores and pickpockets and stickup artists. But Captain Kittleberger, who is lord and master of the Lower East Side, has assured me that the problem can be solved. He'll declare a *dead line* on Grand, and that street will soon be stripped of all vermin. They'll have to run elsewhere."

Gottesman, president of the Jewish bank, wagged his head. He must have become Woolworth's silent partner, and it bothered Cahan. The pennies saved by the poorest Jews in the Ghetto would help finance this project, and then these Jews would find themselves without a home. Cahan listened as Marcus Mendelssohn told how the Kehilla had met with Captain Kit and promised to enforce the dead line.

"With our own bodies," he said. And still Cahan was silent. He shouldn't have been the last to learn about the proposed rebirth of Grand Street. He could have prepared better for this onslaught from the other side—bankers, detectives, merchants, landlords, and Captain Kittleberger.

"And I will hire salesgirls, hundreds of them, all from the Grand Street area, I promise you that," Woolworth said, looking right at Cahan with his bullet eyes. But Cahan knew all about Woolworth's hiring practices. The emperor was a martinet. His girls had to wear black shirtwaists during the winter months, and white all summer long. He would enter a five-and-ten unannounced and look for wrinkles in a girl's uniform. Wrinkles in "a white waist" could get a girl fired. And he didn't like any kind of politicking behind his counters. He got rid of every girl who tried to organize a union. "Cheap goods demand cheap labor," he told his generals. And Frank Woolworth had his wish.

"Bruno," he said to one of the toy manufacturers, "tell these folks about our master plan."

"Aw, shucks, Mr. Frank," said the manufacturer, a tiny man with thick eyebrows, "I ain't much of a talker. You tell it."

"Well, it's a rattling good plan. We aim to build our factory right above the Grand Street store. We'll manufacture everything in one place. That will cut the cost in half. And none of our workers need worry. My lofts will be a hundred percent fireproof. We won't have a repetition of the Triangle tragedy."

He shouldn't have mentioned the Triangle fire when he was so heartless with his own employees. Cahan sat there and sulked as Woolworth's young lieutenant, Paul, who had bits of gray in his mustache, took his crayon and sketched in six stories of lofts above the five-and-ten.

"Gentlemen," Woolworth said, "can you imagine the jolt to the economy of the Jewish streets? All local hires, and shoppers coming in from every part of Manhattan. I'll have cantilevered stairs. I'll have a luncheon counter that runs the entire length of the store. We'll capture the cafeteria crowd. Grand Street will return to its old glory. The cadets will be gone, and the streetwalkers swept away. Families can march together into my thirteenth Manhattan store without being molested."

"Sir," said Paul, still clutching his crayon, "we already have a thirteenth store—on Tremont Avenue."

Woolworth scoffed at his lieutenant. "The Bronx is a separate county."

But Paul was like a windup toy. He couldn't seem to stop himself. "Not until next year, sir."

"That's when the five-and-ten will open—next year—as my thirteenth store in Manhattan. . . . And my old friend Lionel Ravage has agreed to manufacture tool kits at a special bargain price. Such items will be found only at the Grand Street location. Lionel, can you give us a couple of details?"

Lionel sat in his bone white straw wig, staring at the door, as Ben Ravage entered the room. Ben hadn't shaved in a week.

"Ah, said Woolworth, "the downtown detective. I invited him to the club. He knows all about the chicanery on Grand Street. But first we have to hear from Lionel about the tool kits."

Lionel Ravage stood up, whispered something in Benjamin's ear, and walked out of the Hardware Club. He had burn marks on his eyebrows, on his wrists, and pitted scars on his cheeks. He was like a ruinous straw man with liquid buttons instead of eyes.

The emperor had lost his equilibrium. No one had ever walked out on him like that.

Cahan readied his attack with a kind of savage glee. "Mr. Frank," he said, "I am irrevocably opposed to your thirteenth store. I advise you to build elsewhere in Manhattan."

The emperor had always wanted to build a five-and-ten on

Ridley's old site. And he couldn't afford to have the most powerful Jewish editor in Manhattan against him.

"What's the matter, Baron? How have I offended you?"

"I'm not a baron."

Woolworth lured him into a trap with a smile of pure ice. "But you are a baron, or I wouldn't have bothered to summon you here. I've seen what you did to Randolph Hearst when he tried to start a Yiddish daily on the Lower East Side. You wrecked him in a matter of weeks."

"He wrecked himself. He wasn't interested in our concerns. And that was clear to our readers."

The emperor almost began to purr. "Why sabotage my project? I told you, Cahan. I want to hire hundreds of local girls."

"At starvation wages."

Woolworth liked to think of himself as the tall Napoleon. He'd trekked across Europe, following Bonaparte's campaigns, and he wouldn't allow this bespectacled baron to trim his tail. "And what do they earn in the sweatshops, breathing in all the dust? My girls will sit at the lunch counter and have banana splits."

"Mr. Frank, that's not the paradise they need. They can't support themselves with what you offer. And when they try to bargain with your managers, you have them fired."

"Well, we ain't Siegel-Cooper, son. You can't sell luxury items in a five-and-ten. How do you expect us to prosper?"

All of Cahan's old anarchist dreams whipped inside his head. "Not on the backs and the behinds of working girls."

"*Behinds*," Woolworth rasped. "I never took advantage of my clerks. They're decent, respectable. A lot of 'em met their future husbands at my counters. Would ya rather see that corner of Grand occupied by a school for pickpockets and cadets? That's what it is, Baron, the Shilly-Shally Club. I could clear it in a minute, have Captain Kit come down on those cadets like a hammer."

It was all true. Cahan wouldn't have to deal with that one-eyed fagin, Moses Brill, who swept Jewish daughters off the streets. Yet he preferred Moses' *mishegas* to the ruthless, antiseptic world of Mr. Frank. Brill he could contain. But Woolworth was a builder of empires who would fillet the Lower East Side, tear off its skin.

Cahan knew he was making an enemy for life. Mr. Frank would meet with the owners of the *Forward*, talk about a barrage of advertising to accompany Woolworth's presence on Grand Street, and hint at having Cahan fired, or at least silenced on this subject. Cahan wasn't much of a gambler, but he'd have to gamble. The owners couldn't afford to fire him, not while the circulation went up and up. And suppose they did? It wouldn't be the first time he'd become a vagabond, or the last.

"Baron, I speak honestly, in front of all these men. I would like to steal you away from the *Forward* for a few months to work with my team. You can have your own office in the Woolworth Building. I'll listen to your objections, one by one. Name your price. I'll meet it."

It was like a nervous ritual. The emperor still believed he could solve the problem by slathering Cahan with money.

"I have no price, Mr. Frank."

And now Woolworth humbled himself and appealed to the others in the room. "Why is the baron against my Grand Street project?"

"He's from another century," said the Jewish banker. "He doesn't understand high finance. He entertains housewives and poets who can't pay their rent."

"Ignore him," said Marcus Mendelssohn. "He can't hurt you, Mr. Frank. He's a socialist with his head stuck in the sand."

"And you?" Woolworth asked Ben. "You have to deal with crime every day. Tell me what ya think of my project?"

And for a moment, Ben looked like that young wily savage Cahan had met at the Hawthorne School—shrewd and forlorn, and utterly out of place as a printer's devil. Then his lips cracked into a smile.

"The baron doesn't object to the store, Mr. Frank. He would enjoy having a banana split at the lunch counter. But he knows about all the locusts that the store will attract—land developers and other kingpins. They'll beautify and modernize, and tear down the tenements. You'll build promenades, and everything you touch will be fireproof. And the poor, who already live five or six in a room, will be cast out. Where will they go? Some damp cellar in Gravesend? The baron would like to keep the Ghetto the way it is—with its little variety stores, where you can still find toys for a nickel."

"Please, Mr. Frank," said Mendelssohn. "This man doesn't talk for the Kehilla. He's a desperado. He spies on the Ghetto for Cahan. He takes bribes, with Monk Eastman."

"But I admire his loyalty," said Woolworth. "I'll build my store without the baron. And I'll break him if he stands in my way."

He rolled up the drawing his architects had made and marched out of the room with his lieutenants and the rest of his entourage. And now Cahan sat alone with Ben, the two of them like a pair of prehistoric birds protecting the last little corner of the world.

"Ben, what was so important to Lionel that he had to whisper in your ear?"

"He thanked me for getting Waldo out of a tight spot in Satan's Circus. And he says he wants to sit down and talk."

"About what? How he abandoned you before you were born? Are you crazy, Ben? He can't bear to look at you. I can see it in his eyes."

"The feeling is mutual, Baron. . . . Gotta go."

Now Ben deserted him, and Cahan sat there, trying to make sense of his own predicament. Perhaps he should have been more diplomatic with Mr. Frank, but he was never the diplomat. They would hound him at the *Forward*, all the little financiers. *We're in desperate need of revenue, Comrade Editor. Wouldn't it be shrewd to have Woolworth as an ally? His five-and-ten could revive the whole district.* And still he'd publish editorials against the store—until they took the paper out of his hands and watched the readership unravel as all the feuilletons disappeared and *A Bintel Brief* became a humdrum catalog of Ghetto tales, without the lyrical bite of the editor's green pencil. But who was he to crow? He tugged at his sleeve and began to scribble.

> *Dear Reader, please write and tell me if you*
> *would rather have a five-and-ten with all the land*
> *grabbers and other jackals who will follow right*
> *behind and raise your rent . . .*

NINE

Manya

I.

*Y*OUNG RAVAGE HADN'T MEANT TO HURT HER, just quiet her down. She'd married a widower, Lazar, and was flagrant with him and his three girls. She wouldn't feed them, and she tore the pay envelope out of Lazar's fist and had her own bonanza at Wanamaker's and other fashionable shops along Ladies' Mile. She would return with bonbons and corsets that only swelled her size, and when Lazar complained to his rabbi, she went to the Talmud Torah on Eldridge Street and dragged the rabbi between the desks of his Talmudists, and told him never to interfere again. She advertised herself as Tillie Norfolk, but she might have used another name before she married Lazar. She beat his three girls when they asked for bread, and when Lazar cried, Tillie beat him, too. That's when Lazar's youngest daughter, Rose, who was twelve, went to the *Forward* and waited in line to meet Cahan.

He could tell how undernourished she was. Her eyes bulged out of a skull covered with wisps of brown hair. He fed her first—bits of strudel from the bakery downstairs—and sent his printer's devils to find the one sheriff he had. They scoured the Ghetto, searched every corner, and then, as if Cahan had a magic button on his desk, Ben appeared with his golem. He was wearing the extravagant scarf of a grandfather he had never met—Mordecai Rabinowitz. The scarf was a gift from Mordecai's lord at Vilna castle, and was the color of ripe raspberries. Manya couldn't take it with her to the madhouse, so she left it for the little boy.

"I beg you, no violence," Cahan said, hypnotized by the color of the scarf. "I think she's some kind of barracuda who looks for widowers, sucks them dry, and goes on to other prey."

"Then what would you like me to do, Baron?"

"Convince her to go away without ruining these children's lives."

"And what if it takes more than one slap?"

"No violence," Cahan repeated like a Talmudist at his desk.

So the downtown detective went to visit Tillie Norfolk of Norfolk Street with Monk at his side. Tillie weighed three hundred pounds, with arms thick as stalks. Her eyes were barely visible above her swollen cheeks. She had Goliath's shoulder span. And Ben realized that no threats would shake her. He might have compromised if he hadn't witnessed the bare bones and bulging eyes of all three girls and the terrible scratches on the widower's face.

"What a cute boy," Tillie said to Ben while she measured Monk in her mind. "Say, don't I know you from somewhere?"

"Sure," Monk said, "you worked for me once. You were my darling at the Dead Man's Dive."

A "darling" was a female bouncer, and the Dead Man's Dive was a notorious dance hall at the turn of the century, when Monk Eastman ruled the Tenth Ward and wasn't beholden to police chiefs or Tammany bosses. He had his pet shop and his dance hall on Chrystie Street. No one starved in Monk's domain if he could do something about it. He didn't believe in settlement houses or nurses' huts. He walked the streets in red suspenders, his canaries perched on the crushed crown of his hat, and dispensed largesse wherever he saw fit. Monk had no appetite for politics. He wasn't looking for favors in return, and he wasn't a shylock. If a peddler needed funds for a new pushcart, Monk handed him a wedge of butcher paper with one word on it—*Monk*—and it was better than currency on the Lower East Side. . . .

The fat witch of Norfolk Street had once been Tillie Ostropol, and she hadn't weighed three hundred pounds at the time, but was a buxom wench with big shoulders. And she didn't have to prey on widowers and their children. She had plenty of loot. But she must have fallen when Monk fell. The Dead Man's Dive was boarded up after Monk was sent to Sing Sing. Tillie grew addicted to her sweet tooth.

And now she kept staring at Ben. "Blondie, what do you want?"

"A simple task," he said. "We'd like you to vacate the premises."

She roared, this Lady Goliath, and the shelves shook; a bowl of sugar crashed to the linoleum. Lazar hid in the corner with his three daughters; he was a skilled sewing machine operator, and he produced the finest boys' knickerbockers for quality stores.

"And why would I do that, Blondie, when I have a marriage certificate, signed and sealed? I'm not a boarder. I inherited three lovely girls, and I plan to guard that inheritance."

Monk couldn't even take the yellow birds out of his pocket to give her a hint of the destruction that would follow. He knew what his former darling was capable of. She would have slapped the birds out of the air and bitten off their heads.

"I understand the legality," Ben said, "but you still can't stay."

Her whole body quaked, and she seemed to burst out of her

corset. "Ask Edward. He can tell you about my talents. I was his best crippler."

Ben knew he couldn't reason with her; she'd stuff herself with bonbons, abuse Lazar and the girls until they landed in the hospital, even the morgue. Without warning, he dove at her, head down, and dug into the taut, complicated strings of her girdle. He'd caught Tillie off guard, and she fell onto the linoleum, her body breaking right through the wall; she sat in a sea of plaster, while a great bellowing laugh rumbled out of her throat.

"Blondie, give the old girl a kiss. I like you more and more."

He could have gone to the courts, gotten a restraining order, but she had the money to hire her own lawyer, and she'd be out on the streets again, a wild, vengeful woman doing more and more damage.

He thought of moving Lazar and the girls to another location, but Tillie would have tracked them down. It was Monk who seized a flowerpot from the windowsill and cracked it over Tillie's head as she was about to rise. She slumped onto the linoleum and lay there, her eyes fluttering, her face covered in black earth.

"Help us," Monk said, appealing to Lazar and the girls. "We can't lift her alone. She weighs a ton."

Ben didn't want to involve Lazar's daughters, but they helped drag their stepmother to the window with a satanic glee, while Lazar wailed from his corner, "I won't be a party to all this. I'm a religious man."

"Papa," said the oldest daughter, "keep quiet."

"Edward," Benjamin muttered, "what are we trying to do?"

"Get her out the window. That's Tillie Ostropol's one weakness. She was always scared of heights. I couldn't even ask her to work on the balcony."

How could they get Tillie halfway out the window? The sill would shatter and she'd fall to her death right in front of the girls. But the five of them tugged on Tillie, nipped at her flesh until her torso was over the sill and the rest of her was anchored on three chairs. The wind must have woken her. She could see the old abandoned privies in the courtyard and the crooked fences that separated the pathetic little gardens that some of the tenants kept.

They bound her up in strips of bedding as her body pitched back and forth and she screamed like a wounded bovine. It was a pitiful cry that almost shook the fight out of young Ravage. But he wouldn't relent.

"Tillie Ostropol Norfolk, will you leave this place forever?"

Her cries grew shriller and shriller and seemed to crack open the murky, pestilential air. Ben had to calm her down. All five held her with all their might and raised her head an inch. And that's when Lazar appeared with a glaze in his eyes and clutching a kitchen knife.

"I want to cut off her head. I'll carry it to the synagogue in a paper bag and beg forgiveness."

Complications, Ben muttered to himself. *Always complications. It's worse than the Yiddish theater.* He couldn't afford to let go of Tillie. He had to become the lightning attorney-at-law.

"Lazar, what will happen to your daughters when you sit behind bars? There's little leeway for a man who beheads his own wife."

"I don't care," Lazar said. "She has to suffer."

"Papa," the girls snapped at him. "Go away! You'll ruin your life and ours."

He returned to his corner, and Benjamin could concentrate on Tillie again.

"It's your last chance. Will you leave this place and never return?"

"*Yes,*" she cried. "Oh, God, I will, I will, I will."

2.

HE'D NEVER BE FAR FROM THAT ORPHANAGE on Ludlow Street no matter where he was. He had to run from location to location, or he wouldn't have survived Ned Silver's jackals. He couldn't trust his old haunts, where he kept stacks of cash. So he collected whatever cash he'd hidden in fire hydrants, knotted his scarf, and now he was ready to meet Lionel Ravage.

He went to Lionel's little empire on Canal, block after block of hardware stores under the rubric *Ravage & Son.* The stalls outside the stores were as random and cluttered as any rag shop; there were mountains of bolts and screws, metal sleeves, compasses, and pliers that were slightly bent; there were carpenter's awls, slide rules, hacksaws with broken handles, paintbrushes, varnish, and tubs of glue. Lionel had bought out the presence of any other hardware man. He'd left no place on Canal for rivals. His countermen stood near the stalls in rubber aprons and hawked Lionel's wares.

"Paintbrushes, five for a dollar. You won't get another bargain on Canal."

The entrance to Lionel's headquarters was as haphazard as the other stands and stores. The windows hadn't been washed in years. The awning was in tatters. Lionel couldn't have believed in that ruthless efficiency of Frank Woolworth's five-and-tens. He thrived in some eternal chaos.

A bell rang as young Ravage entered a warehouse packed with an endless inventory of pipes. He felt a strange comfort here, amid all the dust and decay, and he couldn't even determine why. Men with shotguns patrolled the ragged aisles. They weren't protecting Lionel's inventory from thieves. They were looking for colonies of rats; rats could gnaw right through lead and suck on copper. They went about their business and ignored Benjamin, who had to climb a spiral staircase to Lionel's office. It had none of the exuberance that ought to have accompanied Manhattan's hardware king. Half the pipes in the Ghetto must have come from him, yet his office was bewilderingly small. His wife, Henrietta, sat behind one desk with a vacant look in her eye, and his daughter sat behind another. Becky Ravage wore a silk blouse that just managed to cover her nipples. Lionel must have had a devil of a time guarding her from those rat chasers downstairs. Her lewdness seemed beyond repair. She embarrassed Ben with her wanton looks, ogling him like some dessert she hoped to devour. Perhaps Becky's imbecilic brother, Waldo, was her keeper. He stood around, jangling the change in his pockets. And Benjamin realized that the Ravages weren't here to help Lionel keep his own books. They didn't have the slightest idea of commerce. They were essentially his hostages.

"Young man, would you care for a cup of tea?" Henrietta asked in a voice that was barely audible.

"Feed him poison," Waldo said with a sneer. "His mama was that blond witch who wrecked your life."

Benjamin wanted to rip Waldo's eyes out, but he wouldn't destroy the one advantage he had. He'd come for Lionel, not his idiotic son.

Henrietta wept in her corner like some old maid in a fairy tale. "You mustn't insult the young man."

Waldo had a laughing fit. "Why not? He's Papa's love baby."

Lionel tossed an iron ruler at Waldo; it spun through the air and would have clipped off half his nose if Waldo hadn't ducked and hidden behind his father's desk.

"Stay there," Lionel said. "If you ever insult a guest of mine again, I'll give you to the rats."

"Papa, I wouldn't mind the same punishment," Becky giggled, but Lionel ignored her. He motioned to Benjamin, and they climbed down that spiral staircase. Lionel wasn't carrying his wolf's-head cane. And Benjamin saw how frail he was. His straw-white hair seemed glued to his scalp. His face was like a corrosive mask amid the swirling dusk.

They went across the street to a tiny café that had no more than half a dozen tables. Other customers cleared out the moment he walked in, and now they had the café to themselves. The waiter brought Lionel a slice of Black Forest cake and a cup of coffee with a cap of whipped cream. Ben had the same.

"I have no regrets," Lionel told him, his mouth cluttered with whipped cream. "I am who I am. But you did me a kindness. You got my son out of a bad scrape in Whoretown. He wanders into one jam after the other and thinks money can cure every problem."

Ben could imagine Waldo on a rampage. "You're his maestro. He learned from you. He's been attacking Jewish girls on Allen Street."

"I've cured him of that habit," Lionel said. "But how can I repay you?"

"You can't."

Lionel kept staring at Ben's scarf. "Where did you get that item? At Wanamaker's?"

"It's an heirloom. It belonged to my grandfather."

Lionel laughed bitterly to himself. "The philosopher with a pushcart. He wouldn't take a penny from me."

"Maybe he didn't want your lucre," Ben said.

"Are you as pure as that philosopher, kid? What if I paid you a thousand dollars for that scarf? It has some sentimental value."

Ben removed the scarf from his throat. "Here, Lionel. It's yours—for free."

Lionel grabbed up the scarf like a little boy and stuffed it into his pocket. He smiled under that reptilian mask of his. "You must be dying to know what Manya meant to me."

Ben plucked at the dark chocolate slivers that sat on his slice of Black Forest cake. "Lionel, if you mention my mother's name again, I'll strangle you inside your own little king's café."

"Go 'head. Strangle. I have to talk about your mother."

Lionel was like a dead man with blue tin in his eyes. And Ben watched all his plans of revenge unravel. You couldn't deprive a dead man of his fortune, even if that fortune was the only life a dead man could ever have.

"I didn't even know you existed," Lionel said. "I swear on my father's grave, and he's the only one I ever cared about besides your mother."

"Shut up and eat your cake."

The reptile smiled again. "Is this the loser's last meal?"

Benjamin stood up, wanted to shove the chocolate slivers into Lionel's eyes and leave, when he heard a whimper that disabled him. It was Manya's cry, that despair she felt when she thought of Lionel. He sat down again.

"Stop crying, or I won't listen to a word."

Lionel wiped his eyes with a filthy rag. "It was our lord and master, Jacob Schiff, who told me about you—and your little trip to Harvard from the Hawthorne School."

Suddenly that mask seemed as animated as any face that hadn't been licked by fire. "I was astounded by my own jealousy. I wanted to tear off your flesh. *Manya has a boy. Manya has a boy.* That's when I took chances, crazy risks. I had other landlords beaten to death."

"You shouldn't tell me that. I'm a detective with the Kehilla."

"Bravo," the hardware king said with a defiant smile. "Arrest me all you want."

Ben couldn't relinquish his hate, or undeliver it, like some package. "You married my mother when you had an heiress of your own—and two brats in an uptown cradle. Isn't that what you did with all your other brides? You even had a regular shamas on your payroll who performed the ceremonies."

Lionel's wig went awry. Benjamin could see the puckers in his scalp that reminded him of the boys at the orphanage who suffered from ringworm; they all had craters in their scalps like Lionel's. And then Lionel repaired his wig, pasted it down, and he had the semblance of a man again.

"I never married your mother—not once. The others, yes. I had my own beadle, and many brides, but not Manya. I never would have married her in a crooked ceremony."

"I'll kill you," Ben muttered, but he was panicking, with sharp splinters of doubt. "Why would my mother make up such a story, and give me your rotten name? Don't tell me it was one more delusion. She wouldn't have lied to me."

"I don't know," Lionel said with a puzzled look.

"But she swore there was a certificate, swore on her life. She said I was the landlord's son."

And suddenly Lionel was the detective, the purveyor of lost souls; his tin eyes darted with blue fire.

"Did you ever see that certificate, Ben? I told her about all the other brides. And once we did pretend. We turned a pillowcase into a canopy and danced under it. I called her Mrs. Lionel Ravage."

Ben couldn't bear to listen, but he did listen, while he imagined Manya dancing under the pillowcase with her blond aristocrat. It was exactly what his mother would have done—gallant and half mad at the same time. He could feel her hot breath on him, as if Manya were dancing with Ben and not the landlord. She swayed and swayed, humming her own melody. But he couldn't keep Manya. She tumbled out of his dream, and he tumbled, too.

"*Mrs. Lionel Ravage.* She used a name that wasn't even hers for the rest of her life. Why?"

For little Ben.

His hatred had blinded him. Manya must have known she was pregnant while she danced. She wanted her baby to bear Lionel's "crest." So she made herself into Manya Ravage. And Ben, the child with an abundance of family names, really had none.

Lionel seemed melancholy under that head of straw. "I knew her less than six months. But tell me about Manya—please."

And what did Lionel want to hear? That they slept at the station house during the coldest nights? That Manya couldn't pay the rent? That cadets wanted to have her work on Allen Street? That she couldn't hold a job for very long? That every shop steward tried to paw her? That they had to move from apartment to apartment with lice in their linen? That later on she didn't have the coherence or the stamina to move? Why should he reward Lionel with the itinerary of such a tale?

"How many other women did you marry after my mother?"

"Dozens," he said. "No—not one. I didn't have the heart. I dismissed the beadle."

"Then why did you abandon her?"

"I never did," he said. "I abandoned myself."

Ben had a sinister glare in his eye; all the violence that brewed in him was about to erupt.

"I don't want your poetry, Lionel, or your preambles. Why did you abandon her?"

And Lionel revisited that winter storm in 1883, after he met Manya on Attorney Street, and was confounded by that first glimpse of her, seductive and shy, with her wild blond hair, and her father, the philosopher who peddled apples whenever he could afford a pushcart, and how they had to fondle each other while Papa Rabinowitz was inside the privy, and how she sent him away because she couldn't make love to Lionel behind her father's back. He went to Attorney Street after the philosopher died, and he told Ben about Uncle Rainer and Henrietta's other relatives, who threatened to tear him to pieces if he didn't return to his wife, and swore to harm Manya if he visited her again, even once, and sell her to the white slavers.

Ben didn't know what to believe. Manya had never taken him near Canal to peek into the clouded windows of Ravage & Son.

"You're a millionaire. You could have had some shamas locate where she was, just for the hell of it."

But Lionel didn't hedge, didn't make excuses, didn't pacify Ben.

"I had to cut her out completely or I wouldn't have survived."

And all this time Lionel thought of the blond dew on Manya's arms, dreamt of the tiny tufts of hair around her nipples, though he didn't reveal that to Ben. He lusted after Manya in his sleep, worried that he'd end up in the madhouse. So he expelled her with a cruel calculation, got rid of her every trace. But he did other damage. His rage spiraled out of him; he humiliated men on the street, attacked with his cane, and sat under the law's protection. He paid off politicians and precinct captains, struck up alliances with men more powerful than himself, had dinner with Pierpont Morgan at Sherry's and Delmonico's, befriended retailers on the rise, like Frank Woolworth, made millions, while Manya gnawed at him no matter what woman he was with. His conquests were like the ashes of a condemned building. But he wouldn't satisfy the boy, wouldn't reveal a lifetime of irrevocable mourning, or that dead paste around his heart.

Despite himself, he blurted out, "I did see her again," as if he were striking Ben with some invisible wolf's head. He saw the confusion in Ben's eyes, the alarm.

"What are you talking about? She died on Blackwell's Island. I am a lawyer, Lionel. I made inquiries. No one could find her death certificate—it fell into the wind. The city clerks think she's buried in a communal grave somewhere; they don't have the authority to dig up a potter's field. I might have succeeded in finding her if I were a loyal Democrat. But I'm not on good terms with Tammany Hall. You know that. Ned Silver's jackals have been following me for days."

Lionel's tin eyes stared out of his own self-inflicted ruin. "Manya didn't die on Blackwell's Island and she wasn't buried in a potter's field."

Ben felt a brutal turn in his brain, as if madness and furor had suddenly crept upon him, and he lacked the capability to read his own past.

"I met with the clerks. They—"

"Clerks," Lionel rasped with malice in his voice. "They shuffle papers and tell you what they've been told to tell. She was ferried to the madhouse on Ward's Island after Blackwell's shut down."

"But why are you so sure?"

"Because once I knew of your existence, I couldn't sleep. I bribed a few officials in the Public Health Department. They found her records in some storage bin. The rest was a snap."

Lionel had papers forged with the Health Department's official stamp. He had men in white coats remove Manya from the island and deliver her to Montefiore, Jacob Schiff's home for Jewish cripples. Benjamin wanted to crush Lionel's skull between his hands. He should have realized that Montefiore was a house of refuge for stray cats, that the invalids on the ground floor were some kind of grandiloquent cover.

"It's the Jewish Four Hundred all over again. Did you drop my mother off in the attic? And did she happen to fall off the ledge, like Leila Montague?"

"She wasn't in any attic. She had a suite of rooms to herself—Jacob's suite."

He could imagine her in that maze of rooms at Montefiore, surrounded by soft cries from the wards; little boys with crooked spines, old men with emphysema.

"And no one bothered to tell me about Montefiore?"

Lionel wasn't even listening.

"I went to her. I abandoned all my plumbing projects. She didn't remember me."

"Manya must have been frightened after all those years of being locked away. She—"

Benjamin felt as if his tongue had been torn from his mouth.

He couldn't recognize Lionel for a moment, with that head of straw hair. The Black Forest cake tasted like bitter dust.

"She didn't remember me," Lionel said. Manya thought she was back on Attorney Street with that pushcart peddler. I have to make pee-pee, Manya told him. She squatted in that prince's suite and flooded the parquet floor. Her urine smelled like cough medicine. He watched her as she got up, wandered across the room, and sat down at a vanity table in her hospital shift. "Guard," she said to Lionel, "brush my hair, or I'll report you to your superiors." Her hair had been clipped in the madhouse, but Lionel pretended she had the same long blond strands. His brush strokes marked her former silhouette. That's what he told his errant son.

Lionel was trembling now, and Ben had to feed him bits of cake with a fork. Suddenly, Ben could hear his own voice rattle in his throat again. "What happened to my mother, you fire-fucked son of a bitch?"

Lionel took over Montefiore, had every nurse and doctor at his call. But he couldn't keep her alive, not with all his money and maddening will. She collapsed while he was brushing her hair, absorbed as he was in the memory of its luxuriousness. The doctors couldn't revive her. Lionel manufactured a death certificate and had her buried next to his father at Woodlawn, near the family plot.

"You can visit her if you want. I wrote the inscription. *Manya Ravage, 39, beloved mother of Benjamin.*"

"Shut up, or you'll never make another sound."

His whole life had come down to this—a hapless duel with a dead man who could still talk. Yet he'd defrauded himself all this time. Lionel was invaluable to him—alive. He wanted to know what Manya had been like before he was ever born, and there were no other witnesses but Lionel himself. A grandfather he'd never met couldn't tell him much from the grave.

"Was she kind?"

Lionel glared at him through that puffed-out morass of skin. "Are we trading marbles now? She could make a man weep. That's the beauty she had. What do I know of kindness? Her eyes ripped into my flesh the first time that door opened and I looked at her. I didn't want to leave. I had a wife I didn't love, children I never wanted to fondle. It might have been different if my father had still been alive. But the hawks swooped down and tried to steal the treasure he had. I was brutal with brutal men. I saw acid and rust until I met Manya. Yes, she was kind. And I was happy with her, and then those other hawks pounced, my wife's own people, merchants and bankers who had a big stake in my treasure."

"They mean nothing to me, such men. Did she smile? Did she laugh?"

Lionel felt as if his skull would crack. He'd never talked about Manya with another soul. She'd dwelled in that long stretch of silence his existence had become, a shriek without an echo.

"I had a cat," he said. "Her name was Chlöe. She was my blond rat catcher. And some pirates from across the river strangled her, left her strung up. I was never the same. I would have fought my wife's relatives if Chlöe hadn't been killed. You wouldn't under-stand the affection I had for the cat. I had no more wind without her. . . . You needn't worry about Ned Silver. There's a moratorium out on you. Ned is in my hip pocket. But you have to keep away from the Essex Market Court, or else the moratorium won't last."

And for the first time Ben could grasp the real fabric behind Lionel's enterprises—the spoils of the Essex Market Court. Lionel was the master of that Manhattan slave pen, not Silver Dollars.

Ben could have been back at Harvard, arguing with his professors over the chicaneries of the law.

"Should I have Ned and his coppers drag people in front of the court who never committed a crime? They're flesh eaters. They'd steal bread from a baby's mouth. And I'm supposed to stand idle and let Silver Dollars steal? I didn't slug it through law school to have him trample on the Lower East Side."

"How many other lawyers are in your little association?" Lionel asked.

"Not a single one."

"And what if I told you that Essex Market is the biggest moneymaker we have in the district? Yes, some people are railroaded. But the profit from that courthouse helps light the lamps in the streets. Would you prefer to have all of Yiddish Land go dark?"

"I'd still have to intervene."

And he left Lionel there with the chocolate crumbs and bits of cherries from his Black Forest cake. He'd lived like Monte Cristo with some real or imagined hate, and the man he hated most was the only tie he'd ever have to his mother. She'd loved Lionel beyond reason, and that love had terrorized him all these years. It was a wound that wouldn't heal. He was no different from Lionel—a lust for violence had passed from father to son. Harvard hadn't civilized him; it had only sharpened his craft. He didn't have a wolf's-head cane, but he did stalk the Lower East Side, and the Jewish criminals he tracked for the Kehilla could have been eruptions from his own past, brother orphans glimpsed through a dark glass.

TEN

Chlöe

I.

"CHLÖE," LIONEL MUTTERED TO HIMSELF when he saw Ned
Silver's ample body glide past the window of the café. Ned
rarely left his fortress on Essex Street. He was surrounded by six
of his men—Ned's entourage, since he never traveled alone. He
stood with his derby in his hands until Lionel invited him to sit.
He devoured an apple dumpling before he uttered a word, having
to manipulate the café's tiny silver fork with his own fat fist.

"How are the receipts, Ned?"

"Divine, boss, divine," and he removed a bundle of cash from
inside his waistcoat.

"Then why are you here? You're not my bagman, Ned."

"Well, sir, we have a problem, see. It concerns the soon to
be departed shamas. Your instructions aren't precise. Do we snuff
him or not?"

Lionel wished he had his wolf's-head with him. He would
have knocked Silver Dollars' derby across the café.

"Your job is to keep him from the courthouse."

"But it's delicate, sir, if we can't do the real number on him,
and he's ruined three of my boys, gave them hernias they'll never

forget. The shamas is attached to you. Sort of an unacknowledged heir, if you know what I mean."

"That's not your business. If he wanders into the courthouse again, you can break his bones."

Silver Dollars scratched behind his ear. "That's a tricky situation, sir. If we break his bones, you might break ours."

"That's a chance you'll have to take."

He turned from Silver Dollars, who left the café and floated into the wind with his retainers. People crossed Canal and fled at the sight of him. Lionel watched Silver Dollars disappear as the café windows rattled. The sky darkened in an instant. Ah, it was an April shower, but the rain that beat on the windows wasn't benign. The first crack of lightning lit up his straw hair. It seemed to halt the run of time, while the past thirty years seemed to slip right out of his palms. He couldn't stop thinking of Chlöe. If he hadn't been remiss and left his blond cat alone in that graveyard of pipes, the pirates from across the river wouldn't have strung her up, with her eyes as burnt-out holes.

He hadn't bought Chlöe from a breeder, or found her at a shelter for strays, or plucked her off the street. She was a feral cat with a brilliant blond coat who prowled his warehouse for six months before revealing herself to him. She'd been clearing the place of rats. She hissed at his watchmen and managers and would have scratched their eyes. His shop steward wanted to blast her with a shotgun. "She's wild, boss. She could attack any one of us. We'll lose customers on account of that blond bitch."

But he liked the feral cat who haunted his warehouse. She comforted him, soothed his own wildness. He named her after a character he'd read of in a foreign book; it was about a demonic woman who ruined one man after another until she got sick of humankind and ran off to the forest—that was his Chlöe in a graveyard of pipes. He didn't buy her affection with whitefish as the watchmen tried to do. Her let her prowl. And one afternoon, she leapt into his lap; Lionel landed on the floor, with Chlöe and the chair on top of him. Her huge green eyes drilled right into Lionel's skull. She ate herring and halvah out of his hand, licking his fingers until they stuck together with a miraculous glue.

None of his customers could approach her. She'd disappear into that nest of pipes and wait until Lionel was alone. He didn't want to run uptown, or play pinochle at the Hardware Club. He let his business slide a little and sat with Chlöe. Lionel wasn't her master; he never wanted to tame his blond cat. They were two primitive souls who moved in and out of the void, and that's how their attachment grew. He couldn't have fallen in love with Manya if he hadn't lived all morning and afternoon with that feral cat. Manya startled him with the amber flecks in her blue eyes and her long blond hair. She was feral in her own way. And Lionel couldn't hold on to her, not after he lost his cat; his will was gone once he looked into the scorched sockets of Chlöe's eyes. And Uncle Rainer could ride right over him. He buried himself in his properties and in his empire of pipes. He toiled in that graveyard. He bought tenements rather than brokerage houses. He seized empty lots. He kept Tammany Hall in line with the hard cash he could deliver. Whatever acquisitions he had made him thirsty to have more. He owned half the clubs in Satan's Circus. He gave gamblers money to gamble with and collected an exorbitant fee. Police detectives were on his payroll. He contributed a fat check to the Captains' Ball. He slid silently into his own sarcophagus of wealth until one afternoon in 1903 Jacob Schiff told him about that blue-eyed boy,

Benjamin Ravage, and the sarcophagus he'd built with such care shattered around him.

He had no more appetite to acquire. He squandered his shares in the Jewish bank. He let his buildings rot. Chlöe appeared in his sleep. He found Manya after twenty years, removed her from her island hospital, and had her sent to a hill on Hamilton Heights. He'd lied to Benjamin. Manya wasn't mad at all. Her keepers had abused her. She had marks all over her body. She wore a white hospital gown. Her beautiful blond hair had been clipped, and clung to her skull. She sat in front of Jacob Schiff's vanity table at Montefiore, her legs wide apart, and looked in the mirror like a bemused clown. She addressed Lionel as she would a servant. "Landlord, comb my hair."

There was nothing to comb. But he held the hairbrush against the fuzz on her scalp.

"Why did it take you so long to visit?" she asked. "Where's your money bag? Have you forgotten how to collect the rent?"

He was astounded and beside himself with remorse. He felt as if she could crush him with a few choice words. She was the clever one, having enriched herself on Ward's Island and Blackwell's in a sea of lunatics, while he lived among aristocrats and brutes.

"Aren't you my Galahad? Poor Lionel, what happened to your hair?"

He hadn't been scorched yet, but she looked at him as if his face were on fire. It bewildered Lionel that she hadn't mentioned her boy, hadn't asked for Ben.

"How's Henrietta?"

Her mind was much too quick. He stumbled for a few words, and found nothing at all.

"Does she ask about the blonde who came out of the closet?

My father didn't belong to a burial society. I had to go begging, or he would have landed in a pauper's grave. And should I tell you how many rabbis' assistants tried to proposition me?"

Lionel thought he was hallucinating, that Chlöe had come back, and could suddenly wail at him. But Manya didn't have a cat's whiskers.

"Landlord," she said, "what are you waiting for? Get undressed."

"Undressed? But this is a nursing home. Attendants walk in and out. We have so little privacy."

She laughed, not to mock him, but to explain her motive. "Darling Lionel, attendants have seen my ass every day of the week. They come into the shower stalls; they peek at us from behind the curtain. I don't have such luxuries. Get undressed."

She unbuttoned his shirt, shucked off his trousers. He stood there with all his scars from pipes that had exploded and floors that had collapsed and buried him in rubble and bits of glass; he could have been some half-baked Minotaur with a bull's balls. And she removed her white gown. Her shoulders were still sleek, even with all the bruises. She had the same tufts of blond hair around her nipples.

"Landlord, did you think of me every day? And when you made love to Henrietta and all your whores, did they possess you, or was it Manya Ravage, the wife you never married?"

He didn't even know what to answer her. She'd stripped him of all his powers, and he lay down with her on Jacob Schiff's parquet floor; he knew there was anger in this little lesson of love, that she was punishing him, that he could never repay her for his vanishing act, yet she moved under him with much of the old desire, with all the little moans he remembered from Attorney Street. . . .

He sat with her every night, often slept beside her in a chair. He waited and waited for her to talk about Ben. He could have told her that the boy was at Harvard, but craven as he was, he said nothing—until he finally said, "Your Benjamin's a real survivor. He went from a trade school for delinquents to college up at Cambridge."

She shut her eyes while he combed her cropped hair. "What Benjamin?"

"Your little boy," he said with a rattle in his throat.

"Landlord, little boys don't drop out of the sky. I'm the wife without a wedding ring."

And then Schiff arrived at Montefiore with all his sentinels, those Jewish bankers and brokers with their Fifth Avenue estates. Lionel was ready for them, convinced that they'd command him to return to his wife, as Uncle Rainer had done. But they had another grievance.

"Lionel, dear Lionel," Schiff said, with a twitch of his white mustache, "you must tell the boy that his mother is alive."

"No," Lionel replied. "She doesn't even remember him. I'd like to keep it that way."

"But you will break his heart. And if he ever finds out, he will throttle you with his own hands."

"Not if I throttle him first."

The Jewish patriarchs stared at Lionel with both cunning and disbelief.

"You cannot be that cruel," one of them said.

"Oh, I'm much crueler than that. An earlier delegation took Manya from me. It won't happen again."

"And what if we should tell the boy?" Schiff asked. "He's an orphan, and he has no one but his mother."

"What are you trying to say? That I abandoned the boy? I didn't even know he was alive. But if you breathe a word about Manya, I'll ruin every last one of you."

"You're a maniac," Schiff said, anger flaring in his blue eyes. "You're the one who belongs in an asylum."

"We'll go to the police," said Felix Warburg, Schiff's handsome son-in-law.

And Lionel did howl like a lunatic. "I stole her from the madhouse, remember? They'll shut down Montefiore in a minute. You're all loyal Republicans, but I'm in deep with Tammany Hall. So how can you hurt me, Felix?"

"We'll pull out of all our property deals," said Schiff.

"Ah, Jacob, did you forget? I'm partners with all your partners and their partners. You'll tell that boy nothing, nothing at all. I won't lose Manya a second time."

"*Gott*," said Schiff, "I wish you and the madwoman had never met."

And the delegation left him there in the vestibule, with some of the invalids wandering out of the central ward. Lionel returned to Schiff's private suite and shut the door. But he had little solace in that battle with the patriarchs. Manya watched him in the mirror of her vanity table as if he, too, were made of glass. He could never recapture those lost years, even if he remained with her for an eternity.

He brought couturiers to Montefiore, had her measurements taken. Dresses and hats and shoes were delivered, and satin underwear. He hired a maid to look after her trousseau. Nothing he could ever do would really tilt her toward him.

He preferred Manya in her white shift, without satins and dark paint around her eyes, without velvet shoes.

"Landlord," she said, "we have to make at least one baby before I die. I don't want to be the only barren bride from Blackwell's Island."

Now he understood her tricks. She was frightened of Lionel; she must have sensed all the rampaging he had done. He wasn't the same cavalier who had sat with her father and talked about Spinoza and Kant while she hid in the closet. He didn't have that musical purr of a cat. He was a hoarder now, a breaker of men. The landlord-poet she had waited for, even on Ward's Island, had forgotten how to laugh.

"I could bring him here—Ben."

"There is no Ben."

But he saw the flecks of terror in her eyes, and it enraged Lionel. She kept him here like a seductive spider, feigned desire to please him, so that he wouldn't harm her boy. Ah, she knew what he was capable of—Lionel Ravage danced with the devil without his Chlöe; perhaps he was the devil.

He planned to run up to Harvard with his wolf's-head cane and bash the boy's skull in, since nothing else could lull that hollow cry at his core, that need to maim. He might have accomplished such a mission, but it would have meant leaving her for a whole night, perhaps two, since he'd have to locate whatever hovel the boy was living in.

"Don't hurt him," she said, as if he were having a conversation with his dead cat. "I promise never to see him, never to leave this room." She was Chlöe, with invisible whiskers and invisible claws that could still dig into him.

And then, after the maid had dressed her in the finest silks, colored her cheeks and called her the princess of Montefiore, she looked in the mirror one last time with a kind of horror, as if she recognized her plight as a prisoner without Ben, that Lionel had become her insane asylum; a shudder went through her body like an electric bolt that could have lit the Woolworth Building, and she sank into her chair.

He buried her without notifying Jacob Schiff. He had a rabbi and a shamas come to the grave. Prayers were sung. He still sat on the board of Temple Emanu-El, wouldn't leave the Educational Alliance. He didn't skip a single wedding of that great fraternal order of Jewish aristocrats. But he went prowling with his silver cane. The detectives who were mortgaged to him masked whatever harm he did. And when he had to pull tenants out of a building he needed to demolish, he hired other detectives to have each apartment vacated. He also could have hired his own arsonists. But when he wanted to collect on insurance premiums without having any witnesses who might blackmail him, he'd walk into an abandoned tenement in the middle of the night, leave a trail of gasoline from the top stairwell to the cellar, light a match, and walk away with his coat collar near his eyes.

Once, just once, he grew careless. He lit the match while he was still on the steps, and the banisters collapsed around him; he tumbled down an entire flight and lay there with a broken knee while the flames licked around him and the tin on the walls crackled. He didn't move. He realized at that moment, as if he'd suffered some memory lapse, that it was Manya's building, a tenement that had once been so sweet to him.

Good. I'll die here. I'll have my own brick grave.

The smoke and heat were unbearable, but he still wouldn't budge. He must have been unconscious when a roundsman removed him with his hair and coat on fire. He lay in Jacob Schiff's Hebrew hospital for months, half the time in a coma. Surgeons had to graft new skin on him. He looked like a lizard. It was a miracle that he hadn't lost his eyesight, that his hands could still move, that his blood could circulate.

He woke to find Jacob Schiff in front of him, with a basket of white roses.

"You'll recover, Lionel. The doctors assured me of that. We've looked after your accounts. We didn't have to sell a thing. You're even richer now than you were before the conflagration."

"And what happened to that little bastard who carries my name?"

"He's with the Kehilla now."

Lionel's face hurt like hell but he still laughed. "A Jewish detective."

And then, only then, he looked in the mirror and saw the great blotches of skin under the bandages.

"Jacob, why didn't they let me die in peace?"

"We couldn't sustain such a loss," Schiff said. "You're our valued brother."

And Lionel fell back to sleep with the sound of Jacob's blessing in his ears like the waft of bitter herbs.

2.

HE'D NEVER GET USED TO THAT HEAD OF STRAW. He had pieces of metal in his back and wrists. He jerked about with a mechanical gait. He could no longer make love to a woman in any natural way. His penis was like a pimple. One of his testicles had been removed. He wouldn't undress in front of a woman. Yet his longings were there, even with that pathetic pimple. Sometimes he'd have a whole harem parade in front of him, or he'd lie down with a buxom wench from Satan's Circus, fondle her with all his clothes on, rut up against her with one knee, lick her from head to toe, delight in the salty taste as he nuzzled her armpits, or skated over the crack of her ass with his lizard's palm; he paid her in hundred-dollar bills, but he was never satisfied.

Lovemaking had to become a blood sport for Lionel. He had to find other wenches, who were desperate for his money. But he beat them without much flair. He had to see flecks of blood on his silver wolf's head. And even that was more like a simulation of desire. What he liked best was when he found a woman who would fight back. Then it was a real sport. They were usually veterans of other wars, mollies who had attached themselves to gangs like the Hudson Dusters, and would laugh away Lionel's blows while they spat a little blood.

"You prickless wonder, is that all you can do?"

He saw them as casualties like himself, ancient relics, and he enjoyed their company. So he often went to Whoretown. And he might sit with these gun molls inside the Haymarket and trade stories with them. They all talked about Monk Eastman and how the world had been different before Monk sat in Sing Sing.

"A girl could make a living when Monk ruled the roost. He was never unfair, never took money from us, Mr. Lionel, and he paid us to manage his clubs. But if you crossed him, he would send one of his canaries to fly over your head, and you didn't even have time to pack. You had to run to Kansas. No one would look at you, or offer you a drink. They couldn't afford to risk Monk's wrath. It was like being invisible inside the Circus. It drove some women bats."

Ah, Lionel wondered to himself. That's the kind of fear he sought. But he didn't have Monk's amplitude, Monk's chivalry,

Monk's generous nature. Lionel was much too mean. He knocked on the window of the café, in the middle of a thunderstorm, and his driver appeared, a police sergeant borrowed from Captain Kittleberger and the Madison Street precinct. The sergeant wore a rubber raincoat and shielded Lionel with the wings of his coat. Lionel stepped into the captain's own Packard from under that rubber coat. Kittleberger sat in the rear, but Lionel preferred to sit up front with the driver. He nodded to the captain.

"Let me do all the talking, Kit. Don't say a word."

"Ah," the captain muttered, "so I'm your personal dummy now. Well, I don't like it."

"Trust me," Lionel said. "I know how to deal with these little lords."

3.

It was like an exalted penny arcade with a barreled ceiling, and lined with shops and steamship companies that could have transported Lionel to Venezuela, Siam, or the South Seas. Woolworth and his flamboyant architect, Cass Gilbert, were grand illusionists; they'd constructed a miniature Manhattan, with subway platforms behind a bronze gate, a subterranean swimming pool, a beer hall and barbershop in the basement, a dental clinic, and an observation deck that revealed how shrunken the actual city was, with all its water routes, in relation to Woolworth's tower. And then there was also the master architect's clever signature crafted into the lobby wall, a grotesque of Woolworth, counting nickels and dimes, like a mischievous dwarf.

Lionel wasn't amused. A lobby meant to look like the nave of a cathedral was just the fanciful cover of a sewer trap. He and

Kittleberger took one of the high-speed elevators up to Frank Woolworth's corporate headquarters. Woolworth's own pages led Lionel to the Empire Room, with the captain tagging behind.

The Empire Room had a Napoleonic grandeur, but Lionel could barely see the décor; all he remembered was working with the electricians and his own plumbers in a barren space without floorboards. Woolworth collected every bit of memorabilia he could from the Old World. He had a copy of Napoleon's "throne chair" from the palace at Fontainebleau, with its cobalt blue footstool and armrests in the shape of a lion's paws. There were also replicas of coronation robes and bronze inkwells with images of Napoleon riding into battle. Woolworth sat behind a gold-and-silver-plated desk, with Cass Gilbert beside him; they resembled a pair of vaudevillians with their mountebank mustaches; Lionel disliked Gilbert's air of an artiste. Woolworth was more roughly hewn, with a plumber's hands.

"We're disappointed in you, Lionel," he said. "You vanished on me, just like that."

"I'm not your servant, Mr. Frank. I found this site, I cobbled it together, bit by bit, bribed inspectors, forced owners to sell."

The architect shivered in his seat, his smooth hands forming a crooked spire. "Show a bit of discretion, Ravage. We're sitting with a police captain, for God's sake."

"He's all eyes and ears," Lionel said. "But he'd never repeat a word of this conversation. Isn't that right, Kit? Just nod your head."

Kittleberger sat in one of the Empire Room's gilded chairs and nodded in silent rage. He didn't give a damn about Lionel's little lords.

"If Kit can't speak for himself, how can we rely on him in a pinch?" asked the architect.

Lionel couldn't afford to alienate Cass. He was grabbing up land all along the subway routes. He would build apartment complexes in the Bronx, where the value of a plot could triple in a day once a subway line was announced. And Lionel had all this information firsthand from the city engineers he bribed. So he tiptoed around the artiste. He didn't want a rebellion among the ranks of master architects.

"Kit is always reliable, Cass. He'll do whatever we want."

"I'd like to hear that from the captain himself," Gilbert said. "We can't invest all our time and money without certain guarantees."

And the captain broke into song, like some monstrous toy with teeth. "Well, gentleman, my own lads will parade up and down Grand Street. All the riffraff will be gone."

"But there are troublemakers," Woolworth said. "We tried to reason with Cahan. I offered him a lucrative position, a sinecure. Any other fellow would have grabbed it."

"Are you frightened of *A Bintel Brief*?" Lionel asked, teasing Frank Woolworth. "They're sob stories."

"We can't just dismiss Cahan. Several of his articles have been picked up by the *Herald*."

Lionel was having the time of his life in Woolworth's pompous headquarters. "Should I tell you a secret, Mr. Frank? I own the land rights to the *Forward* building. I could shut down his shop whenever I want. But I like having him around. He's my court jester. He imagines an endless sea of immigrants. That sea will dry up, and I'll still be here with my sewer pipes. And why worry about the *Herald*? I can have every janitor in the building stay home. If I call in my plumbers, the *Herald* will be swimming in shit within a week. That's the power of the press."

Woolworth wouldn't laugh at that plumber's tale. He didn't understand the Jewish quarter, with its noise and constant haggling. No one ever haggled at a five-and-ten. The prices never varied; that was his trademark, the sign of his astounding success. "Lionel, will the neighborhood welcome my store? Bad publicity can spread like wildfire."

Fire. Always fire. Didn't they look at his face?

"I have a brand, Lionel, and I won't risk it with one rogue store. Wasn't that Jewish detective against us? Can't we silence him?"

Everything backed up around Lionel. He had Chlöe's pungent odor in his nostrils like an unbridled perfume that made him want to run from Woolworth and return to his graveyard. But he had to hide his own turmoil from Mr. Frank.

"The boy doesn't even have a badge. We could arrest him whenever we want."

Woolworth brooded for a moment while the rain beat behind the silver-threaded curtains. "Lionel, isn't the boy related to you?"

"He's my son."

The silence around him crackled like the corrugated tin walls in the tenement that had nearly swallowed him alive. He would lose Mr. Frank and Cass Gilbert if he wasn't careful now. He saw Chlöe's green eyes in the deep shadows of the Empire Room. The cat was prepared to pounce.

"The boy has no claims on me. We'll deal with him. You have my word."

"But those are blood ties," the architect said, far shrewder than his boss in a gigantic bin of memorabilia. "Would you be willing to sacrifice your own boy for one five-and-ten?"

We're strangers, Lionel wanted to say. *We never lived together.*

But he'd have lost his purchase with these traditional family men, who would have seen him as a renegade they couldn't rely upon. Only a brute would abandon his boy.

"We'll bring my Ben into line."

The architect was still suspicious. "And what about the property rights? I can't redesign Ridley's until we chase that one-eyed shylock off the premises. We've presented him with a contract, and he tears it up."

"I've been remiss. I haven't visited Moses Brill."

"Mr. Ravage," Kittleberger said. "Moses has turned the Shilly-Shally into a fortress. We can't—"

Lionel cut him off. "You'll have your contract, Cass, by tomorrow."

"But how do we know that one visit will be enough?"

"Ah," he said. "It always is."

4.

LIONEL WASN'T NAKED NOW. He had his walking stick. And he was prepared for whatever mischief Moses had in mind. The shylock had been strutting around like a one-eyed rooster, haggling with the Royal Packet Co. and other steamship lines as he smuggled listless, lonely, half-brained orphan girls in and out of Odessa. Lionel had warned him to quit the racket, but Moses had aggrandized himself as an impresario of human flesh. He had the impertinence of Odessa. He was now a rival who thought he could bury his boss in a graveyard of pipes and have the rats feast on him. It was Lionel who really owned that skeleton of Ridley's department store, but he'd put the property in Moses' name, and the shylock wouldn't give it back.

Lionel himself had helped design the icebox doors of the Shilly-Shally Club. They were meant to withstand an army. And Kittleberger's own squad had stood like foolish boys outside the club with their sledgehammers; the icebox doors were reinforced with six inches of steel. So he couldn't rely on Kit and his buffoons. And he couldn't use his walking stick as a burglar's hook. But the shylock had never even bothered to look at Ridley's floor plans. He was too involved in the contours of his own self-portrait. He favored a parrot green shirt and yellow shoes that seemed to match the skin around his hollowed eye socket. He always carried tea bags and bars of Peter's milk chocolate in his pocket. He paid his gang a pittance but demanded the strictest loyalty from his men.

Lionel slipped in through a rear delivery door that hadn't been sealed up. He remembered every detail. Ravage & Son had installed the pipes at Ridley's department store palace on Grand.

Lionel found Moses Brill behind his mahogany desk at the club. Moses wasn't even startled to see him. He mocked Lionel in front of his own men. He had five scrawny girls standing naked near his desk, their wrists tied together with pieces of ribbon; they were as bald as mannequins. Their skulls and pubic hair had been shaved, probably as a protection against lice. Lionel couldn't tell how old they were. They didn't flirt or hiss at Lionel. None of them had the least adventure in her eyes.

"Lionel, I kept them for you. I shaved their cunts so you could have a good lick."

He laughed, expecting a loud roar from his own lackeys. But his men looked at Lionel, not at Moses Brill. Still, he had his audience and wouldn't let go.

"Say, Lionel, didn't you once have a wild cat, a real rat chaser? What was her name?"

"Chlöe," Lionel whispered, looking at Brill's loveless love dolls with a rage that was unbridled now.

"Well, these little pets can replace your Chlöe. I'll let you have them—for free. Kill them, cut them up, but I want to keep my club."

"You never had a club, Moses. My hand was always behind your signature. Where are the documents that Woolworth's people gave you?"

"I tore them up," Brill boasted to his lackeys, but he didn't have time to laugh.

Lionel used his walking stick like a rapier, tearing Brill's cheek with the silver teeth on its wolf's head. Brill sat there, sobbing with pain.

"Boys," he screeched in a girlish voice, "grab that silver club. And finish him."

His men moved away and stood behind Lionel.

"You arrogant prick, they were always on my payroll," Lionel said.

Brill reached into a drawer, pulled out a sheaf of papers, and signed the last page. Then he stared into the tinlike reflection of Lionel's eyes that seemed almost colorless to him, with a touch of blue.

"Boss, don't hit me again."

Lionel might have left him alone on another evening. But Moses shouldn't have mentioned his cat. He didn't care about witnesses. These girls couldn't even remember where they were. And his rage had been building around Moses Brill, the arrogance of his parrot green shirt, the stupidity of trafficking in orphan girls who couldn't even spell their own names.

He struck the shylock on the bridge of his nose, struck him again and again. It wasn't the same as hitting the gun molls, who always fought back. And he never really tried to damage them. He left marks on their behinds. Years ago he'd black out in the middle of a rampage. A detective from the local precinct would have to wake him and assess the damage. But he knew the damage he was inflicting now.

He called Jacob Schiff at his banking house. Jacob would know what to do with these listless orphan girls. No one had ever equaled Jacob's philanthropy. He wouldn't allow Jewish girls to be caught in some municipal maze. And even if they were Gentiles, he'd still help. Lionel didn't bother wiping the blood from the mirrors, nor did he swear the girls to any silence. They didn't have enough language in them to write down or retell whatever they had seen. Jacob would probably legalize their status, and have them placed as domestics, or put them in a Jewish orphanage. One day, Lionel might find them on the ward at Montefiore, accompanying an old man to the toilet.

There wasn't a soul in the main gallery. The female pickpockets had all scattered after Moses went to war with the coppers, and they'd pilfered whatever they could from his clothing barrels. So Lionel had to dress the orphans in the few rags he found at the bottom of the barrels. They could have been mannequins in the window of some relentless variety store. And Lionel was like Monk Eastman, who could sign his name on a chit. He wrote a few words on his business cards and sent Moses' former lackeys off to work as watchmen on the sites of those apartment mansions he intended to build in the Bronx.

Lionel heard a rap on the icebox doors; it sounded like the knock of a child—that's how solid the doors were. Jacob Schiff had come alone to Brill's nest without his agents. Lionel hid the shylock and opened the icebox doors. Jacob looked at the five orphans in their rags with such pity that Lionel felt ashamed.

Jacob couldn't converse with them. He tried several languages—Hungarian, Spanish, Dutch—but they were bewildered by every word.

"Lionel, it's a miracle that you rescued them. They would have been nameless in another week."

"They're nameless right now."

"But we will discover who they are—with a little patience. . . . I have my man outside. Where can I drop you?" he asked, trying not to notice that he'd blundered into the scene of a crime. Schiff had become a pragmatist. He'd saved five girls from a life of misery, and he didn't care how it had to be done. "Where, Lionel?"

"Satan's Circus."

And for one terrifying moment, Lionel had an itch to strike all the civilized stuffing out of Jacob Schiff, to smash his brains once and for all in this charnel house and rid Yiddish Land of its chief philanthropist. Jacob must have seen the mad gleam in Lionel's tinlike red eyes, but he didn't flinch. Lionel Ravage had become the fallen angel among Jewish aristocrats, an angel who was necessary to them, even with all the Ghetto fires, the unscrupulous land deals, and the blood on his walking stick. Who else would have rescued these bald girls from oblivion?

5.

HE WENT THROUGH THE HAYMARKET and found her in her little opium den, where she always loved to hide, far from her Poppa. She lay curled in a corner with her pipe, that French ghoul beside her, Franz, who turned the opium den into a cabaret at night for other hermaphrodites like himself and their dancing partners. Lionel had financed the cabaret; it was his headquarters above Canal. He'd also financed Babs; he was much less stingy with her than her own father. He had to catch her before her eyes were completely closed.

"Does Ben know about Leila yet?"

Babs blinked at him, came out of her torpor. "You should have been more careful, Lionel, and had *two* idiotic sons. This one is much too clever. You shouldn't have used Montefiore as your playground—and your dungeon."

"What better camouflage could we have had than a home for chronic invalids? Jacob is master of the ground floor. He isn't curious about anything but the clinic. He's never even visited the laundry room. . . . Go back to sleep. You're always cranky after a few puffs on your pipe. Jacob's servant is in our pocket."

"And everybody else's," she said. "He's a whore, that Marcus Mendel-s-s-s-ohn," and she fell back into her opium dream, while Franz prepared Lionel's pipe. The female man locked the doors of the cabaret and strapped on the Colt that Buffalo Bill had sold to Lionel for three hundred dollars during the Wild West Show at Madison Square Garden; Bill had shot at wooden jackrabbits all afternoon, while wearing a blindfold, and never missed once; Lionel treated that gun as if it were a religious article, when he knew that the Colt's handle was made of mock pearl and its silver barrel wasn't silver at all. Franz still had to carry that relic around whenever Lionel smoked a pipe. Cody's Colt comforted the hardware king while he slept. He recalled Bill's dyed yellow beard, the mascara on his cheeks, the white paint on his throat. The bullets had all been blanks. Bill's Wild West was a tepee and a few trick riders in the depths of Madison Square Garden.

Lionel sucked on his pipe like an Indian chief. He'd always wanted to visit Wyoming and the Dakotas, but he never had the time, and he didn't believe in the penny dreadfuls about ruthless gunfighters and desperadoes. There were probably more desperadoes at police headquarters than there ever were in the Badlands. Lionel ought to know; he'd hired every one.

Chlöe often visited him in his opium dreams. She sat on his chest. And she didn't have hollow holes for eyes. But she wouldn't come to Lionel on this occasion. The blond cat had abandoned the king of Canal, left him in a room with an unreliable Colt. It wasn't Manya who popped up with a cat's paws. Lionel was back on the Lower East Side as a boy. His papa was tied to the Bavarian princes who had settled on Chrystie Street, near a rebuilt Methodist church they turned into Temple Emanu-El. It was right after the Civil War, and the Tenth Ward was a mishmash of German immigrants and Irish toughs. The princes kept a kind of order by hiring some of these toughs to watch over the shul.

Lionel's father provided the primitive drainage and one workable sink at Temple Emanu-El. Father and son had to wear hip boots as they swam around in excrement under the shul. His father was a lesser prince, while the other Bavarians were really ragmen and tinkers with great ambition and a sense of industry. They looked down upon this plumber with shit on his pants, but he was still a member of their congregation, was still invited to their wedding feasts. He became the de facto janitor of the shul. And when toilets were installed, it was Lionel and his father who installed them; the congregation haggled over the costs, and Lionel listened to all the haggling, watched his father's back stiffen with a rage he had to quell. Lionel was only seven when his father put the handcrafted signboard above their little shop: *Ravage & Son.*

He'd come here to conjure up Chlöe, and all he could summon were hip boots in the shit-clogged cellars of Emanu-El. Then he saw a little blond boy, and it wasn't Lionel. The boy could have been five or six. He was with his mother, who wore a tattered winter coat. The love on her face alarmed him—it wasn't for Lionel. He'd held himself hostage all these years, cut out the one family he could have claimed. The fires hadn't burned deep enough. The wig he wore was as pathetic as Buffalo Bill's painted throat and dyed yellow beard. "Manya," he moaned.

Lionel blinked. The hermaphrodite and Babette were standing over him.

"Boss," Franz said, "you were crying, and . . ." He had Buffalo Bill's sham Colt cradled under his arm. Why did Lionel care about that showman with his suitcase full of Colts? Was Bill as much a prisoner as his papa, both of them with some illusion of grandeur? One was an aristocrat with shit on his pants, and the other a hunter and scout who shot at jackrabbits that sprang out of a board.

"Jesus," Babs said. "You scared me, Lionel. I thought you were having a heart attack."

And just as Lionel was about to rise from his pillow, he could feel Chlöe leap into his lap. It was like that first time, when she knocked Lionel out of his chair. He didn't have to ask Franz to heat up his opium lamp. He'd sucked in enough vapors through the bowl. Lionel curled up on his pillow with the least bit of a smile.

Eleven

Bad Babette

I.

SHE'D BEEN RAISED TO MARRY A CROWN PRINCE within that incestuous circle of bankers and bankers' sons, to read *Middlemarch*, paint or sculpt for a few years, travel to Europe on the *Princess Cecilie*, wander through the Louvre, then sit at home and have babies until she delivered a male heir to the same incestuous circle, so that she, too, could have a possible crown prince. She would be rewarded with her own charity after that—a home for boys and girls with rickets, perhaps—or she could volunteer at the Henry Street Settlement and the Hebrew hospital.

It was everything that Babs did not want, girls of privilege with no privileges at all. She could attend one of the elite preparatory schools where the daughters of Jewish barons were tolerated, even desired, such as Miss Gordon's of Central Park West, and go on to an elite women's college, or she could marry a crown prince at seventeen if she were buxom enough and came with a fat dowry. Babs went to Smith, a college with its own settlement house on the Lower East Side. It was there that she met Leila, not at the campus monastery in Northampton. Babs had been drifting until then, uncomfortable and out of place, pursued by male predators interested in her father's fortune.

Leila had never graduated from Smith, had left as a senior to take charge of a project at College Settlement on Rivington Street—it looked like an old Greek temple with fire escapes and a crumbling roof. Leila didn't teach disabled Jewish children, didn't run kindergarten classes in the Ghetto. She had assembled a crew of young women with hammers hooked to their belts and wet plaster on their faces. They weren't licensed by any landlord. They were mavericks who arrived at a tenement and repaired whatever they could—doorknobs, window frames, crooked fire escapes, clogged toilets, electrical outlets. Leila always wore a black undershirt and baggy trousers; she was as muscular as a crown prince; her biceps glistened whenever she climbed out from under a sink. Leila had black hair and somber eyes, and Babs loved being a member of the crew. She didn't have to worry about bankers' sons chasing her with marriage proposals.

"Oh my God, Leila, where did you get such a physique?"

"At the women's farm in Massachusetts," Leila said. "And my real name is Lily Pringle."

"But why would you need an alias? You went to Smith."

Leila laughed. "I escaped from the prison farm. College was the best cover I ever had. I'm a forger, Puss. I invented Leila Montague. I like her a lot. But the state police might have caught up with me in Northampton. The Lower East Side is perfect camouflage."

The landlords didn't want their tenements repaired by a phantom crew of college girls. It made them look meager in the eyes of their tenants. So they hired bullyboys to frighten these Smithies away. But Leila went at them with her hammer, and the landlords lost the battle. They couldn't even protect their own terrain. After one of these little wars, Babs sat on a tenement rooftop with Leila

and licked the blood off her biceps with some kind of rapture—
they were lovers before their first kiss.

They lived at the settlement house, where Leila was both king
and queen. But their honeymoon on Rivington Street didn't last.
One of the landlords interrupted their bliss. Lionel discovered
them up on a roof, licking each other like a pair of toads.

"I could break your neck," Leila warned him.

Lionel clapped his hands. "It won't be the first time, Lily Pringle. I could have you all cuffed up in fifteen minutes and sent to
Massachusetts on a private train."

Leila looked at him with those somber eyes. "Mister, you don't
have fifteen minutes."

That's when Babs whispered in Leila's ear. "You can't hurt
him. He walks right out of fires."

"He's a guy with half a face," Leila said, "and a straw mop over
his ears. He'll fall down if I blow on him once."

"He's still Lionel Ravage. My own father is afraid of him."

In the end, they had to barter with Lionel, who wanted to
usurp their talent to fix up tenements.

"We can't deal with you," Babs said. "We've been fighting
landlords."

Now it was Leila who relented. She'd never survive her cap-
tivity if she had to go back to the farm, she said. So little by
little the entire crew turned into Lionel's slaves. College Settlement was almost an annex of Ravage & Son. The Smithies
reworked the corrugated tin of the tenement halls. They repaired
the plumbing. Lionel paid them in cash. Babs would have tossed
that lucre at Lionel, but she couldn't afford to anger him, at least
for Leila's sake.

Then she realized that the landlord and her lover had a lot

in common. The two of them conspired together, and sometimes they brought Babs along. They went into dark corridors, danced in some thieves' den. Babs puffed on her first opium pipe. She floated above the roofs of the tenements, a hammer attached to her heel. It was more than an addiction. She liked to lick Leila after shaking herself out of a dream. But Leila was always whispering to the landlord.

"Are you performing stunts with Lionel?"

"No, Puss," Leila said. "We're both artists, your uncle and I."

"He's not my uncle," Babs insisted. "What kind of art does Lionel produce? He's a plumber."

"Yes, a plumber with bigger pockets than I ever had. I'm an amateur next to him. He doesn't have to forge a few checks. He fleeces other landlords, buys and sells properties faster than you could ever blink."

Babs felt lost, in and out of her opium dreams. "Have you fallen for him?"

"Puss," Leila said, her eyes widening with contempt, "I'll let you in on a little secret. He's a man."

But their lovemaking was like sandpaper now. There was always a rough edge, as if Leila had too little time. Babs saw herself as a trinket. She was almost embarrassed as she undressed. She couldn't even lick Leila's tattoos, the marks of her sojourn in Massachusetts—barbed wire with tears of blood, a hat with a spike in the middle. Leila managed the landlord's properties, and the former angel of mercy hammered eviction notices on tenants' doors and bludgeoned rival landlords.

"I'm saving up," she said. "We'll run when we have to run."

And she wouldn't even dig into Babs' mouth with a proper kiss. Her tongue lay dead in her own mouth. She'd stopped exploring Babs. They were like a married couple among the Jewish millionaires. Babs had even less to do than her own mother. And so she became Leila's little accomplice. She collected receipts for her at the cabarets of Satan's Circus, following Leila around like a lapdog. And then Leila brought in another crew, women with razor cuts under their eyes, who must have been her bedmates at the penal farm. They descended upon the Circus like a swarm of locusts, and soon they were gone, Leila with them, and every cash box that hadn't been nailed down.

Babs was still living at that Greek temple on Rivington Street when Lionel knocked on her door.

"Your sweetheart stole from me."

"Well, Lionel, you can ask my father for reparations."

He slapped her with that lizard's skin of a hand, and one side of her face swelled up like a cantaloupe.

"Idiot, she used you and all the other Smithies as bait. You must have known that she was a jailbird. Did that excite you, Babs? Did you keep a record of her prison tattoos? You're on the pipe now. You'd better come with me."

She hated Lionel, and did whatever he asked. She fell in with his enterprises, not as a seductress, but as a bookkeeper, almost. He trusted her with money, and she carried around wads of cash in a belt under her blouse. He liked to say that she was too rich to steal, though her father kept her as a pauper. Lionel trusted Babs, told her his vilest acts. Soon he was paying her a salary. She ran his clubs in the Tenderloin, and she had her pipe. She still flew above the tenements with a hammer tied to her heel.

2.

BABS WASN'T EVEN SURE WHY SHE RETURNED every night to her
father's apartment-palace. It wasn't to see her mother, who wandered about, a skeleton in a silk robe, neutered years ago by her husband's neglect. "Where's my Meyer?" she would wail. But Meyer
Bristol was never there. He couldn't have built his fortune without
her family's enterprise, yet he avoided her, cursed the sound of her
footsteps. She chattered like a demented magpie, often wept for no
reason, and withdrew into her own solitude.

It was Babs' misfortune to find her on the stairs.

"I have one daughter, and she's a whore."

Babs bowed like an ingenue. "Aw, Momma, thank God I'm
not a princess who's lost at sea."

"What sea, dear?"

"The one you're drowning in."

Babs swept past her mother and ran to her own room. She
locked the door behind her. She'd always preferred a brick wall
to a river view. Her dorm at Smith had faced a deserted orchard,
with the roots of trees that resembled gnarled bones. And the
room she'd shared with Leila on Rivington Street opened onto an
abandoned coal bin. Babs could sit for hours and brood when she
wasn't sucking on her pipe or reading *Pride and Prejudice*, with its
whirlwind of marriageable daughters, and that abominable bachelor, Mr. Darcy, with his ten thousand pounds a year. And as Babs
was about to settle in, she saw a shadow flit past her bed, and she
screamed, "Mr. Darcy."

It was the downtown detective. "I could never be your Darcy.
I have no manners."

"How did you get in here?"

"I walked right past the butler."

"You have no business . . ."

He shook Babs, as if she were a rag doll he had discovered in the street, and he mimicked her. *"Find Leila Montague.* And all the time you knew she was dead. Did Lionel hire you to play the victim? She dropped you long ago, didn't she?"

"Yes," Babs told him.

"Why was Lionel trawling so hard? He's not afraid of the police. He uses Montefiore as his own asylum and punishing ground. He had my mother taken there, the son of a bitch. Rescued her from the madhouse, he says."

"He did."

Ben stared at Bad Babette. "How would you know?"

"He found a letter in her pocket after she died—a letter to you. He wanted to burn it, but he's superstitious. He let me have the letter."

"Why you?" Ben asked. "Why, why?"

"He trusts me. I'm his conscience, the keeper of his accounts."

Manya had written on scraps of toilet paper. Babs handed him all the pieces, and he had to unpuzzle them, like a scattered poem.

dearest ben,

once

upon the lower east side

a woman loved a man

more than her own life

and gave up

her sanity and her son

He held the crumpled scraps, each with its own sad line. It was all the history he would ever have, his mother's lonely archive. He folded the pieces into a cigarette case he sometimes used as a purse; he knew his mother's words wouldn't last—the toilet paper would crumple beyond recognition, and he would be left with a few signs that made little sense, but he would have a picture of what she wrote inside his brain.

"Mr. Darcy is beholden to you," he said.

And Babs was beholden to him. It wasn't her father who had really introduced them. She'd heard about the vagabond lawyer when she was with Leila's crew, this detective from the Kehilla who would tear up eviction notices and write scathing letters to landlords. His address was a post office box in the *Forward* building. He would ride into night court out of the wind. . . .

"You killed Leila, didn't you?"

"Yes."

"Was it anger, jealousy, or spite?" he asked.

And Babs didn't know how to answer. Leila had come back to her old roost. She should have gone to Alaska, where she would have been just another face. But she had Manhattan in her blood. Her new incarnation was as a stickup artist. She went after messengers on Wall Street and was picked up within a month. Leila could have rotted in some cellar at police headquarters, but her yellow sheet disappeared, and she landed in the attic at Montefiore, with other lost souls who had disappointed Lionel. And here, on Hamilton Heights, he might beat you with his wolf's head, challenge you to a game of chess, talk about Hamlet's ghost, or have you copulate with his other guests. It was as if Lionel had corporealized one of his opium dreams.

She knew how insane it was, but it seemed to satisfy Lionel's hunger to hurt. And she couldn't resist her own rides uptown to the attic. Lionel had broken Leila's will. Her biceps shrank to nothing. She was a gaunt ghost in a woman's gown. Yet she still believed in her power to seduce.

"I missed you, Puss."

They could have made love in a little room. Babs might have summoned up the urge, if she shut her eyes and recalled those glistening biceps under a tenement sink.

"Leila, does he have you fixing toilets?"

"I'm Lily now."

But Babs couldn't bear to have her use that name, even if Leila Montague was counterfeit. She liked to think of Leila's crew at College Settlement, because there was nothing counterfeit about the windows they repaired.

"And I'm Bad Babette."

Lionel's guests in the attic preyed upon one another, since the warden of the attic, Marcus Mendelssohn, distributed so little food. Babs despised that fastidious little man in kid gloves, who was far crueler than Lionel. He fed Lionel's guests scraps from Montefiore's kitchen; there were never more than nine or ten at a time, and none of them ever lasted very long, these renegade bookkeepers, bondsmen, or landlords who had cheated Lionel. Mendelssohn spat at them, kicked them like wild dogs; he was always methodic, while Lionel had a mercurial nature. He might arrive with jars of baby food for a guest who had lost her teeth in the attic. And he allowed Babs a little sway.

She'd become protectress of the attic. The little martinet never went anywhere without the Colt strapped to his side, but Babs kept a kitchen knife tucked inside her blouse.

"Mendelssohn, if you hit Leila one more time, I'll stab you

right between the shoulder blades when you aren't looking. Your Colt can't save you. I'm a bad girl, or did you forget?"

He laughed in her face. "You wouldn't dare," he said, and never hit Leila again. Babs didn't have the skill or the desire to help Leila escape. She was frightened of Lionel. She also enjoyed the sudden power she had, with a prisoner of her own. She once brought Leila a meal from Schrafft's. Lionel's other guests nearly ripped Leila apart for a dollop of mashed potatoes. Mendelssohn had to hop about with his Colt, or there might have been a mutiny in the attic.

"You little bitch," he said to Babs. "You could have caused a riot. Nourishment is my department."

"Shut up, Mendelssohn. You make me puke."

Babs would sneak in crumbs of food, and Leila licked these hidden crumbs out of her hand. It excited Babs, and they'd kiss in some secret corner, though Leila didn't have the strength to do much more than that. She was a bag of bones under her tattered gown. "I loved you," Babs said. "I would have done anything you asked—stolen for you, hit Lionel with a hammer, and you left me flat."

"I'm a thief," Leila said.

"That's no excuse. You dazzled me with your prison tattoos, and excited yourself with a cash box between your legs. You're not really a thief, Leila. You're a whore."

Babs would visit every afternoon, and then, for some reason, she stopped. Was it out of perversity or too many puffs on her pipe that she fell into oblivion for a week? And when she returned to the attic, Leila was gone. . . .

That's what she told her Mr. Darcy.

"But you didn't kill her."

"Every day I left her there was another nail in her head. I could have pleaded with Lionel. He might have listened. But I didn't want her roaming about with new accomplices. I wanted her in *my* spiderweb."

And suddenly Ben thought of Henry James, patrolling Manhattan in his worn cuffs. The Master might have had a renaissance writing about the daughters of German Jewish barons.

"Why did you have me go chasing after a corpse?"

"Because you're the downtown detective," she told him. "And I wished her alive through your graces. I still loved her, even if I was one of her marks."

"You were her pigeon," Ben said. "Lionel was her mark. She could have slit your throat, or strangled you on a rainy day. That's how close you were to dying."

Babs wouldn't have cared if Leila had accompanied it all with a kiss. But she said nothing. And Ben vanished just as he'd appeared, out of the ether. She kept thinking of the crumbs she'd fed to Leila in the attic, and her own erotic bewilderment at the wetness of her hand as Leila licked, strands of black hair falling in her lap like rough silk as she hid her own deep sighs, because she didn't want her prisoner to feel the least bit of power.

Twelve

Lady Hamlet

I.

*M*ONK EASTMAN HAD FITS OF MELANCHOLY after he returned from Sing Sing in 1909. He could not decode who or where he was. He might have suffered from bouts of amnesia, provoked by the beatings he took from the warden's men. He couldn't recognize the streets he had ruled for so long. The old gangs were gone, with all their swagger. The girls of Allen Street didn't dance under the El. They lurched about, like figures in a puppet show. The coppers had their own sway, collecting swag from merchants, pushcart peddlers, and prostitutes with missing teeth. The Tammany Tiger ruled now, but Monk wasn't going to take his marching orders from political bosses and their henchmen in the precincts. Luckily, he still had his pet shop on Chrystie Street. And his yellow birds went wild with wonder when Monk walked in and whistled one of his old tunes. Half his crop had died waiting for Monk, molting all the time and refusing to drink water. He opened all their cages, and the canaries that had survived serenaded Monk and nestled in the brim of his hat. He was content with his canaries until a man with scars around his eyes walked into the shop and introduced himself as Benjamin Ravage, a detective from the Kehilla.

Monk didn't know what the Kehilla was, and he'd never been fond of detectives, so why should he listen?

"Come on, Edward, I was your scout."

Monk squinted at this young detective with all the shrewdness of a man who'd once had his own kingdom on the Lower East Side.

"Aren't you that squirt who looked after my canaries when I was mixing it up with the Five Pointers? I'd never have held out if I had to worry about my yellow queens."

And they formed a partnership on the spot, a camaraderie that had nothing to do with the spoils of war, though they did earn a sizable reward catching horse poisoners and other recreants. But Monk didn't care about the swag in his pocket. They'd become guardians of the Ghetto—retrieving kidnapped daughters from suicidal social clubs, finding rabbinical scholars who'd gone astray, pummeling wicked stepmothers—and it almost seemed to Monk that he was recapturing his terrain, bit by bit. He might become a king again, with canaries hovering over his derby.

So he didn't utter a sound when the detective walked into Kehilla headquarters on East Broadway and pulled Marcus Mendelssohn right out from behind his desk. Ben was quite the cavalier with his own chief. He dragged Marcus by his collar in front of secretaries, other investigators, accountants, and clerks.

"You'll pay for this," the chief investigator snarled. "You're finished here."

"What will your master say when he finds out that you've been running your own punishment club at Montefiore?"

Ben saw little bullets of fear in Mendelssohn's eyes. "It's not my attic," he moaned. "It's Lionel's."

"But you're the one who starved Leila Montague. And there

are no escape routes from that attic. You beat her to death without soiling your delicate hands."

"The boss said—"

Ben dragged him like a crumpled bag in his cutaway and white spats sprinkled with dust.

"How many bosses do you have? You're Jacob Schiff's bodyguard."

"Everybody works for Lionel," the chief investigator said. "You, too, but you don't know it yet."

"And what about Monk? Is he also Lionel's little man?"

Mendelssohn smiled like an evil gnome while his body bumped across the room. "Every cent Monk earned came from Lionel's coffers. He was just a lonely copper without a badge. Monk and his gang policed the Ghetto for Lionel and Silver Dollars."

And suddenly Monk awoke from his bout of amnesia. He was Ned Silver's enforcer in the old days. He broke heads for Tammany Hall . . . until the Wigwam abandoned him.

"I would have lost my pet shop without Silver Dollars. He paid the rent while I was in Sing Sing."

Mendelssohn was seized with laughter. "Ned's the worst chiseler at the Essex Market Court. Lionel owns your pet shop, sonny, and Lionel paid the rent. He had you cashiered. You were 'omnipresent,' that's what he said to me. 'We'll give Monk Eastman a little rest.' But he always looked after your birds."

"You're still going with us to Montefiore," said Ben.

And he dragged Mendelssohn right out of the Educational Alliance.

They rode up to Hamilton Heights in a hired car, a silver Packard with an engine that buckled like a half-savage horse, while the chief investigator shivered in his seat.

"The boss will murder me. The attic's his domain. I'm his watchman, that's all."

They went through a gate and stopped at Jacob Schiff's palace on the Hudson for chronic invalids. But Lionel Ravage was the real curator of the grounds—and the landlord of Manhattan, not Woolworth or the Astors. Mr. Frank could have the tallest skyscraper in the world named after him, but his signature wasn't on the underlying lots. No wonder Lionel put Monk out of commission. Monk had become too recognizable as a prince of the streets and threatened Lionel's secret hegemony. Frank Woolworth was only a five-and-ten merchant, a purveyor of trinkets, and it didn't matter to Lionel what fortune he amassed. He would never be loved and feared and adored the way Monk had been at the turn of the century. And that kind of power might topple a man, even with all of Lionel's minions. But he couldn't erase Monk's aura, Monk's own myth. Monk had become a lone gang leader with half a dozen canaries. And that's how he entered Montefiore, with birds in his pocket.

While Jacob Schiff was down on Wall Street, Montefiore didn't have the same resilient calm. The doctors and male nurses had cigarettes in their mouths. The cook was carrying a pistol under his gown. The patients were locked away somewhere; none of them wandered about. The double doors of every ward were lashed together with chains.

"What's this?" asked the cook, who must have been the chief lieutenant while Schiff was away. "Marcus, are these guys kosher?"

"They're with me," Mendelssohn whispered.

"That's no excuse. They can't visit the premises without a paper slip."

Monk let the canaries out of his pocket. The cook was startled as the canaries chirped and flew under the chandeliers. Now he recognized Monk's battle scars, his tiny hidden eyes, and the bird's hypnotic songs. And he stood like stone while Ben, Monk, and Marcus mounted the stairs. There were other doctors and male nurses on the balconies, and still they climbed. One of the nurses tossed a cigarette at Mendelssohn.

"Mendie, this isn't their house. Isn't that guy from the Kehilla, with Monk Eastman? What's the boss gonna say?"

The canaries followed them, flew round and round Monk's hat, and those warlike nurses blinked at the birds and got out of Monk's way, scratching their beards.

Ben climbed another flight and must have arrived at the doctors' dorm. He met women in kimonos parading in the hall. They were bold with the three intruders, revealing strips of flesh from their navels to their kneecaps. Ben cursed Lionel Ravage. Montefiore was another cabaret.

Marcus grew more and more frenzied as they reached the attic. The ceiling was very low and they all had to stoop. Ben expected guardians with shotguns. There wasn't a soul in the hall. The lights were very dim. They entered the attic rooms; Ben couldn't find a piece of material; not a truncheon or a thumbtack. The floors were bare; the commodes and sinks in the bathrooms were gone. Marcus was as startled as his downtown detective, though he masked his bewilderment with a smile.

"Didn't I tell you? It's clean as a whistle."

Babette must have talked to Lionel after her little confession, and he changed venues, found another attic, but Lionel's venue was everywhere; his warehouse on Canal, that wonderland of pipes, was some kind of canteen. Lionel was as much a vagabond

as Ben, but he had properties all along the routes of his vagabond-
age, and Ben had none.

2.

BEN WAS STILL ABLE TO CATCH THE MATINEE at the Thalia. He'd
missed the first two acts of Clara Karp as Hamlet. But it didn't
really matter. Clara bent Hamlet's life and death to her own
desire and will. Her Hamlet might become defunct in the first
act and rise out of the grave in the second, matching his dead
father, ghost to ghost. She didn't usurp Shakespeare; she limbed
his lines, repeated soliloquies, attacked time and again with her
rapier, like some colossal assassin. The corpses kept piling up.

"To kill," she sang in Yiddish, "to kill and kill again."

And that's when he noticed Lionel standing at the rear of
the orchestra, enraptured, and repeating Clara's lines, like some
prompter, or a playwright who'd also risen out of the grave. The
performance lasted six hours. The white cap she wore to cover her
hair was drenched. Her black tights revealed every heave of her
bosom, every mold of her buttocks and hips. Clara herself was a
kind of rapier. She pinched her mother, the queen, spat in the face
of her stepfather, while the king's men stood about, mummified.
There was no one on the boards to counter her. If she drank a poi-
soned goblet, the poison only made her twice as potent. She had to
die sixteen times before the crowds let her off the stage. Yes, she'd
appeared in the *Follies*, but she'd never have thrived uptown. She
would have driven every dramaturge insane. She needed a primitive audience, people who would cry and laugh and hurl back her
lines, and wouldn't tolerate any barriers between themselves and
Clara Karp. They caught her sadness in every whisper, her sense

of homelessness in America, as if Lady Hamlet relived their own travails on Ellis Island, and the corpses onstage were really the custodians, doctors, and clerks at the induction center, and not the royals of some foreign court.

Ben couldn't enjoy the performance while his father stood there, his mouth bubbling with Clara's words. After her nineteenth curtain call, Clara crept under the boards to her closet. And Lionel followed her.

Ben waited in the dark outside Clara's dressing room.

If he stays with her more than ten minutes, I'll knock down the door, and beat him worse than that midget with the kid gloves beat Leila. And if Clara is naked, I'll beat her, too.

He stood in the dark, immobilized. Ben couldn't break in on Clara. She would have pulled his hair out in front of his own father. Then the door opened—Lionel crawled out of the closet, and Ben could see him in a cusp of light.

Kill him, kill him right now.

But there was such despair on Lionel's fire-fucked face that it served as a shield. Ben was inches away from his father in the shadows; their shoulders nearly rubbed.

I could snap his neck. The Angel of Death would probably reward me with a kiss.

He waited until Lionel's footsteps grew fainter and fainter, and then he rapped with his knuckles on Clara's door.

"Go away," she growled.

He knocked again.

"Are you deaf? I need my beauty sleep."

"Madame," he intoned in a mock voice, "you are beautiful enough."

There was a moment of silence.

"Who the devil are you?" she asked in a much more seductive voice.

"The Angel of Death. I've come to devour your bones."

He could hear her giggle behind the door. And Ben entered that little paradise under the boards.

"Darling," she whispered in that hoarse voice of hers, "you should have been a playwright. You're much too clever for me. I can only memorize other people's lines."

She was still wearing her white paint and black tights. She stopped smiling after she saw the little explosions in Ben's blue eyes. She was startled when he tossed her onto the divan like a brigand.

"How often have you entertained my father?" he shouted.

He hadn't even caught her by surprise. "You don't have a father. You're an orphan. That's why I fell in love with you. You have an orphan's eyes."

And now Ben himself was all confused. "What, exactly, are an orphan's eyes?"

"Sad beyond measure," she said, leaping up from the divan. "Suddenly I wasn't homesick. They reminded me of certain clowns and acrobats in Odessa, who risked their lives with every performance, every step they took."

Ben's legal palaver was lost within the precise and brutal eloquence of the Bowery's Yiddish Shakespeare.

"How long have you known that prick?"

"Longer than I've known you, dear."

He felt trapped in a corner with his painted lady. "And you never told me once?"

"I have a million admirers," she said, removing her white cap so that Ben could see her rush of black hair. "Should I catalog every one for you?"

"But this is different," he groaned. "This is personal."

And Clara told him how she and Lionel had met. It must have been in 1901, while Ben was an apprentice printer at the Hawthorne School. She was having lunch at Rector's with Pierpont Morgan, who was quite virile in his walrus mustache, even if his nose was as big as a flowerpot. He wanted to buy her a villa in the South of France.

"I'll strangle him," said Ben.

"Show a little respect. The man is in his grave. Besides, I couldn't take him seriously. He never saw me at the Thalia."

"Then he's a damn fool, and he doesn't know what he missed."

"You're so harsh, my love," she said. "He missed nothing. J.P. didn't know a word of Yiddish."

But another man did—Morgan's nemesis, Master Jacob, who showed up at the table, introduced himself, and spoke to Clara in fluent Yiddish. He bowed in his cutaway and kissed her hand.

"Your Hamlet is perfection, Madame Clara. And your Medea frightened the wits out of me."

There was a third man, blond as a god, with rough hands and harsh blue eyes that glanced at her bodice without shame. He was Schiff's partner in certain enterprises. He never bothered to introduce himself, but she'd heard of this heartless landlord-plumber who terrorized his tenants.

"I haven't missed one performance," he told her. The orchestra at Rector's was very loud, and Morgan had complained to the manager. Suddenly, the music stopped, and the restaurant was as silent as a roomful of cadavers; every diner was looking at their table.

"And what was your opinion, Herr Ravage?" she asked, invoking his name with a little of her own sauce. She had J.P. as her protector in front of this beastly man, who kept staring at her bodice.

"I trembled, madame. You were very daring with the text."

She wanted to humble him. "How so?"

"Hamlet in a woman's tights. It mystified me at first."

"But he's a prince, monsieur. I do not give him feminine airs."

"Still, there is a mystification," Lionel said. "And that's what delighted me."

Then he walked away without excusing himself. He began sending her roses with twisted stems, and his plumber's card, inviting her to midnight suppers. She wouldn't dine with him. He persisted. She refused—until she met her young admirer from Harvard, this blondish boy in a ragged coat, who could barely afford his seat at the Thalia. And the resemblance between Lionel and Ben alarmed her. He'd knocked on the door of her dressing room.

"Child," she growled, appraising the magnificent lines of his chest, "did you come for my autograph?"

"No," said Ben. "Madame Clara, you changed my life. This was the Hamlet I imagined in my head and never saw onstage— as wild and mysterious as rhythm itself."

She invited him into her closet. They talked for ten hours, until the sun rose. Exhausted, half delirious, she asked him to share her divan.

"Like comrades," she said. "You mustn't take advantage of me while I sleep."

He couldn't stay; he'd already skipped one final exam, and he had to return to Harvard Square. He fled her closet without kissing her once. She ached for this boy, who was like a lost lover-son. He didn't knock on her door for another month. He nearly broke her teeth with his first kiss. He tore her tights. He was like a greedy vampire who drank from her body, and she realized with a certain hesitation that she'd never been in love until she met this Harvard boy. She'd been courted by millionaires and penniless poets, and none of them could touch that quaking world inside her belly. They liked to quote themselves, hear the sound of their own voices, make speeches meant to move her toward some manufactured bliss. They promised marriage, or at least the bottom floor of a mansion. The poets promised her their patrimony, the rights to all their unpublished texts. They scribbled odes to Clara, insisted on reading them aloud, when she had Shakespeare—and this silent boy—to breathe a little fire into her loins. He might talk about his mother, who had died in the madhouse, but he had no sonnets to give her, just his loving hands. And she understood the danger he was in, even if he did not.

That's why she was twice as cunning with Lionel Ravage. She encouraged him up to a point, allowed him to kiss her in the dark, went to dinner with him at Delmonico's, where she had to fight not to fall asleep at the table, since she couldn't replenish herself after so much leaping about on the boards. It was Ben, only Ben, who could rouse her from her natural slumber.

But she was like a clairvoyant across the table from Lionel, with oyster juice on her lips.

"If you ever harm the boy, I'll ban you from the theater for life."

"What boy?" he muttered.

"Shut up."

He would have adored Clara forever if she'd whipped him

once or twice. He couldn't thrive without their groping in the dark. And the melodies she served up on the stage, fueling Hamlet's madness, had become his elixir. After he'd nearly torched himself, she visited Lionel at the Hebrew hospital, in front of all the patriarchs and their wives. No one would dare accuse her of being Lionel's whore. Some of the wives had seen her play Hamlet in an uptown production, and she had to give them her autograph.

"Madame, madame, what a privilege."

Lionel basked in his hospital bed. She preferred his mottled face and hands, his straw hair. That much she told her Adonis.

"And you allowed him to visit after he was all healed up," said Ben with a frozen face.

"Lionel never healed, but he would bring caviar and blue wine from the Russian restaurant on Rivington."

There were no Russian restaurants on Rivington Street. And he was quite skeptical about blue wine.

"That's what we drank in Odessa," she told him. "More than one distillery prepared blueberry wine."

He stared at her stevedore's shoulders. "Was that part of your ritual?"

"Yes."

Now Ben had to play the shamas. "What about tonight? Did he see you naked, Clara?"

He watched her wicked smile. "Lionel's the one who undressed. He was desperate to show me his little dingle. And I indulged him. It's smaller than a fishhook."

"And did you bathe it in blue wine?"

He could sense the anger build under the white paint. She wasn't Hamlet, spitting fire in the court of a fratricidal king. She was Clara, the female acrobat, who walloped Ben with all her might; he landed on his rump, among the mousetraps, the dying roses, the moldy jars of mayonnaise.

"I do it all to save your life. I'm his Scheherazade. Only it's not me he wants to kill. He can't bear the idea of your existence, that your mother loved you more than she could ever love him. He dreams of your blood, darling Ben. I can almost smell it on his hands. And while I entertain him, he'll leave you alone."

Ben rose up from the mousetraps. "And you think I can't protect myself from that straw man?"

She walloped him again, and he crashed into Clara's lamp, his arms curling awkwardly around the column.

"He owns the courts, the mayor, and the coppers. Benjamin, every street you walk on has a murderer-in-waiting. All he has to do is signal once."

Ben balanced himself against the erratic swings of the lamp. "I could leap first and break his neck."

"That wouldn't stop his bloodhounds," Clara said. She was crying. "I'd rather show that maniac my nipples than mourn you the rest of my life—it's a very small price."

"Small price," he muttered, mimicking her. "And what if he tires of those rendezvous in the dark? He could thrash you with his cane out of some whimsical idea of fun and find his real delight."

"Ha!" she said. "Let him try. I'll make him swallow that fancy wolf's head of his."

But Ben had seen that stark nakedness of the attic. He understood the wind inside his father's head, void of every human feeling. Not even Lady Hamlet was a match for Lionel, no matter what courage she had in her closet under the boards. Still, Clara clung to Ben with a crinkle in her brown eyes and a softness that wasn't part of her usual repertoire. She had no repertoire with Ben, the vagabond lawyer who seemed to have a hunger to rescue Yiddish souls. She trembled at his touch, as she always did, was moved by his strange valor. He wasn't a café socialist. He had no wish to change the world. But he went into night court, battled the little lions who preyed upon the poor—and all he had was words, words, words, to pry Yiddish lambs lose from that corrupt den.

He had her naked with three flips of his hand. She was covered with sweat and the white paint of her performance. But he wouldn't allow her to climb into her tiny tub or wash off the paint. He reveled in the sour perfume of her armpits, kissed her until her mouth was raw with the taste of his saliva and his eyebrows were covered in white paint, like some gentle demon.

"Darling," she said, "it's lucky you didn't inherit your father's prick."

"The man was in a fire," said Ben as he pinned Clara to the divan. She'd never in her life been swallowed up by such sweet passion. She'd made love with the acrobats of Odessa after bacchanals of blue wine. She'd been rough on the acrobats, and they'd been coarse and greedy with her, boasting of their conquests while they sucked on black cigarettes.

"Clara," they'd scream, "let's fuck."

It was a bit of rowdy exercise, nothing more. But this boy floated above her limbs. He plumbed her belly like a navigator in the middle of a dream. Still, she could never hold on to Ben. He might plot and scheme, prowl the Ghetto with Monk Eastman, but he'd never truly survived his mother's death. That's what first drew her to the boy, that sense of mourning in his soul.

When she woke on the divan, she was certain that the

vagabond would be gone, but there he was, in his flannel under-wear, cutting up slices of apple as a morning snack.

"Let's go to the Pinnacle," he said, "and have some breakfast with all the anarchists."

Clara wasn't pleased at all. "There are no more anarchists at the Pinnacle," she said. "And suppose Cahan is having coffee at his table? He'll crucify me in the *Forward* if he catches me with another man. People will talk. Poets love to gossip about my exploits. That's why I play the nun at the Pinnacle."

"Then you'll play the Odessa acrobat this morning."

"But we can't hold hands at my table," she said, "or kiss. Will you promise?"

"Certainly not," he muttered, stepping into his pants.

3.

IT WAS BEN WHO SEEMED LIKE THE ACROBAT as they marched along Rivington Street in a sun shower. Clara was meek, with-drawn, under this boy's spell.

Luckily, Cahan was still somewhere at the *Forward*, or out in the field settling a dispute among warring factions of garment workers. And she had the café to herself. Tea arrived at her table before she had a chance to sit down. The Pinnacle had never been an Orthodox café, and she could have tidbits of ham with her French toast.

Ben had become a local celebrity, sort of a Jewish knight, but like everyone else, he listened while Clara held court. Every poet at the Pinnacle bowed and kissed her hand. She'd abandoned her tea with strawberry jam and slurped from a bottle of slivovitz as she talked about her life as a tramp and a clown. She sat like a

Cossack, with her knees wide apart. Her eyes could no longer focus. She garbled half her sentences.

Ben whispered in her ear. "Clara, you have to perform tonight. You'll slur all your lines."

"I will not, sweetie pie. I'm perfectly coherent."

And she was. Her drunkenness was the real disguise. She was worried about her Adonis. He'd never spent this much free time with her—yes, he'd lived with her while he was wounded. But that was on account of Ned Silver and his murderous band. And here he was as her consort at the Pinnacle, as if it were an announcement of some mating season—practically an engagement party in front of the poets. It was a bad sign.

"Where are you going?" she growled.

"Nowhere," he said. "I've been sitting here with you for hours."

"You're going somewhere. I can see it in your eyes, you blond devil."

"Yes, I'm taking you back to the Bowery. I have to sober you up."

"I'm sober as a saint," she hissed at him, having another slug of slivovitz.

He had to carry her in his arms across the rain-swept streets, kicking at garbage pails and a flurry of rats. She was snoring when they arrived at her closet. She had less than half an hour before her first entrance. He fed her cups of cold coffee and applied white paint to her cheeks like the fanciest uptown dresser. Her black tights were bedraggled; the dagger she wore was tilted upside down. But the audience rumbled with pleasure when she pranced upon the stage.

Now she understood the boy's own stagecraft; squiring her everywhere, he left little room for Lionel. She could feel his absence. It was almost palpable. Lionel wasn't in the house tonight. She performed, ripped with her rapier. Bodies crashed through the trapdoor. Casualties mounted. Soon there was no one left to kill.

He'll leave once he drives out Lionel, she sang to herself while she mouthed her lines. *He's more of a ghost than all the ghosts I kill.* But he was there when she returned to her closet with beads of sweat under her white cap. He made love to her before she had a chance to sprinkle her armpits with *eau de rose*; she felt as if she'd gone through some delightful massacre; only this boy could warm her bones while breaking her into little pieces.

And then he vanished without a word while she crouched in her tub. He knew all her tactics as only a detective could. She'd have clung to him had he kissed her good-bye, so he left without a kiss. And for the first time in her career, she canceled a performance. The house was packed. She went into the manager's office.

"Breitbart, you'll have to put up the sign."

"What sign?" he asked, shivering under his derby.

"My sign," she said. "*Hamlet too ill to play.*"

"There will be consequences," he said, trailing her out onto the carpeted sidewalk in front of the Thalia. "All the lost receipts will come out of your salary."

She laughed and flung his derby into the air. "Half my salary goes into your pocket, you fat crook."

And she spun away from him, wearing a long cape. She had adorers on every block, women, men, and even little boys, who pronounced her name like a magic token.

"Bless you, Madame Clara, you have found a voice for all of us."

Yes, as a killer in black tights.

She was desperate, in a hurry, but she had to sign her name on shopping bags and cardboard briefcases that nearly crumbled in her hands.

Affectionately, Prince Hamlet

She was gone before they could decipher the curlicues of her script. She arrived on Essex Street with hardly a pinch of air in her lungs. She heard a great commotion inside the Essex Market Court, and her heart shivered for that Jewish knight of hers. The coppers at the door doffed their caps like all the king's men in her play.

"A pleasure, madame, a real pleasure."

They winked at her and never smiled once; they had nothing but malice in their eyes. And she had herself a fright the moment she stepped inside the courthouse; delirium and panic filled every aisle; it was like a synagogue gone insane, where the chief rabbi sat behind a tall bench in his black robes and kept shouting, "Order, order, before I clear the court."

She noticed Ned Silver and his enormous girth; the king of the bondsmen was raw with rage. The object of his derision was her Jewish knight, who stood alone among that angry red sea of faces, while Silver sat on a divan in the middle of the court, like some grand pasha, his left foot dangling over a pillow, with the threat of mayhem all around him.

"Hey, Clarence," he shouted at the judge, "will you get rid of that infant? He comes here in his diapers and fouls our little nest. He has no business here. Send him away with his army of pickpockets and prostitutes. Jesus, you can't even convict a Jewish soul for larceny around Lawyer Ben."

Silver's acolytes stamped their feet. "Lawyer Ben, Lawyer Ben."

The judge winced at each rattle of the floorboards.

"Are you accusing this court of impartiality, Mr. Ravage?" he asked, phlegm in his mouth.

"Oh, much more than that, Your Honor," said her foolish boy, as if he had his own champion in that hot, boisterous room, when he had none. She let out a gasp that no one heard. Clara had never seen so much hate in a single room.

"Counselor, I've set all your clients free, all those damn Yids. What more could you ask?"

Shut up, she wanted to say to Ben. *Shut up and run before you're swallowed up by all the crocodiles.* But he wouldn't have listened.

"Your Honor, they were kidnapped off the street and brought here under duress."

"Well," said the judge, peering down at Ben like some tin colossus, "what do you expect? It's Yiddish Land. And it's packed with whores and thieves."

He'd never been more beautiful to her, this fanciful boy, in Ned Silver's courtroom, full of hissing men and frightened Jewish housewives, who'd been plucked from their doorways as prostitutes and would have remained utterly voiceless without Ben, while every scavenger in the building bled bail money from their husbands, fathers, sisters, and aunts, and Ben's blue eyes shimmered with ferocious heat under the leaden lamps.

"Your Honor, I have the right to expect a bit of mercy and a modicum of justice, not the posturing of a Tammany hack."

The judge wanted to hurl his ink bottle at Ben, but he could do nothing without a nod from Ned Silver.

"I've cleared the docket, Mr. Ravage; now move on."

But her darling remained in front of the bench in that lurid semidarkness, where faces moved in and out of the shadows, and the judge sat between his oval lamps like some disheveled Buddha.

"Move on to what, Your Honor? Another day's docket, when you preside over a robber's den?"

"Ravage, you are out of order, sir," said the judge.

Clara wanted to whistle, lure the boy back into her own den, but there was so much shouting as little packets of money flew from hand to hand. She hadn't come to a crazed synagogue. The Essex Market Court was a circus where the condemned mingled with the clowns, and the clowns wore badges and mustaches and bowler hats, their pockets stuffed with cash. She'd never encountered such perfidy in her life.

A little boy of nine with dollar bills pinned to his hat managed to weave through the crowd and whisper in Ned Silver's ear. The bondsman smiled and signaled to the judge, who pulled on the pleats of his robe with a sudden sense of triumph.

Run, darling. But she couldn't save her Ben.

"Your Honor, I'd rather plead against a jackanapes. We'd have a much fairer chance. A monkey might be impartial, and wouldn't have his pockets weighed down with a fat man's silver."

The judge hawked up some phlegm and wiped his mouth with a crumpled handkerchief before he uttered a word. "Counselor, I'm holding you in contempt of court. . . . Sergeant Pat, remove this man. He is to be kept in custody without bail."

A burly policeman handcuffed Ben, and Clara couldn't even get near him. Ned's runners hurled broken pencils and apple cores at Ben's eyes, while Silver himself seemed to savor the moment.

"Boy-o, you shouldn't have come into my territories without that baboon of yours. But not even Monk and his canaries can save you now."

And Ben disappeared from the courtroom, within a swirl of bodies, while Ned's runners poked at him with their filthy thumbs. Clara couldn't even catch Ben's eye.

"Darling," she said, but he was gone.

Silver drew his thick, leonine head back on the divan and roared. Then he noticed Clara, and his little narrow eyes surveyed the fullness of her form. He'd never been to the Yiddish theater, but he still knew all about this Lady Hamlet who drove customers wild. Lord Lionel was sweet on her—that's what his spies had told him.

"Mrs. Hamlet, stick around. Judge Clarence has a samovar near his private toilet. I can fix you a superb glass of Russian tea."

Clara wound up and struck a blow that would have crippled a lesser man than Ned, but he stared at her for a moment in disbelief, then toppled over the divan. His runners wanted to tear at Clara's flesh, perhaps even pluck out her eyes, but Ned Silver shouted, "No, no. She's the boss' merchandise."

"Fat man," she said, "I'm nobody's merchandise," and she swerved around all those milling bodies as the ominous shadows of coppers and Democratic clubmen climbed the crooked walls. She couldn't rely on Jewish lawyers in the Ghetto; even the best were under Ned Silver's thumb. So she ran to East Broadway and banged on the front door of the *Forward*. The night watchman undid the latch. She must have roused him from his evening nap.

"Madame Clara," he said, with one eye shut, "what's the occasion?"

"I must see the baron," she said; she knew of Cahan's habits, since all his writers practically slept at the Pinnacle Café. The baron spent many nights inside his tenth-floor lair. The wife he had uptown seldom warmed his bones.

"Is our illustrious editor expecting you?" the watchman asked with an obscene smile.

"Yes."

She would have smacked him on any other occasion, but she had to get to the tenth floor. They rode upstairs together in the rickety elevator. The car lurched, the lights went out, and Clara's heart beat with a crooked rhythm.

"Don't be afraid, madame."

They arrived on the tenth floor in the dark.

"Who walks?" a voice shot out of the shadows. Cahan must have thought that one of his competitors had come to haunt him.

"It's only Beryl," said the watchman, "with the actress."

"What actress?"

And Clara sang one of her soliloquies just as the lights came back on. Cahan was clutching a candlestick. He dismissed the watchman, who returned to his own lair on the ground floor. Cahan put on his spectacles. She wasn't ignorant of his anarchist past. The czar's secret police had chased him across Europe. He'd carried a price on his head, this meek, half-blind man who was once a bomb maker.

"Baron, your boy has been arrested."

He trembled at the first quaff of her *eau de rose.*

"Please, Madame Clara, I never had the good fortune to have a child."

"Ben Ravage," she said. "He was taken out of the Essex Market Court in handcuffs, and God knows where he's being held."

And Cahan wept with his hands over his eyes.

"It's my fault. I sent him to monitor the Ghetto behind the Kehilla's back. And he tilted against the worst windmills, ones with razor blades."

When the baron opened his eyes, Clara stood without her corset and her cloak, like some bountiful Eve. How many times had he sat in the balcony and dreamt of Clara's aromas under her black tights? He stared at the magnificent sweep of her bosom and the undulations of her belly and blacked out. He'd never swooned before, not even when the Okhrana was chasing him from town to town. When he awoke, he was lying on the floor, with Clara kneeling beside him, fully corseted now. She tilted his head and had him sip some water.

"*Maître*, I did not mean to frighten you. Am I such a monster?"

"Yes, yes," he muttered, "a marvelous monster," and rose to his feet without Clara's help.

"Baron," she said like some crafty caller of cards in a gambling den, "we've sat across from one another at the Pinnacle for twenty years. And what did I see in your eyes?"

"A man who wanted to ravage you, to bite every piece of your body until nothing was left."

Clara was all business with the baron, yet his words did excite her a little, even while her Ben hung in the balance. "Well, ravage me."

She feared his silences more than his swoons.

"I cannot," he finally said. "I'm not a tradesman, madame. You love that boy, not me."

And Clara wondered if she would have been better off with acrobats rather than editors and detective-poets. But she knew he wouldn't abandon the boy. Cahan called police headquarters, the Madison Street precinct, and the Essex Street jail. Even with all his cachet as editor of the *Forward*, and his shrewdness as an ex–crime reporter, he still couldn't break into the labyrinthian codes of incarceration. There was no record of Benjamin Ravage, Esq., in any lockup.

"It's past midnight, madame. He probably hasn't been processed. We'll have to wait until tomorrow. Meanwhile, I'll walk you home."

But she wouldn't allow him to accompany her to the Thalia. His nostrils flared as he kissed her hand. Ah, what could she do about all these men? Thank God Pierpont Morgan couldn't rise up from his grave to offer her a villa. Clara always seemed to strike the fancy of one millionaire or another. But she preferred her closet under the boards. She rode down in the same feeble elevator car that lurched from floor to floor.

She was nauseous and dizzy when she got to the sidewalk. The streets were deserted now, under a sliver of moon. There was no one to court the downtown diva. The lamps hissed and died with the last flicker of light. She began to sob when she arrived on the Bowery. Cardboard signs were strung across the Thalia's marquee like piratical eye patches.

THE HOUSE IS DARK

HAMLET IN DEEP MOURNING

WE AWAIT ANOTHER TROUPE

Breitbart had been prescient. She was in deep mourning. But he also liked to bluff. He had no other troupe in mind. He was trying to bully her into her black tights. She was the one who wore the dagger, and drew the crowds in, not Breitbart in his manager's box. She nearly lost her way through the Thalia's serpentine tunnels.

She fumbled with the keys to her closet—the door was open. What could a thief have found of any worth? She had nothing but old costumes in her armoire, a few trinkets here and there. Everything was strewn on the floor; her dressing table had been smashed, her mirror turned to silver rubble, her divan cut into macabre ribbons. It was no robbery. The intruder had wanted to rip her guts.

Lionel Ravage.

THIRTEEN

Old Sparky

I.

*I*T WAS LIKE THE HOOD HE'D OFTEN HAD TO WEAR as punishment at the Hebrew asylum. The hood had a pair of holes for his nostrils and was buckled tight at the neck. The guards claimed it was an old hangman's hood from Sing Sing, used before the warden and his men installed Old Sparky, the prison's own handcrafted electric chair. One of the guards had built a replica of this chair at the Hebrew asylum, and it was Ben who was strapped in most often, Ben who wore the hangman's hood, and nearly choked to death with the constraints around his neck, while this guard and his cohorts fondled him and rapped his knees with their batons.

"Dance for us, little sister."

While he sat in Old Sparky and wore that hood, Ben plotted the demise of every single guard at the orphanage. It helped him pass the time and ration his breaths. And now he sat in another chair, with another hangman's hood over his head, and it felt like he had returned to the orphanage, fifteen years after his first stay. But it wasn't the old punishment cell, with cockroaches crawling on the walls. Ben heard the sound of crickets.

He remembered being dragged from the courthouse in cuffs.

One of Silver Dollars' lads must have slugged him with a black-jack. He'd been with Clara. That much he recalled. He still had the melodies of Hamlet inside his head. Yet he couldn't sit in one place—he never could, as much as he loved her aromas, the little comforts of her divan.

Ben had to go back one last time into that thieves' paradise. He knew Ned Silver would pounce, and still he had to go. He was more like Lionel than he dared admit. He had to rush into a house on fire. He couldn't permit Ned to steal and steal and steal, to manipulate the Ghetto, lure grocers and tailors into a legal web that would turn them into paupers. . . .

He heard the patter of feet break into the explosive roar of crickets. The buckle was loosened around his neck, and Ben could suck in bits of air. The hood rose above his ears like some leather crown. He recognized Marcus Mendelssohn and his kid gloves, and Ben realized where he was. They couldn't risk taking him to police headquarters. They would have had to record his arrival on some ledger. And so they fixed up a kind of doll's house in the attic at Montefiore and borrowed Old Sparky without all the burden of electrical bolts. Ben's wrists and ankles were strapped to the chair. He watched Mendelssohn pluck at the fingers of his kid gloves.

"We wanted to make you comfortable, Ben. It's like old times, isn't it? We borrowed all the stuff from the orphans' asylum. That was my own idea. We have your whole history in a little black book at Kehilla headquarters. I never miss a trick. That's why we catch so many deviants like you, troublemakers who want to stir up the wind."

Mendelssohn laughed at his own good luck; he had Ben where he wanted, in an attic dungeon—no one, uptown or downtown, could hear him scream.

"You shouldn't have interfered with our honeypot," the chief investigator said.

Ben couldn't control his rage. He tugged against the straps that tied him to Old Sparky.

"Ned can talk of honeypots, not you. You're an agent of the Kehilla."

Marcus chortled at Ben. "You should have been kinder to me, kid, and not dragged me uptown in front of my inferiors."

"And you shouldn't have picked the pockets of your own people."

"My own people," Marcus said with a sneer. "I have nothing in common with the downtown Yids. They live like rats in their hovels. They deserve whatever they get."

Ben stopped struggling, as the strap bit into his ankles. Now he understood why Cahan had been so adamant about having his own secret service inside the Kehilla. The baron had to penetrate an endless hall of mirrors, but it was impenetrable; he was chasing phantoms in the dark. Not even an entire café of anarchists could topple the Essex Market Court and all its paths of patronage.

"The downtowners don't deserve you, Marcus; they don't deserve you at all."

That's when Marcus struck him with the smooth, tight leather of his gloves; at first it felt like an angry kiss, and then Marcus' knuckles grew sharper and sharper under that soft jacket of pigskin. Ben's cheeks began to split after the sixth or seventh blow.

"What a sweetheart," Marcus said. "You're bleeding like some damn hemophiliac—hey, Ben, are you the czar's own little boy? What's his name?"

"Alexei," Ben muttered.

"Ah, you're a bleeder, just like him."

Prince Alexei, the little czar, was the one hero of the Russian court, and constantly appeared in the Yiddish press, a nine-year-old saint on a pony, who softened the news of the latest pogrom in Kiev. There were photos of "Alyosha" in kosher butcher shops and restaurants; somehow, little Alexei could paint over the sins of an empire with his own spillage of blood. Cahan published feuilletons about Alexei in the *Forward* every other month. Ben recalled the latest feuilleton, "Alyosha's Secret," written by the baron himself under his nom de plume, Max Vilna.

It was a fantastic tale. The boy is lost in the woods outside the czar's summer palace, abandoned by his own bodyguards. He wanders the countryside, nibbling on wild berries, and is kidnapped by a band of army deserters, who hope to ransom the little czar or bleed him to death. Among the deserters is a Jewish soldier, Joshua, who was conscripted into the Russian army from a Lithuanian village when he himself was nine. The villagers sold Joshua, an orphan, to save themselves from conscription. Joshua is scarred from years of war. He has raped and robbed, given himself over to pogroms, even sacked his own village without a second thought. He can't recall the number of women he's sodomized, or the number of necks he's broken. But this little boy in the sailor suit touches him. Perhaps bleeders are like orphans, whose bodies have become their own sad little cage. No matter. He rescues the boy from his own band, and returns Alexei to the czar's summer palace. The czar rewards Joshua, makes him captain of Alexei's bodyguard; he's the lone Yid at the summer palace, except for a few of the czar's financiers.

Certain pundits considered Ben the model for Joshua, that Jewish orphan turned savior, but Ben saw "Alyosha's Secret" as a fairy tale about the reconciliation of a lost father and son: Cahan's masked voice, Max Vilna, was dreaming of Lionel Ravage. And Ben had to laugh bitterly at Cahan's secret wish. Reconciliation was the fairy tale. Old Sparky was Lionel's own sinister song.

Ben's imprisonment made more and more sense. Lionel hadn't wasted his time at the Thalia. He'd turned the attic at Montefiore into a stage, his props a hangman's hood and a discarded electric chair out of Ben's own past. His actors were also his audience; they did double duty in the attic. The doctors checked Ben's pulse, the male nurses applied some sulfurous balm to his cheeks after every beating. And Ben was also an actor and a witness in Lionel's theater; the last act would be Ben's own annihilation.

The chief investigator thrashed him at regular intervals. The nurses would undo the straps, feed him caviar and dark bread, drag him to the toilet, scrub his testicles and armpits, and return him to the electric chair. The beatings didn't occur without some sort of conversation. Marcus never really tried to probe, nor did he ask the downtown detective to confess his sins.

"Dummy, didn't the boss give you fair warning? You and Monk could have been the little kings of the Ghetto. Yiddish Land was yours. All you had to do was keep away from the courthouse."

If Ben lost consciousness, Marcus would caress him with a sponge.

"Did I hit you too hard, darling?"

And the beatings would start all over again. Ben had to hold on to the bits of brain he had left. "You were Schiff's bodyguard and fix-it man. When did Lionel crawl into the picture?"

"Ha!" Marcus said. "And you call yourself a detective. It was Lionel who sent me to Master Jacob. I worked in his shop on Canal. I was his rat chaser, and I lost out to a miserable cat."

"Chlöe," Ben whispered, with blood on his cheek. The image

of Lionel's blond cat soothed him much more than the sulfur some nurse applied to his cheeks. He could thrust himself into the picture, imagine the cat prowling in that huge warehouse of pipes. Chlöe must have been as savage as Clara, who also prowled.

"Tell me more about the cat."

"What's there to tell? That wild bitch nearly chewed my arm off. She wouldn't let anyone near Lionel. So he recommended me to the Old Man."

"And you've been serving two masters ever since."

Marcus struck him again; he was a maestro at this art. He knew how much punishment to deliver with each blow, to cut Ben with surgical precision, break his spirit before his blood let out, so he could keep a dead man alive. That's how he would minister to a horse thief at headquarters and have him give up all his accomplices. Only Ben wasn't a horse thief.

His vision was blurred. Marcus seemed to dance in his own fog. One of Ben's ears was clogged with blood.

"Come on, Marcus, when does Lionel make his grand entrance? We've all been acting out our parts."

"The boss is finished with you. He's written you off."

Ben stared through the fog in the attic. He'd tried to keep count of the days. He couldn't even count the number of times they'd let him breathe without the hangman's hood. But there had to be a finale, a fifth act.

"Then why am I still alive?" Ben asked.

"Because you're the lucky one," Marcus said. "But you won't be lucky much longer."

And the process began all over again—the methodical beatings, the little walks to the toilet, the clipped breathing under the hood. Perhaps they wanted to bleed the sanity out of him. So he had to guard the few fixtures he still had. He tried to recollect all the rooms he lived in with his mother, but he couldn't hold on to that particular thread; the rooms unraveled in front of his eyes, and Ben had to carry all the bedding on his back, as he and Manya rushed to yet another address—with landlords chasing them for the rent, leering at Manya all the time, poking at her with their hands. He started to cry under the hood.

"Stop that."

He couldn't recognize the voice; his ears were whistling as the hood was pulled off. Lionel had sent his messenger, Bad Babette. He could only pick at pieces of her with his damaged eyes.

"Tuscany," she muttered. He tilted his head toward her and watched as best he could. She'd been smoking her pipe. Babs couldn't stop blinking. She must have come from Lionel's private cabaret and opium den.

"Are you listening? He'll let you live. But you have to go to Tuscany and promise never to come back."

"Why Tuscany?" he asked, to lure her deeper into the conversation. She couldn't stand straight without clutching the back of the electric chair.

"How the hell should I know? He has enemies—or friends—who own an entire village. And that's where they banish all their undesirables."

Not quite. Untouchables, those who can't be touched.

That's what he had become in Yiddish Land, a threat to all the visible and not so visible players on Lionel's grandiose stage. But there was no mysterious town in Tuscany, or anywhere else. It was a fairy tale that Lionel had spun, and Babs couldn't have understood that in her own shrunken state. She was a messenger without a message, like most of Lionel's flunkies.

"You can tell my prick of a father that I'd rather not retire in the sun."

She must have jolted herself out of her pipe dream. She no longer had to lean on the electric chair. She licked her lips like some predator about to abandon its prey.

"Marcus," she shouted, "he's all yours."

Babs leaned over and kissed Ben on his bloody cheek. Her face was a grim mask. "Good-bye, dear downtown detective."

Ben couldn't comprehend how she'd drifted into Lionel's orbit, even with all the opium. She didn't need his money or his power. She was an heiress, not a feral cat.

"Tell me, Babs, were you in this same crib when Marcus beat Leila to death?"

Her grim mask seemed to soften in that fog surrounding Ben. "I watched every blow," she sang in a child's voice as she exited the attic.

2.

THE NURSES HAD PUT A BLOOD BUCKET near Old Sparky, and that's how they captured the boy's teeth. There was no longer much rationale behind Marcus' repeated wallops. He wore out several pair of kid gloves. The nurses had to keep checking the boy's pulse. None of them could believe Ben was still alive. They checked his pulse several times as he lay in Old Sparky, the hangman's hood over his head.

Mendelssohn might disappear for several afternoons, and one of the nurses would think, *Hey, the kid has won. Mendie's given up.* And he'd return to deliver a far more severe beating.

"Come on, kid, say something."

It was impossible for Ben to speak with so much blood in his mouth. He spat into the bucket and realized that he had lost another tooth. But he wouldn't give this crazed executioner the smallest satisfaction.

"Mendie, I dream of you every night."

He slept fitfully under the hangman's hood, and his dreams were as disconsolate as a dead cat with scorched eyes. Shadows bit his ear—Clara perhaps. And then Manya wandered about in an actress' black tights.

This beating was as senseless and random as the last. Marcus lowered the hood again.

"Sweet dreams, kid. That's what's keeping you alive."

The nurses came, scrubbed his balls while he sat in his chair, and left. He must have drifted off; when he woke, he heard the light slap of ballet slippers and the tremor of wings.

"Who is it?" he asked, wondering if some angel had come to shut his eyes forever.

"Bad Babette."

Babs plucked off his hangman's hood and tossed it into a corner; she was wearing a yellow cape that flew around her like agitated wings. She loosened the straps around his ankles and wrists.

"Idiot," she said, "run while you have a chance. I'll guide you down the stairs."

Ben hadn't lost his detective's guile, even after all the beatings. But his mouth was swollen, his tongue was raw, and his voice sounded like a series of whistles, with all the wind between his missing teeth.

"Why are you doing this, Babs? What master are you serving now?"

"Shut up," she said.

But he wouldn't leave with Babette. She kissed him on the forehead, wrapped those porous wings around her, and left him there. He clasped and unclasped his fingers, fiddled with the straps so the buckles were still loose, slipped the hood back onto his head, and waited for Mendelssohn. He didn't want to stray too far from Lionel's script. But Lionel had a coauthor now.

Mendelssohn seemed to arrive out of a dream. Ben had to raise his own hooded eyes as the hood was lifted off his head.

"How are you, kid?"

Marcus didn't even move as Ben rose up out of the electric chair. He still had the Colt strapped to his chest. But he'd lost all his markers of what was real and what was not. Ben didn't say a word. He ripped off Marcus' holster straps with his thumbs. He saw the traces of urine on Marcus' bone white spats. The executioner had peed in his pants.

"Don't hurt me," Marcus squealed. "I'm only the middleman."

Ben had a terrible case of vertigo; he begged God that he wouldn't fall. He dug his hand under Marcus' collar and shoved him down onto Old Sparky.

"There's your kingdom, Marcus; there's your throne. Let's see how much it's worth."

Ben didn't bother with the straps. But his hands were much too brittle, and several of his fingers were broken. He put on a pair of kid gloves that Marcus had kept in reserve on a shelf behind Old Sparky, and it took him several blows to smash the executioner's windpipe, since he could barely make a fist. Marcus' throat churned like a sick steam engine seconds before he died, and he had the same look of absolute terror in his eyes as the horse thieves he'd pummeled to pieces in the cellars of police headquarters.

Ben walked down from the attic, clutching the banister rails. He had blood splattered all over him. He'd lost one of his shoes. The nurses and the doctors and their whores kept out of his way; he looked like a wolfman with a beard of blood. He managed a toothless smile when he saw Jacob Schiff at the bottom of the stairs. The patriarch was about to begin his rounds of the central ward, but he was repelled by all the blood and dirt on the downtown detective.

"Master Jacob," Ben muttered, "I don't think you can rely on Marcus anymore."

"Young man," the patriarch said. "I cannot understand a single word."

"It's a pity, that. Your majordomo is dead."

Ben seized Schiff by the collar with his broken hands. His voice still sounded like whistling in the wind, but he'd learned from Clara to capture his own cadence, despite the missing teeth.

"You can prosecute me if you like, sir, bring all your witnesses to bear, but you'll have a hard time explaining Old Sparky in the attic."

"You're a raving lunatic, like your own mother."

Ben struck the patriarch; it was a feeble blow, but no one had ever touched his face before, not even his own father. The lord of Kuhn, Loeb could finance a battleship with the curl of a finger, ruin a rival banking house.

"Mention my mother one more time, Master Jacob, and you'll join Marcus."

The patriarch stood there, shivering with rage, as Ben lurched out of Montefiore with one shoe. The doctors and nurses were in a panic; patients were howling for Schiff.

"Shouldn't we make our rounds, sir? Your presence will calm them."

"No," said the master of Montefiore. He'd started this clinic so that the chronic invalids of the Ghetto could breathe some fresh air and heal themselves in a countrified manor. "What's upstairs?"

"Nothing, sir. It's a wasteland—just our quarters and the kitchen."

He shoved his own vassals aside and mounted the stairs. He didn't blink when he noticed women in kimonos on the balconies. They smiled at Master Jacob and pressed their own nipples, as if they were feeding some phantom child.

"Out," he said, "pack your things and get out."

"Hold your horses," said one of the kimono-clad women. "Couldn't we come to an agreement? We have a lawyer, grandpa, and we're entitled to reparations."

"Not a dime," said Jacob Schiff, who continued up the stairs; it felt like his annual hike in the mountains with the president of Harvard, but Charles Eliot didn't hide a band of thieves behind his walls. Schiff arrived in the attic, and discovered Marcus' corpse in the wireless electric chair. The Kehilla's chief investigator sat like an obedient boy, with blue marks under his lips. Schiff noticed the hangman's hood and the discarded pairs of kid gloves; otherwise, the attic was empty.

He'd been to the Death House at Sing Sing, and was one of the first to see Old Sparky. He'd gone upstate with the governor, when a young accountant from the Ghetto, Julius Goldbaum, had strangled several of his clients and absconded with their funds. One of the victims was Schiff's own niece. And he felt a kind of moral obligation to be her witness at the accountant's execution. He was not a man of violence, but his father, a rabbinical scholar, had instilled in him a sense of piety toward all Jews, the holy and the unholy. And so he shared the condemned man's last meal; the warden had borrowed a kosher cook for the occasion.

"Will you pray for me, rabbi?" Julius asked.

"I'm not a rabbi," the patriarch insisted.

The accountant smiled. "I know who you are. The king of the Jews."

The patriarch wasn't amused. "Have we met before, young man?"

"Many times, rabbi. I was always at Kuhn, Loeb—I blended in. One of your associates introduced me to your niece."

"That's impossible," Schiff said. "Who are you?"

"The prince of darkness," Julius said, and slurped his chicken noodle soup.

Schiff ended the meal right there. He watched the accountant being strapped into Old Sparky, with a metal pan on his head, like a silver crown. He didn't turn away from the electrical bolts as the accountant writhed like a man struck with lightning. But he did intone the prayer for the dead. Perhaps it was out of habit. And he paid for the accountant's burial service.

"Marcus, you fool," he muttered to the dead man in *this* electric chair. He couldn't afford a scandal at Montefiore. The gates would be shackled, and the home shut down. The invalids here would be put in some inferno, and all these years of labor and trust reduced to ashes.

Schiff marched downstairs and fired his entire staff, giving doctors and nurses twenty minutes to pack. They looked at him with murder in their eyes. But he didn't back down. His own cook had been in charge of these rogues. Schiff had borrowed him from his mansion.

"Peter, if you aren't gone within the hour, none of you will have any future."

"And what about your future, sir?" said the cook, who'd grown fat at Montefiore.

"I've taken liens out on your lives," Schiff said, his own flair for invention far in advance of these men. "If anything untoward should happen to me, you'll be hunted like wild rabbits."

They'd all seen the unbroken line of his power. They scattered as fast as they could with their whores, their belongings stuffed into pillowcases. And Master Jacob was all alone in this house of invalids. He marched once through the wards, his presence calming boys who had coughing fits, old men with unlit eyes. Then he withdrew into his little office. He phoned his allies at certain Jewish agencies, and assembled a new staff in a matter of minutes. He made no threats. He wasn't harsh. No one could deny his gentle commands. That was always how he conducted business, unless his temper flared.

Then he called Captain Kittleberger, the one friend he had among all the coppers in Manhattan. He'd never bribed the captain, but he did set up a "college fund" for his children and all his nephews and nieces. They referred to that little deal as "Noah's ark," but it was rarely mentioned. They had a kinship of mutual respect, nourished over the years.

The captain arrived well after dark, without his driver.

"Kit, I have a problem in the attic. Marcus Mendelssohn. He's suddenly expired. I'd like him buried somewhere."

"With a cantor's blessings?" the captain asked.

"Yes, of course. He's a Jewish boy. But the cantor has to be selected carefully."

The captain nodded his head.

244 *Ravage & Son*

"Did you know about this establishment, Kit?"

"I did."

And now the patriarch's temper did begin to flare. "So I was looked upon as the blind old fool with sacks of money."

"Sir, I have no authority up in Hamilton Heights. I can't stray too far from Yiddish Land. But this is the plumber's doing. I could close his shops on Canal—at least for a little while."

"I'll take care of Lionel," the patriarch said.

And Kittleberger climbed upstairs. He returned with Marcus bundled in a blanket he'd found in the doctors' dormitory. The chief investigator looked like an infant in the captain's arms.

"Don't you worry, sir. I'll have him all waxed up and buried in no time."

Soon the captain himself was gone from Montefiore, with that corpse under a blanket, and Jacob was left with his old guilt. He'd contributed to Lionel's derailment, had belonged to the society of uncles that visited his warehouse thirty years ago, all relatives and friends of his wife, descending upon Lionel like some lynching party. Schiff's own great-uncle had been in charge, Rainer Weiss, patriarch of what they called the Teutonic Knights, who were willing to pluck at Lionel for Henrietta's sake. They didn't care about Lionel's whore, the daughter of a philosopher who peddled apples in the street. These Knights were all pious men, and they hid their cruel jests within their piety. They could never forgive Lionel for the happiness he found with this girl, for the passion that had always eluded them.

Uncle Rainer also had a mistress, a niece he kept under wraps. But she never interfered with his marriage and never would. Perhaps that's why he was so vehement about Lionel, so bitter in his pursuits. Jacob shouldn't have gone along with that lynching party. But he was just as brutal, whacking Lionel as often as he could. It was Rainer's idea to murder the cat. "We must divest him of whatever props he has, or he will not give up the girl."

Rainer hired some Hoboken pirates to crucify that blond cat. It was Jacob's mission to spy on the apple peddler's daughter. Did he covet her? Perhaps he did. But he wouldn't have devoured Manya Rabinowitz, magnificent as she was. He could have warned Lionel, told him to run with the girl from Uncle Rainer. He did nothing, went along with the plot. And they broke Lionel, sent him back to Henrietta and his imbecilic family. It was Jacob's fault. That's why he was so distraught when he discovered that Manya had had a child, a little boy named Ben, who'd grown into a delinquent with an impossible quest, nourished by that anarchist Cahan, to find a place at Harvard. Jacob Schiff found him that place, working behind the scenes like some diabolic puppeteer. . . .

It was Marcus, his own man, who had tortured Ben, and in Jacob's attic at Montefiore. Who was the criminal here? He should have gone against Rainer, not sided with those other torturers, the Teutonic Knights. Now he would have to be his own Teutonic Knight.

He went back into the central ward; the new doctors hadn't arrived yet, and he had to calm the patients, ease their fears. It disheartened him to see boys who would never grow up because of some spinal injury, old men who couldn't even recollect where they were, tailors and former shop owners with blood in their spittle. They shouted at him from every corner.

"Uncle Jacob, what was all that noise? Where's Nurse Freddy and Dr. Ted?"

"On a long siesta," he told them. But they weren't blind, even if their long stay at the home had confused them and dulled their wits. They watched him tremble.

"What's wrong, Uncle?" asked Henry, the boy with a battered spine, whose father had accused him of opening Montefiore as an act of penance for his capitalist crimes.

Manya.

He alone had ruined that girl, driven her mad with a love that consumed her. What would the Vilna Gaon have said? *The girl was shamed.* Would the Teutonic Knights have beaten Lionel into the dust if he'd been married to this Lithuanian girl and Henrietta of Fifth Avenue was the woman he pursued on the sly? No, the Knights would have rejoiced. They'd have danced at Lionel's wedding after some miserable rabbi produced the divorce papers and the Russian Jewess was sent into the cold with a bagful of silver.

"Shame," he muttered. It was another sad tale of Ghetto queens and Fifth Avenue squires. And Jacob Schiff had always been caught in the middle, with a piety that crumbled at his own feet. He himself was half mad. He wandered through the ward, his goatee wet with tears as he hugged each invalid in his wake, like some medical wizard from the Old World.

"We will cure you, Avram. . . . Cough into my handkerchief, Joseph. It will clear your chest. . . . Don't hunch your shoulders, Yankel. Your heart will move to the wrong side."

His litany grew louder and louder, and when the first new doctor arrived, he thought he had come to an insane asylum.

FOURTEEN

Manhattan Mayhem

I.

NED SILVER SAT SLUMPED IN THE BALCONY at the Haymarket, his enormous bulk captured in a Napoleonic chair, his suede boots leaning against the rail. He rarely left his kingdom opposite the courthouse, but he had his bodyguards and his yes-men with him. The Haymarket would soon be shuttered, and he'd never have another panoramic view of harlots and their cadets dancing in a great circle. There must have been a thousand children of the night, in a dance hall that belonged to another era, when all the ruffians arrived with their gun molls, and each gang had its own etiquette. Ned had once lived in that rough-and-tumble world. But there wasn't much cash to be made. So he underwent a metamorphosis, became some judge's disciple, pinning dollar bills to his robes, until all the swag went to Silver Dollars himself as master of the Essex Market Court.

The orchestra was playing "My Gal Sal," and he hummed the sad lyrics about Sal's demise. At heart, Ned Silver was a sentimental man, despite the lads he'd kicked and clubbed to death, and he wondered if he'd ever meet Sal or another darling on the other side. He could hear a faint sound, like a birdcall that wove in and out of the orchestra's roar. Ned lost that silent composure of a fat

man. Something was amiss at the Haymarket. He growled to his
bodyguards, but no one answered. That's when he saw the yellow
birds on the balcony rail. And what they warbled had nothing to
do with "My Gal Sal."

He'd planned every step to the Haymarket without telling a
soul. It was a bondsman's holiday. He'd brought his bodyguards
at the last minute, stationing them around him like the points of a
spectacular star. And then they were gone in a whisker, not a sign
of them, as if they were part of an illusionist's act, and were stuck
in a secret pocket somewhere, with all the other martyrs, gang
lords and their mollies who never made it out of the dance hall
alive. Ned did not want a similar fate. He had too many capons
he still had to devour, too many quiet dinners in a private room at
Delmonico's with a sweetheart from the *Follies*, too many suckers
he had to separate from their hard cash at the courthouse. But the
birds kept accumulating on the balcony rail. And Silver Dollars
had no need of a clairvoyant. The birds were a prelude to some
disaster—his own.

Ned was fleet enough. He could have run from the balcony
and hollered blue murder, but he wouldn't have gotten very far. So
he sat. He hadn't been to shul since he was a *pisher*, and he couldn't
pray for his own deliverance. The Lord wouldn't deliver Ned.

"I'll retire," he sang into the dark. "I will leave my bondsman's
cage and move to Westchester with the wife."

And a voice sang back to him out of the dark. "Ned Silver,
you haven't seen your wife in seven years." It had all the authority
of Jehovah, even if it was as familiar as the basso in a barbershop
quartet.

"I know you're there, Edward," he shrieked as a canary hopped
onto his shoulder. It was like a death warrant. He couldn't escape

Monk Eastman or his birds. And Monk stepped out of the dark like a slippery angel.

"You're a reasonable man, Ned, and you've always been cautious. Couldn't you reckon that I'd find you *anywhere* after you kidnapped the shamas? I would have pulled you out of your wire cage. And yet you walk right into one of my old roosts."

The bondsman started to blubber as a second canary hopped aboard his shoulder. He stood up to shake himself free of the birds. He might still have a chance. He had an ice pick in his cummerbund.

"I'm willing to bargain, Edward—for my life. The shamas is still breathing, ain't he? No harm done. I'll build playgrounds for crippled kids. I'll . . ."

The canaries clung to him no matter how hard he shook. He tried to swat at them, but they hopped right under the blade of his hand. He squinted at Monk, reached into his cummerbund, and pulled out the ice pick with a snarl. It wasn't clear what happened next, whether he was pushed or he tripped on some peanut shells and plummeted over the balcony rail on account of the unfortunate distribution of his own weight. His body spun as he clawed at something—the fat man seemed to hang forever in midair. Finally he crashed into the floorboards, and the entire dance hall seemed to buckle. He was rushed to St. Vincent's in an ambulance and died on the way there.

2.

POLITICIANS DECLARED A DAY OF REST on the Lower East Side. Packages of food were distributed in the poorest neighborhoods. Ground was cleared on Hester Street for a playground in honor of Ned Silver, a son of the Ghetto. Money was given to local synagogues in Ned's name. His consummate greed was stricken from the folklore surrounding Ned, but he couldn't be replaced at the Essex Market Court. Magistrates bumbled along like blind men without Ned. Coppers lost their magic touch. The downtown detective had dug deeper into the Ghetto's mythology than Silver Dollars ever could, despite the food packages and the proposed playground.

Still, no one could find Ben Ravage. Cahan wrote about him in editorial after editorial, wondering if the Kehilla had conspired to kidnap him again. "It wouldn't surprise me none if these so-called Jewish detectives were attempting to silence one of their own."

Cahan slept on a table at the *Forward* with all his manuscripts, and was awakened at seven in the morning. His secretary, Matilda, rang from the newsroom. She seemed delirious, almost out of control.

"Comrade Editor, you have an important guest—the god of the German Jews."

"I'm tired," he warned her. "Don't talk riddles."

And Jacob Schiff climbed upstairs to that falcon's lair of Cahan's with his white spats and impeccable mustache.

"*Gott*, I spent half the night waiting outside the Pinnacle for you."

"What could be so important, Jacob?"

Cahan had to remove a pile of books from his only other chair, with its worn wicker bucket.

"Baron, you must stop attacking the Kehilla in print. Marcus was an aberration. You will ruin the last chance we have."

"What last chance? Benjamin is still missing. And your coterie of detectives will never find him. But I can't think without my morning strudel."

Cahan grabbed his hat and coat from a peg on the wall and they marched to Rivington Street, the wind climbing up their backs. The usual clamor of the café halted as Cahan entered with the patriarch in his astrakhan hat. Cahan's table was cleared of coffee cups and drowsy poets. Strudel and fresh coffee were carried to the table by the owner himself.

"Herr Schiff, would you like some *Schlag* with your strudel?"

"Don't pamper him," the baron said. "We have some important business to discuss—life and death."

But it didn't matter. Every poet at the Pinnacle had to shake Schiff's hand and palaver in Yiddish with the patriarch.

"Comrades," Cahan said, "you're dulling his mind. How can he buy and sell the world if you keep pestering him? And there will be nothing but a few crumbs left for me."

But Schiff had to write a whole parcel of names on a piece of paper—daughters who needed an apartment, sons-in-law who could use a job in the bond market. He was patient with them all.

"Enough!" Cahan said. "What is it you want from me, Jacob?"

"A permanent truce. I can't afford bad publicity at Montefiore."

"Then you must rid yourself of all the rotten apples—and prevent Mr. Frank from building his thirteenth five-and-ten on Grand."

The patriarch was deeply puzzled. "I'm not an anarchist, Baron. Should I bomb the building site for you?"

Yes, Cahan wanted to say, *yes, yes, yes.* "But you could discourage Mr. Frank. We do not need another pharaoh. He will seduce other builders into buying up lots. He dreams of his own Ladies'

Mile. A luncheon counter for debutantes and their grandmothers in satin veils."

The patriarch picked at his strudel with a tiny fork. "Another merchant will come along—and you'll have Wanamaker's instead of a five-and-ten. But without Mr. Frank or someone like him, the Ghetto will become a morgue of abandoned tenements. You'll have miles and miles of rubble."

"But poor people will still have gas to cook with, and they won't have landlords and pharaohs crawling on their backs."

"You're impossible," the patriarch said, wolfing down his third portion of strudel. He felt comfortable in this café of luft-menschen. He preferred it to the sepulchral silences of Kuhn, Loeb. "Do we have a truce, Baron? We cannot survive with Jews devouring Jews."

"Then you'll block Mr. Frank's excursion onto Grand Street."

"I will try," the patriarch whispered, knowing his partners would eat him alive if he tampered with Woolworth's finances. Schiff was about to leave, when Clara Karp entered the café with that feline prowess of hers. She'd stopped performing after Ben was plucked from the Essex Market Court. The Thalia had been dark ever since; no other troupe would have dared replace her. Breitbart tried to bring in a gang of Yiddish jugglers and clowns, but he couldn't sell a ticket. The Lower East Side mourned its Lady Hamlet. Flowers were delivered to her dressing room, but she was never there. She wandered the streets in a trance without her Ben, didn't sign one autograph.

She wouldn't sit at her own table, where the usual loafers would have courted her. She sat with Cahan and Jacob Schiff. She was as striking as ever in her pallor, her dark eyelashes softening her sadness. A bottle of slivovitz was waiting for her.

"Ah," she said, "the two earth shakers. Where's my Harvard boy?" She would have given herself gladly to both of them right on the Pinnacle's hard floor if they could bring back the boy. She'd taken part in drunken revels with her troupe of Odessa clowns, had even slept with a dwarf. It was Ben, only Ben, who could warm her bones.

"Comrades," she said, "why haven't you offered a reward? Some desperate gang could be holding him."

"Clara," Cahan said, "haven't I reached out *everywhere*?"

"He's hurt," she said. "And there's no record of a visit to any hospital. I have my own spies. But you, Herr Schiff, should be ashamed of yourself. Your own people kept him locked up in that mausoleum you advertise as a home for chronic invalids. Well, you've turned Ben into an invalid. Find him, or I'll tear your eyes out."

The patriarch couldn't stop marveling at her acrobatic airs; her anger stirred his loins. "Madame Clara, we will do our best, the baron and I."

He rose from the table, wiped the crumbs from his mouth, kissed her hand, and left the café, juggling crisis after crisis in his mind.

3.

HE MET THE KING OF CANAL at the Hardware Club, one of the few places in Manhattan that didn't treat Lionel as an outlaw. They sat in their own alcove, where Jacob wouldn't be bothered by petitioners for money. A waiter brought them slices of honeydew melon, shipped in from South America.

"I must beg your forgiveness, Lionel," the patriarch said. "I was *there*."

"What are you talking about?"

"With Uncle Rainer," the patriarch said. "When he made you give up Manya."

Lionel stared through the eyeholes of a face that would always be a burnt mask.

"You'd be wise not to mention that name, Brother Jacob, not ever again."

"I was there, with the other Teutonic Knights. I beat you every bit as hard as they did."

Lionel sipped from a glass of water. "I would have remembered. No, one of us is dreaming."

"We should have left you alone. We could have found another husband for Henrietta, another father for—"

"Quiet," Lionel said. "It's not your affair."

"Oh, but it is, very much so," Jacob said. "If we hadn't visited you that day, you wouldn't have tried to murder Ben."

Lionel writhed under that mask of raw skin. "The boy walked out of Montefiore, didn't he? If I had really wanted to murder him . . ."

"And where is he now?"

Lionel gobbled some honeydew that dribbled on his chin. "Hiding, I suppose. And he has every reason to hide. Now what else do you want?"

"Babette."

Lionel's bitter laugh sounded like a lament. "Babs doesn't belong to me."

"But you have her, Lionel. I want you to shut that opium den inside Satan's Circus."

"I can't," Lionel said, "even if you offered me a million. It's where I go to rest, where I dream of my dead cat. Those Teutonic Knights of yours had her killed. I might have resisted Rainer with Chlöe at my side. . . . You can't have Babette."

4.

LIONEL DIDN'T REALLY HAVE TO STRAY FAR from his kingdom on Canal. He might meet that pious patriarch of the Jewish Four Hundred at the Hardware Club, or sit with one of Mr. Frank's magician-architects in a corner of the Woolworth Building, or ride uptown and puff on his opium pipe somewhere in the womb of Satan's Circus, but he didn't have to stroll to the Bowery and watch Lady Hamlet perform, since the theater was dark and would stay dark while that mongrel boy was missing. And Lionel took a perverse delight in the Thalia's demise. If he couldn't have Clara's rumbling music, her pouncing on the boards in black tights, then why should anyone else? He loved to ruin whatever he could. Endings always enticed him. Let others learn to live with his scars, find their heads on fire.

And then he noticed the signboard on a sandwich man near his domain.

LADY HAMLET RETURNS TO THE THALIA

GALA PERFORMANCE

FEW TICKETS LEFT

Ah, they couldn't rob him of all his pleasures. He strolled to the Bowery, stood on the Thalia's red carpet, and went to the ticket window, but whatever luck he had disappeared with the sandwich man. He couldn't even use his charm on Sophie, the ticket vendor.

"I'm sorry," she said. "We're all sold out."

"That's preposterous. Girlie, do you realize I'm the principal investor in this music box? You couldn't stay open for five minutes without me. Where's Breitbart, the manager?"

Breitbart arrived, with his fat hands and surplus of flesh. He didn't seem alarmed, even with that ominous cane of Lionel's.

"If I pull out, Breitbart, the house will go dark again."

"Not at all, Mr. Ravage," the manager said. "Your shares have slipped through your fingers."

"Since when?" Lionel growled, rubbing the wolf's head on his cane with his own brand of quiet menace.

"This afternoon," the manager said. "They've been assigned to certain parties at Kuhn, Loeb. I've been informed, sir, by a reliable source, that you're out on your ass."

"One phone call," Lionel said, "and the electricians will sabotage all the fuse boxes."

"I doubt that," said the gruff voice of a much larger man. Kittleberger loomed behind Breitbart in his captain's coat. He was six feet four.

"Kit," Lionel said, "if you play the emperor's game with me, you're liable to lose. There's a good amount of my money in your pocket. I kept Madison Street warm every winter."

"And we're all grateful," Kittleberger said. "We'll put a plaque on the wall. But you're still not welcome here. I'd hate to cuff you right on the red carpet, Mr. Ravage."

"Cuff me," Lionel said. "I couldn't care less."

And then another figure rushed past Kit with a rage that startled Lionel—it was the Thalia's own feral cat, Clara Karp, and she slapped him with such force that he crumpled into the police captain with his silver-toothed cane. It was the slap of a lifetime. A current ran through his mottled face like an electrical spark. He hadn't experienced such delight in ages, and the pimple between his thighs suddenly awoke.

"You come here," she said. "Not even a crazed animal would plot the murder of his own son."

Lionel rose to his feet with the help of his cane. His mouth was bleeding. He caressed it with Mordecai Rabinowitz's raspberry scarf.

"Madame," he said, in front of Kittleberger. "I'm not an amateur. Ask Kit. If I wanted him dead, he'd be dead."

She slapped him again. Kittleberger grasped Lionel before he fell, and he hung there like some puppet on a human peg.

"I love that boy," she spat into Lionel's hooded eyes. "Next time, play your Russian roulette with someone else's life."

She ran toward the stage door, while her admirers clutched at her arms. She was almost as savage with them as she had been with Lionel.

"Not now," she said, brushing them away; a few tumbled to the ground, mystified at the ferocity of their idol, and loving her even more.

Lionel watched her disappear into the bowels of the theater. He lingered for a moment and then had to consider the parlous state of his fortune. He should have anticipated Master Jacob crouching on his left flank.

He returned to Canal Street and clutched the silk scarf, his own blood mingling with the rich raspberry color. He could conjure up Manya and old man Rabinowitz with the soft wound of that silk. He didn't climb the spiral staircase to his office. His wife and children were gone for the day. He stood in that graveyard of pipes, still the master of a mountain of rust. Not one of his rat chasers was around with a shotgun. He preferred his isolation, but it was still curious. He smiled to himself.

How quickly the giants fall.

He didn't need an accountant to tell him that he was worth more dead than alive. He could no longer generate cash—the insurance companies and all his creditors would profit from his imminent mortality. It didn't really matter who the instruments were—retired detectives, burglars from Odessa, members of the Baxter Street Dudes. They'd already be waiting for him upstairs. The market couldn't coddle Lionel like some prima donna. Dollars disappeared with every one of his breaths.

He kissed the raspberry scarf, kissed his own blood. "Manya," he moaned as he climbed the staircase. He couldn't switch on the light. His killers had cut off the circuitry. He saw their shadows. There were three of them. He wished he had Chlöe's talent to see in the dark.

"Gentlemen," he said, "what about some scotch before the slaughter begins?"

He twisted on his toes and lunged into the darkness with his wolf's head. He heard one of the killers yelp like a sick toad. But he couldn't twirl his cane around fast enough. He could feel his left shoulder crush.

Louisville Sluggers.

His killers had come armed with baseball bats. He still parried with his cane. And one of the bats fell out of a killer's hands. He wasn't thinking of romance or revenge, but of his conversations with Mordecai before he ever knew that Manya existed. The old man couldn't pay the rent; he offered to become Lionel's valet, said he'd once worked for a prince, an educated man, and they'd read Pascal together. And Lionel told him that he'd exchange Rabinowitz's own thoughts for the rent money, Mordecai's *Pensées*. He had no idea that Manya was listening all the time in the closet. That's how she fell in love with the landlord, watching him through a keyhole as they discussed Pascal, who imagined all men trapped inside a single room, waiting there until they died. That was Mordecai's own premonition of the New World. Lionel had laughed, said Pascal had a peddler's point of view.

And now his cheek was crushed, and Lionel was still arguing with a dead man. Pascal's room, he should have said, had no closets, no Manya hiding behind a keyhole. . . .

The third blow crowned Lionel, crushed his skull. His killers examined him with a flashlight. They were all burly men. They were used to looks of horror on their victim's faces, bulging eyeballs and twisted mouths. But Lionel didn't have a regular face, and they could have sworn that his mouth was curled into a smile. They wiped the blood and bits of brain from their bats with hand towels from the Plaza and one of them flicked off the flashlight. They had no urgency. They smoked Sweet Caporals in the dark, more interested in the baseball cards tucked inside the packets than in the cigarettes themselves. And they tiptoed down the spiral staircase with the Louisville Sluggers, which were much too precious to be left behind in a plumber's paradise.

5.

HE COULDN'T WALK WITHOUT A CANE, and he looked so much like Lionel now, with his face raw as an open wound, that people mistook him for his father. He sat in Clara's box at the Thalia. No one had seen the downtown detective in months. He'd gone from the attic at Montefiore to Monk's pet shop on Chrystie Street. He had a nurse around the clock, Monk himself, who'd healed many a gang member in the golden age of his rule over the Ghetto. He was as good as any sawbones or surgeon at St. Vincent's. No gang leader could survive without such skills, since the coppers were always looking for any trail of blood. And Monk's infirmary was the best in Manhattan. It had something to do with the birds. They serenaded Ben while Monk unwound the bandages. They sat on his shoulder. Monk had to discourage them, or they would have pestered Benjamin all night.

"Delilah, be nice. Stop flirting with Mr. Ben."

Monk had to rely on all his resources. He knew that Lionel owned the coppers, and the informants Monk once had were out of circulation. He had to send a shiver where and when he could. Silver Dollars was the last of the clever ones and would have seized upon the pet shop sooner or later. So he caught Ned unawares inside the Circus and sent him to the angels—suddenly all the bondsman's soldiers were in disarray.

Monk was embarrassed for Ben. His warblers nested in Ben's scalp, and hopped about in a panic whenever blood oozed from a wound. It wasn't only the birds. The dogs would howl in their cages, and the cats would leap against the wires, trying to absorb Ben's agony. Clarence, the pet snake, would sleep coiled around Ben's ankle. And Monk had to quiet the whole shop like some sorcerer of caged animals if a customer rang the bell. Ben's cot was in an alcove behind a curtain. Monk waved his hand, and time froze on Chrystie Street until Monk could talk that customer out of buying a snake or a bird. His pets weren't really for sale. Monk had his menagerie.

The wounds healed, but Ben had a disquieting lack of balance; he would topple for no reason. Sometimes he stuttered. He'd forget a word; his face would contort and he still couldn't summon it up no matter how hard he tried. Monk understood. Ben had been banged around once too often by that maniac with the kid gloves. He had only one guest—Clara Karp. Ben scribbled a note in pencil—"I'm on Chrystie Street with a bunch of yellow birds"—and Monk dug it into Clara's mailbox uptown.

She arrived that same afternoon, screamed at Monk and Ben, while the canaries squawked and flew around her in dizzying circles.

"So, my darling, I'm the last to know if you're dead or alive."

"The first," he told her, and she hid behind the curtain with Ben, licked his wounds with the salt on her tongue, undressed among the chaos and squalor, but she couldn't block out the infernal racket of a pet shop; Fatima, another snake, climbed on her as she clung to Ben. She stayed amid that filth for a week.

"How can you bear it, Ben? I've had more quiet in a carnival."

"I like . . . the noise," he said.

He might have remained on Chrystie Street forever with Delilah and Clarence if she hadn't coaxed him out of there with the promise of *Hamlet*. One phone call to the theater was enough.

"Breitbart, I'm back. . . ."

"Darling, you'll have to take a cut. We've had bills to pay in your absence. We had to keep an entire cast on retainer."

"Don't talk about money or I'll hang up. You'll cheat me as much or as little as you ever did."

And so it was settled. Monk let Ben have one of the canes he'd kept around for his wounded warriors. It was a hickory affair he himself had used when he broke his leg in a monthlong battle with the Five Pointers. It was a stick that wouldn't tilt in the wind, and could support Ben if he had a sudden case of vertigo. And Clara had a tailor from Attorney Street come to measure her Ben for a cashmere suit. He showed up at the Thalia in that suit, with Delilah on his shoulder and Monk Eastman at his side. People compared him to the Prince of Wales, who also had a fondness for cashmere, but the current prince didn't have a swollen face with dark ridges. Still, Ben sat in Clara's box and waited for the diva to appear.

It took two hours before the lights even dimmed. There was a great hush, and then a sigh as Lady Hamlet leapt onto the stage in her black tights, menace in her dark eyes. She nearly stumbled, but caught herself in one lyrical sweep. The boy was on her mind. She couldn't stay in America. Ben wouldn't survive 1913. The baron could write his articles, sing from the tenth floor, but he was compromised by the *Forward*'s creditors. He was tied to his gilded cage, and the housewives of that lonely hearts column, even with all his eloquence as he attacked the oligarchs and the criminals who cannibalized the Ghetto. But Ben had no gilded cage. He was a lone detective within the Kehilla and its Bureau of Morals, with its police spies. Ben couldn't interfere with the plunder at the Essex Market Court. He'd become slow of speech. But he could make war on the gamblers and cadets, upset the equilibrium, and rip into the vital flow of cash. And the guardians of that cash would get rid of him now that Lionel was in the grave.

"Grief," she cried. "I sing my grief." And she tore into one of the king's men with her rapier. It would be her last wounds in America.

6.

JACOB KNEW WHAT WOULD HAPPEN once Lionel's enterprises began to unravel. But he had little choice. He felt that first stab of guilt as Lionel was undone—found with his skull bashed in. Could he have prevented it? *Yes.* But he would have put his family and Kuhn, Loeb at risk. The patriarch paid for the funeral, for the whole cortege to the Ravage crypt at Woodlawn. He wasn't blind. He saw Manya's grave on the very next mound. Lionel's own death had stopped the hemorrhaging. Jacob himself was the executor of Lionel's will. Henrietta went into a rest home, a Jewish nunnery, where she would remain for the rest of her life. Waldo went berserk within a month and was confined to the madhouse. Lionel's lascivious daughter was the real problem. The patriarch couldn't leave Becky to prowl. He would have been blackmailed by a hundred false husbands and fiancés. And he didn't want one of his own to end up in some high-priced bordello, where she belonged. He couldn't frighten the wits out of her; the girl loved danger. He told Becky that he would sell her to a gang of pirates on an opium run to Shanghai, and she laughed in his face.

"Uncle, when should I pack?"

So he married her off to a lesser baron, a distant relative of the Four Hundred, and knew that he and his heirs would have to support them until the day she died. And should they divorce, he would find an even lesser baron. Jacob had sealed up that leak, but then there was Babette. He'd cut her out of Satan's Circus, but she was still an opium addict. For a moment he wished that he had Uncle Rainer's Teutonic Knights. Then he might have visited the downtown detective and convinced him to marry Babette. Who else would have her? Hadn't she saved his life in Lionel's attic at

Montefiore? Ben owed her *something*. Jacob could bribe Clara Karp with a packet of money, build a theater for her, make her rich. But he would only have revisited his own sins, and it would have been Manya, Manya, Manya all over again.

Soon he had Meyer Bristol on his back. And his fellow patriarchs supported Meyer.

"Jacob, there are no other suitors. My daughter cannot live in shame while the man she rescued from oblivion cavorts with an actress. You must bring young Ravage to her bed."

"Stop it," he shouted. "She's a *lesbianke*."

"Then it's up to him to cure her of that affliction. It's a family matter. Lionel's little bastard is responsible for her now. It's just as valid as a marriage contract. He cannot have the actress. I swear to God, I'll burn down her theater."

"Meyer," Jacob said, a fierce will in his eyes, "haven't we had enough fires in one lifetime?"

"It's your duty," Meyer said. "I demand this of you. She's your goddaughter."

The patriarch groaned. He scribbled a note to Clara. He didn't threaten. He simply begged her to meet with him at Kuhn, Loeb. She demanded more neutral ground—the Pinnacle Café. And little machinations spun around in his head. He'd battled Pierpont Morgan over the rights to certain railroad lines, and won. He'd subdued the czar. Now he went to see Captain Kittleberger.

"I'll need a favor, Kit. You'll have to come with me to the Pinnacle on Rivington Street and swear that you're about to send Monk Eastman back to Sing Sing."

"*Jaysus*," Kittleberger said, imitating his own Irish detectives, "would you like to wear my shield, Jacob? You Yiddish princes demand honesty and a bit of freewheeling in the same breath."

"But didn't he hurl a man off the balcony at the Haymarket? That's what I have in my notes from the Kehilla."

"No one could place him there," the captain said. "There were rumors about his canaries. . . . Sing Sing it is."

Kittleberger arrived with Jacob and the other Jewish princes at the Pinnacle and completely overwhelmed the little café. The Yiddish poets moved to tables in the back, and couldn't even hold on to them as the number of princes swelled. Clara felt surrounded at her own table; she slurped from her bottle of slivovitz and sat with Ben in his cashmere suit.

"Clara," Jacob said, "Benjamin belongs to Babette. He wouldn't be alive without her."

Ben was all confused by this babble. He kept staring at the captain. "Why is Kit here?"

"Because there have been certain improprieties relating to Monk Eastman," Jacob said, "and he might have to go back to Sing Sing."

"I want to hear it . . . from the horse's . . . mouth," Ben said. "Tell me, Kit." He could sense the captain's discomfort.

"Well," Kit mumbled, staring at his own huge feet, "Monk was spotted at the Haymarket fifteen minutes before Ned Silver's demise."

"Who . . . spotted him . . . exactly?"

Jacob steered the conversation toward Clara. "There will be compensation for your loss, Madame Clara. We can promise you your very own theater."

He'd expected her anger to ripen. It wrenched his bowels to watch her brush away a tear. "You men," she said. "You know the boy will never abandon Monk."

Ben sprang up from his chair and meant to leap on Kittleberger, but landed in his lap. Kit had to carry the boy back to his own chair. Ben sat in silent reverie as his mind wandered off.

"Then it's sealed," Meyer Bristol said. "Babs will have her husband. And the actress will grow rich."

Meyer shouldn't have intervened. Jacob saw Manya's stone at Woodlawn in front of his eyes, and it seared him worse than any fire Lionel had been in. He could not tolerate his own Teutonic Knights. He remembered following Manya around, on Rainer's orders, the musk of her, the blondness, and how jealous he was of Lionel. He'd ruined the father. He wouldn't ruin the son.

"*Gott*," he said, "I'm getting out of here."

Meyer was in a panic. "Wait, wait. We haven't clinched the deal."

"There is no deal. . . . Kit, you can go back home to Madison Street."

And as he marched out, someone grabbed at his sleeve.

"I'll kill you," Jacob growled. He'd never uttered such words, not even during the worst calamity. Cahan stood near him in his rumpled editor's coat.

"Jacob, have you met with Mr. Frank? Will there still be a five-and-ten on Grand Street?"

"I can't work miracles, my sweet Baron. It takes time."

And he rushed from the Lower East Side as if a cyclone were attached to his tail.

7.

CAHAN COULDN'T EVEN RELISH what small victories he had. A day after that encounter at the café with all the Jewish princes, Ben and his diva disappeared from the Ghetto like some infernal vapor. His own subeditors were twice as shrewd as the baron. "They've gone into exile, Comrade. And that's how exiles behave."

Even as he sulked, the baron had his printer's devils march along Grand Street, looking for Mr. Frank's building engineers. He marched, too, after a morning at the café. He could sense the upheaval around him, the ruinous state of affairs—the king of Canal bludgeoned to death in his own office, while speculators ran rampant with Lionel Ravage's former properties; the new landlords were as bewildering and cruel as the old. He thought of quitting his falcon's lair and becoming a tramp—or a bomb maker again. He'd lost the two people he loved most, Clara and her boy detective. He understood their maneuvers better when he glanced back at his own days as an outlaw. He couldn't have survived without becoming invisible, forsaking his own parents and younger brother, as his two delinquents had forsaken him.

Then Mr. Frank's wrecking crew came to Grand Street. Working like gifted ants, they gutted the interior of that old pink elephant, Ridley's, leaving a skeleton outer wall in their wake. Next they built their own wall around the dusty ghost of the department store, with a signboard at least six stories high.

GRAND OPENING
WOOLWORTH'S OF GRAND
SUMMER OF 1914

There was a mural of the five-and-ten, like another one of Mr. Frank's terra-cotta mountains designed by Cass Gilbert, where the muralist allowed you to peek through the front window, rimmed with fire-engine red, and glimpse at "the smartest luncheon counter in all of Manhattan." And Mr. Frank must have used some devil with a paintbrush, because the men and women outside and inside the five-and-ten were greenies in shawls and Russian boots. Only one woman at the counter was wearing a cloche hat.

The baron went to the site on an August afternoon. He'd forgotten the complexities of building a bomb, and he was never good at it, as he would imagine the torn limbs while he tinkered with the wires. He stood in front of the workers' entrance, sealed it off with five of the *Forward*'s printer's devils as his accomplices. He hadn't proselytized them. They weren't even anarchists. They adored this old man with the gray hair. Mr. Frank's workers wouldn't shove them aside. They hadn't been paid enough to rough up five kids and an old geezer in thick glasses.

Reporters began to arrive at the site, but Cahan wouldn't give interviews. "I'm not representing the *Forward*. I'm a private citizen."

"Don't act so innocent," said an editor from the *World*. "You've brought five lads from the composing room."

"That's an anomaly. I couldn't form a human chain on my own."

Kittleberger had to march over from Madison Street. "Baron, be a good boy. You're disturbing the peace. Do you have a court order to stop construction of this enterprise? If not, you'll have to come with me."

Cahan accompanied the captain to the precinct, where he was booked by Kittleberger himself. No one bothered to fingerprint the baron.

"*Jaysus*, Kit, what does a man have to do to have his own proper yellow sheet?"

"Commit a crime."

Cahan played chess with Kittleberger for part of the afternoon.

"It's an embarrassment," he said, trapping Kittleberger's queen. "Ben Ravage leaves without a note."

"It was a wise move. He was as unpredictable as his lately departed dad. No one knew where the boy would go next."

"He's an invalid, nearly beaten to death," Cahan said as he chased Kittleberger's king around the board.

"He was still upsetting the balance of power, Baron. I'm fond of Ben. I wouldn't have wanted to discover that boy in some ditch."

Cahan slept on a couch in the captain's office. He realized soon enough that Kittleberger had locked the door. Cahan peed in the captain's private toilet. He had the morning to himself, with coffee and cake sent over from the Pinnacle. Kit arrived in the afternoon with a copy of the *Forward*. Cahan's sunken cheeks took up the front page, except for a two-line banner.

A Manhattan Pogrom
Editor Seized on Grand Street

"Damn you, Baron," Kittleberger said, "we're the villains now. Go about your business."

Cahan walked into the glaring sunlight, women kissing his hand. He was serenaded in the newsroom, but his bitterness against Mr. Frank was still there. The next day, all work at the building site suddenly stopped. The mural was torn down. There was never a news conference, never an article by Cass Gilbert about the thirteenth store. The baron wondered if Jacob Schiff had interfered with Mr. Frank's financing of the project. How would he ever know? But he had read that Lionel's empire of toilet seats now belonged to Kuhn, Loeb. He published another installment about that young hemophiliac, Prince Alexei, and his Jewish captain of the guard. The czar's heir was still popular in the Ghetto despite the pogroms. Cahan wrote and wrote. He'd reconciled with Anya again, but in his dreams the actress appeared without a stitch, her breasts rising over him as she manipulated his trousers with her toes, like the acrobat she had once been. He hated to rouse himself from such slumber. And then she, too, disappeared, perhaps as a kind of punishment. And the editor had nothing but his feuilletons and *A Bintel Brief.* He went to rallies, sat at the Pinnacle, wrote about ingenues who couldn't warm his blood. He was invited everywhere, and felt like a dead man dancing in the wind.

A package arrived at the *Forward*, addressed to Cahan, with a whole catalog of foreign stamps. He couldn't decipher exactly where the package had come from. He tore it open with his hands and found a pair of black tights with Clara's perfume and sweat. One whiff, and the master of *A Bintel Brief* rose from the dead and returned to his latest column.

> *Dear Reader,*
>
> *Mrs. R. of Forsythe Street has a boarder who writes hymns to her but can't afford to pay the rent. She floats above the tablecloth with such finery she can feel the stars, but her husband says that hymns can't put bread on the table. What should she do?*

CODA

1919

I.

She lived in a courtyard that abutted the Montparnasse Cemetery. This alley didn't even have a name, so the concierge had her mail delivered from a building on the rue Cassendi. But Clara liked her masked address. She didn't want anyone to find the boy—he was twenty-nine, with a law degree, and would remain a boy all his life. It was that orphan's flush of his. Clara had never wanted a child—she was an artiste, after all, and artistes couldn't be bothered with morning sickness and such. Yet here he was, her Ben, who feasted on her nipples like a wolf cub. She hadn't come to Paris on a whim. She opened a bank account and rented a room in this alley without a name on her last tour of Paris, where she was fêted as the Yiddish American diva who'd been with the *Follies* and played Hamlet uptown and downtown. She met with impresarios. All their talk turned to dust.

She became an acrobat at the Vélodrome d'Hiver, a coliseum with a skylight made from shivers of glass, where indoor bicycle races were held. It was also a roller-skating rink, a wrestling arena, and a home for touring circuses. The Vél' d'Hiv' was a great barreled vault as large as the Hippodrome. And there was always work for an acrobat, even during the bicycle races and wrestling matches. Clara would paint herself white from head to toe, with blue dots under her eyes and a smear of red on her mouth, and perform in a tutu and ballet slippers. She leapt like Nijinsky, her managers said. What did she care about the lies? She did somersaults six or seven times a month and made enough for the boy and herself. When the circus was in town, she performed twice a day under the tents.

Men always left their cards outside her tiny dressing booth, whispered into the curtain, and talked of dinner at Fouquet's, where all the actresses and star performers congregated between gulps of white beer. Clara laughed at the cards and the proposals. She'd rather have wine and cheese with her little wolf than sit over a tub of oysters with these mustachioed men. The boy still walked with a cane, and his balance grew worse. She worried about leaving him alone, and she counted every minute while she rode the *aérienne* to the Vél' d'Hiv'. There was also a band of Yiddish painters and poets with their own studio and club near Montparnasse. The painters had seen her march across the cemetery; they whistled a tune and invited her to pose in the flesh at their studio. She bantered back and forth with them.

"Is it correct, madame, that the Jews of Manhattan have their own little state, with lawyers and judges and—"

"*Banditen.* It's not a state within a state, Chaim. It's row after row of churning streets, where swindlers thrive and families grow poorer every day."

"But it has its own prince, we hear."

Yes, she could have said. Lord Lionel Ravage, whose reign was ended with a baseball bat. And she was living with Lionel's own boy, a prince of sorts. But she said, "There are no princes, Chaim, only police captains and mayors who don't mean very much—chaos is the one and only king."

"Don't destroy our illusions, madame. Everyone here dreams of Yiddish Land."

They invited Clara to their café, the Rotonde, right on the boulevard; it was the preferred canteen of local artists and their models, philosophers, poets, pamphleteers, and vagabonds with mansions in Montparnasse. The waiters and barman were also artists in this bohemian enclave, where customers could pile up enormous bills, drown themselves in absinthe and Karl Marx. It reminded Clara of the Pinnacle, but the coffee was much better here, and the tables on the terrace were tiny and round, so that everyone sat nose-to-nose and knew everyone else's business. And once, after she drank a little too much of that bitter green-and-white poison, which she had to mix with an enormous absinthe spoon, Clara agreed to model for the Yiddish painters of Montparnasse; she accompanied them to their studio, banging into walls along the way.

These artists were unprepared for the ripe lines of Clara's body as she stumbled out of her clothes; her eyes were bleary, and she couldn't even strike a pose, but now they understood what audiences at the *Follies* had seen—a Russian goddess with the rounded calves and clever toes of an acrobat; her navel seemed to have a magnificent depth, while her buttocks hadn't dropped an inch.

She was bored after an hour, missed her Ben, and wouldn't accept a centime from the art club. These lunatics were in love with her. They babbled in Yiddish and French. She ran out onto the rue Schoelcher half naked and returned to her boy on the dead-end street. He must have sniffed the absinthe oozing out of her pores. He'd developed aphasia after all the beatings in the attic. Her Ben was blind to words. He could still speak, but he couldn't write a letter or read a book. And she'd brought the little library he kept from his Harvard years, books he'd often hidden in his pockets or placed on her shelves at the Thalia—a short novel, *The Red Badge of Courage,* by some boy wonder who died of the tailor's disease long before he was thirty; and weather-torn editions of the Master, who suffered from a kind of self-inflicted aphasia after he abandoned the art of writing novels. . . .

Ben worried how Monk would survive alone in his pet shop. As a graduate of Sing Sing, Monk had lost the right to vote and travel abroad. The Ghetto had become his graveyard. He couldn't venture far north of Manhattan, where his mug was known to every cop. Twice he was picked up in Scarsdale and escorted to Spuyten Duyvil Creek by state troopers. He was told there wouldn't be a third time. He would have to rot in some village where the judge appeared only once or twice a month. So he roosted in Manhattan, where letters would arrive at his pet shop in envelopes as delicate as tissue paper, with a strange perfume. The letters were from Ben, but in Clara's looped handwriting. He had to squint hard and search for his magnifying glass. He thought he might be going blind, until he realized that her writing was irregular, that words would grow larger and smaller in the same paragraph, and slant in different directions. He had to clutch the letter like a steering wheel and keep turning; sometimes the tissue paper tore in his hands, and he lost forever what little sense the letter had.

> . . . *Edward, I miss Delilah every day. But I couldn't have smuggled her on board. They wouldn't let a bird like her through customs. And those bastards would have left her to rot with the contraband. Still I—*

All these waves and inkblots weren't Clara's fault. Her handwriting deteriorated the longer she cried over the boy, who had nothing to stare at but a cemetery wall. Yet he found some solace in the sepulchers, in the smooth, graying stones. Clara doted on Ben. Perhaps he was her prisoner on that dead-end street. She bought winter coal in the huge bin on the boulevard, where the owner served bits of honey cake at the counter. And she made love to her winter boy; he was as tender and wild as ever, even as his mind unknit.

2.

SHE SHOULD HAVE PAID MORE ATTENTION to the Huns. While she was at the Vél' d'Hiv', wearing her tutu, the Germans broke through Belgium, and were forty miles from Paris. The Rotonde had become a ghost's café. Absinthe was banned from the menu; the government swore that the green poison made soldiers and civilians insane. Suddenly, there were no more cigars and cigarettes; people had to smoke dried cabbage leaves. Coffee disappeared from the cafés and the market stalls, no longer imported from the Caribbean; some kind of ground chicory was served at the Rotonde—it tasted like shit.

There was less and less work at the Vél' d'Hiv'. Most of the wrestlers and bicycle riders were at the front. And the circus came to town with ragged tents and without tightrope walkers. Clara's salary was cut in half. But she and the boy survived. She read Henry James to him; he listened, as if he could still slice the sounds with some knife inside his skull. They spent the first winter of the war scavenging for coal. The matches she bought in the shops broke in her fist; only one in five would ever strike;

and the blue flame died in a whisper; they spent most of the day wearing blankets.

Her French bank account was frozen for weeks at a time. Paris began to swell with every sort of swindler. A few of the Yiddish painters hadn't been mobilized, and she did have to pose for them to pay the bills. But she hadn't grown scrawny that second winter of the war, when half the population starved and the other half flourished in some improvised black market of goods that were impossible to find. Clara grew stout on a diet of turnips.

The women on the boulevards were still chic. Clara watched them parade in officers' uniforms, wearing kepis, boots, and Sam Browne belts manufactured by fashionable tailors; others wore flared skirts, as if Paris were made of magical glass that wasn't forty miles from the front. Victory cries were announced every other week, while more and more churches, museums, theaters, and five-star hotels became clinics and convalescent homes. German airships floated above Paris with an irritating roar and dropped little bombs that landed in the Luxembourg Gardens and left craters near the tennis courts.

The circus suddenly became popular again during the third winter of the war. The clowns taught her to ride bareback in her tutu, and after she began firing cap pistols at the clowns themselves, she was likened to Buffalo Bill, who had appeared at the Vél' d'Hiv' in 1906 and captured Paris like a rifle shot. She now had all the coal she could want. She took the boy to Fouquet's, where she had to sign autographs for an hour. Ben was wearing the same cashmere suit that she'd had hand-tailored for him. He was still the most seductive boy in the room, even with the welts on his face.

There was a photograph on the wall of Sarah Bernhardt, another Jewess, playing Hamlet in spangled pantaloons, and Ben noticed how much Clara resembled Bernhardt, with her deep frown and puzzling eyes.

"She's . . . your double," Ben said, biting into his goblet of champagne. "She's your twin."

"Stop that," Clara said. "Your mouth will bleed . . . I'm an acrobat with big shoulders and bigger tits, Hamlet with a horsey grin, who recited in Yiddish for apple peddlers and tailors as they littered the floor with peanut shells, and Bernhardt was with the Comédie Française."

"But she didn't . . . rise up . . . from the dead sixteen times . . . during a mat-mat-in-ee."

"That's because I mixed Shakespeare with *shund*."

She watched him collapse on the velvet banquette. "You must . . . never . . . say that . . . madame. I did not . . . f-f-fall . . . in love . . . with *shund*."

It was their first and last meal at Fouquet's. All the other clowns kept waiting for America to enter the war; they expected an entire nation of Buffalo Bills, with pearl-handled revolvers and silk mustaches. And finally, in 1917, the doughboys did arrive in their tin hats. The slaughter didn't stop. It only grew worse. And a few months before the armistice there was a knock on Clara's door in that dead-end street that even the postman couldn't find. She wondered if the French coppers had come to collect her Ben for some insane crime.

She undid the latch, and there was Monk in a Sam Browne belt and a soldier boy's puttees. Clara blinked, and Monk wouldn't go away. Ben leapt out of bed, propelled by the force of his cane.

"Edward, how . . . did you ever . . . find us?"

"There's a safecracker in our unit, and he knows every hidden alley in the district. . . . Delilah's dead. I sang to her every day, tickled her feathers, but she was your sweetheart."

Monk had enlisted with a whole troupe of former convicts. He served overseas with an Irish regiment, O'Ryan's Roughnecks; his tactics as a gang lord had served him well with the Twenty-seventh Division. Once he'd drifted in and out of the Five Points like a ghost to deliver mayhem at will, and now he was a one-man army who would wander across no-man's-land to retrieve a wounded comrade or materialize behind German lines to obliterate a machine-gun nest. But he couldn't even sit with Ben and Clara at a local café; he had to return to his unit. He and Ben hugged like two chieftains from an earlier war. And Clara could see for herself how much the Lower East Side was written into Ben's blood.

3.

THEY RETURNED ON THE MOST LUXURIOUS *paquebot* in the entire French fleet, the *Rochambeau*, in the summer of 1919; Clara had a cabin that took up almost half the ocean liner. She could have remained forever at the Vél' d'Hiv', but she was an actress, not an acrobat in a tutu. Reporters met her at the dock. Yiddish theater had become the rage of Manhattan during the war, and the Eagle himself, Jacob P. Adler, had invited her to join his troupe. Adler didn't want this Lady Hamlet to undermine his reputation as King Lear. So he abandoned the *shund* of a Yiddish *Lear*, set in Russia, with a whole catalog of cousins, and promised to return to the original text, with his own scribblers rewriting Shakespeare, of course. Clara would play the Fool as some kind of *schmendrick* in tattered clothes, mouth a word here and there that would feed into his magnificent lines. She would be invisible onstage, as she had been for the past six years.

Ben might have warned her if he could have read the script. But the words danced off the page like a scatter of ribbons.

"Clara, why . . . would the Eagle . . . h-h-hire you? He hates . . . your guts."

"But his ego got in the way of his good sense."

The performances were sold out for months in advance. Broadway producers shivered in their bones. The Eagle himself had arranged special fares from Philadelphia and Washington for Yiddish Theater Night. Clara was given a closet near the men's toilet as a dressing room. The pipes hissed and leaked. She could hear the Eagle hawk up phlegm and dribble on the toilet bowl. She didn't complain. The Eagle had a dresser, paid for by the New National. Clara had to dress and undress on her own. That way, she wouldn't have one of Adler's spies in her lap.

Cahan had come with Anya on opening night. Anya cried when she saw how diminished Ben was, a bag of bones. She loved the boy, sat next to him, clutched his hand. His blue eyes seemed to gaze at some distant point beyond the New National. She blamed her husband. He shouldn't have mingled Ben with his own affairs, turned him into some forlorn hero of his own feuilletons, the guardian of a Ghetto that couldn't be guarded. Such a fairy tale had nearly gotten him killed.

Sitting beside her was that other guardian, Monk Eastman, who'd been exonerated by the governor himself, had his full rights restored, and become the hero of Manhattan.

"Abraham," she whispered, "you must help Ben and that golem before the Ghetto eats them alive."

"Please," Cahan said, "the lights are dimming, Anya. How can I concentrate?"

The curtain rose, and there was Adler as the king, magnificent in brown leather, his hair a startling white. The audience cheered. He made the least little motion to reveal his age; his hand trembled slightly. And the play unfolded as his scribblers had prepared it for him. He fights with his daughters, snarls at the universe. And suddenly the lights deepen and we notice the Fool dangling on a wall—Clara in motley clothes, with bells attached to her slippers. And in an instant, the focus on Adler was gone; Cahan couldn't take his eyes off Clara, with her languid motions. She'd turned the king's ranting into pomp. He talks to the Fool. Clara smiles like a wicked cat and doesn't answer. The king waits and waits. And what was meant as repartee becomes a stuttering monologue. He asks and answers his own questions. It was as if Clara had used Ben's aphasia against the Eagle, or had become aphasic herself, a Fool without a Fool's vocabulary.

The action unraveled around her. She'd managed to turn Shakespeare himself into *shund*, while she jangled the bells on her toes to break the silence. The Eagle wanted to fire Clara after the first act, but the audience thumped and begged for Shakespeare, more and more. There'd never been so much static on the stage, such an electrical storm. The Eagle took fifteen curtain calls, while Clara wouldn't even acknowledge the audience; her legs continued to dangle.

Playwrights and critics besieged Adler, said his *Lear* was a masterwork, the event of the season. It was Cahan who saw how Clara had sabotaged the Eagle's entire career, had used herself as a kind of distorting mirror to reflect Adler's bombast and great love of himself. There was talk of moving the production to Broadway. Ziegfeld was interested in adapting a few scenes for his *Follies of 1920*. Adler declined; he was a stage actor, not a vaudevillian, he told the *World*.

Clara moved with the boy into that same sunless apartment on Attorney Street where he'd been brought into this world with the help of a midwife. The current landlord was a criminal who charged her fifty dollars a month. She scoffed at the price. Adler's *King Lear* was floating in revenue on account of her. It was difficult for Ben to climb the stairs. The building had been gutted after Lionel was trapped in the fire he himself had started. There were new electrical outlets, flush toilets on every floor, but still corrugated tin in the halls. The boy didn't remember much. Manya had moved when he was three. But it was the first real address he'd had in the Ghetto since the day his mother was stolen from him and put in the madhouse. Some kind of rhythm was coming back to his movements. He didn't sway so much, didn't fall. He made his own circuitry while Clara was at the theater. He visited the pet shop. People stopped him on the streets. He was recognized as the son of a prince. No one called him Herr Ravage, because everybody hated the Huns. But housewives curtsied to him, told him about landlords who had exploited them. He couldn't write the names in a little black book. Words still exploded like a scatter of ribbons in his head. But sometimes he could memorize portions of a name. He'd march into the pet shop and a cluster of birds would dive from the ceiling in a great yellow swirl and sit on his shoulder while he erupted into his own staccato song.

"Edward . . . I think we have to visit a l-l-landlord."

"On what street, Mr. Ben?"

"Ah, I can't recall, but . . . it . . . will come . . . sooner . . . or later." And that's how they learned to proceed, with a stutter and a step.

4.

YET SOMETHING WAS WRONG. The canaries often seemed agitated, as if the pet shop had been burgled—or violated. Sing Sing's most decorated ex-con was conducting another line of business on Chrystie Street. Ben recognized shylocks and opium dealers. Monk had recaptured bits of territory while Ben was away, and he rifled the Ghetto like any other gangster or gyp.

"It got lonely," he said while Ben inhaled the odor of bird shit.

"I don't get it—you had all those medals, a pardon . . . from the g-g-governor. You risked your own life s-s-saving soldiers."

"That part was fun. No-man's-land was like the Five Points. The governor said I ought to open a garage. Well, I'm a different kind of mechanic."

"But we helped clean up the Ghetto, and . . . you got rid of Ned Silver."

Monk made a sound halfway between a cough and a sneeze. "Ah, they were all laughing at us, Mr. Ben, saying how the whole damn city was one big racket—baseball included."

"Christy . . . Mathewson was no r-r-racket."

McGraw was involved with all the gamblers. The Giants could have won the pennant six years in a row if Fred Merkle hadn't dropped mothballs in Mathewson's water cup before a big game to make him a little groggy, according to Monk.

"Big-time gamblers hired the heavy hitters who put Lionel to bed. They couldn't count on him. He was bleeding money from his eyes and ears. So they plugged the holes with hickory sticks. Those hitters were Giant fans. They all sat behind the dugout at the Polo Grounds. They wouldn't miss a game."

It was as if Monk had never returned from no-man's-land, and still wore his puttees in the pet shop.

"Why didn't you . . . tell me about the h-h-hitters?" Ben asked.

"I couldn't. I had to steer them away from you."

Ben began to shudder, as if his brain had been singed in some flash of fire. Monk wasn't meant to survive Sing Sing. He hadn't really been paroled. It was Lionel who had arranged his release.

"You worked both sides of the fence—as a shoofly. Did Lionel offer you a free ticket?"

A sudden silence seized the pet shop; the birds could sense Monk's disrepair.

"I had no other way out, Mr. Ben. I would have rotted in that hole for the rest of my life."

Mr. Hyde was even more diabolic than Ben had imagined. "But we d-d-did him a lot of d-d-damage."

"A drop in the bucket," Monk declared.

"It was . . . more than . . . a drop. You got r-r-rid of . . . N-N-Ned."

The birds plunged blindly now, as if they could no longer read Monk's mind and were frightened of their own imminent isolation.

"Lionel went too far, laying you away in an attic like that, with his chief torturer. I'm still a general, ain't I?"

"Yeah," Ben said, "and both of us were shills in Lionel's amusement park."

He limped out of the pet shop, leaning on Monk's cane, with a blur of yellow creatures behind him. He could barely recognize his own native quarter. The horses and stables were gone, and a midnight blue touring car loaded with petty gangsters cruised Eldridge Street, honking at pushcarts and trying to lure young Ghetto girls in bright blouses into the back of the van.

"Ride with us, sweetheart. We'll take you to the end of the world."

They could have been the members of some thriving Jewish gang. They had nicks under their eyes, and Ben wondered if they'd graduated from the same orphanage he did. But they didn't even have the gallantry of cadets. They reached out the rear window of the van, like heartless trawlers, clasping at the arms of a girl who couldn't have been more than sixteen. For a moment, Ben wondered if he were living in a feuilleton, where Jewish Cossacks with a downtown swagger had suddenly invaded the Ghetto. He knocked at their wrists with his cane, and they had to release the girl, who tumbled into the gutter, upsetting a pushcart full of apples, picked herself up, and ran away with a shriek that rippled through his eardrums, while apples rolled along the gutter.

The peddler cursed at Ben as the Jewish Cossacks climbed out of their touring car with knives and brass knucks, prepared to pounce on Ben.

"What are you, the shamas of Eldridge Street?"

And that's when they saw that familiar old-fashioned derby come toward them with a rhythmic rise and fall. "Nix," they said, and returned to the touring car.

"You clowns," Monk Eastman said, "go on back to the garage. You're supposed to act like a local ambulance, helping people in distress, not chasing skirts."

The midnight blue van disappeared with all its occupants, and

Monk Eastman got down on his knees with Ben, who held the cane like a crutch and picked apples out of the gutter. They worked in silence until most of the apples were piled onto the cart. Monk didn't dare utter a word.

It was Ben who broke the silence. "Thank you, Edward. This is the l-l-last time I'll require your services."

That Jewish gang hadn't been so wrong about Ben. He was like a shamas, a beadle with the Lower East Side as his shul. Those beatings had ruined him for the art of a detective or an attorney-at-law. His hair turned white one day. He looked more and more like his father's ghost. Gangsters were afraid of him. Landlords and bondsmen wouldn't cross his path. Yet he had nothing but his cane and his diminished flair. The coppers saluted him. Kittleberger was long gone from Madison Street. Each new captain was a lesser man, tied to the mayor like a ragged kite. Clara had to give Ben pocket money.

Adler's *Lear* had moved to Broadway. He kept the lion's share of the purse, had his name in lights, but it was a childish trick, and Clara had her own child to deal with. He spoke less and less, and limped about, yet his passion never waned. She was fifty years old, and feared losing him to some immigrant princess on the immigrant streets, but he always returned home before midnight, always warmed her bed; she would bathe the scars he had earned at the orphanage, and never interfered with whatever quest he was on.

A feral cat had been his real ancestor. Ben was another Mr. Hyde, with a cudgel rather than a silver-headed cane. Children stared at his scarred cheeks. He'd never have been born if Manya hadn't come out of her closet to glimpse at that blond landlord. How many times had he imagined himself in that closet? It was as if he had been created and demolished in a single glance.

He limped across the narrow lanes; pushcarts swerved from his path. Sometimes he'd wander into a stuss house and retrieve a grocer who had an itch to gamble his tiny fortune while his children starved; Ben always got the grocer's money back. It wasn't Ben's cudgel that intimidated the gamblers; they carried the picture of Monk's canaries in their eyes. "Would you like a bagel, Mr. Ben?"

It annoyed him that he was still wedded to Monk no matter what he did. A yellow queen would come out of nowhere and alight on his shoulder for a second or two. "Ah, you little bandit, go on," he'd growl, but he didn't have the heart to send the warbler away. And the yellow queens that clung to the boy lent him a certain stature—the shamas was also some kind of a sage, like the Gaon of Vilna, with a distinct stutter. He settled disputes between brothers and sisters, fathers and sons. He'd sit in Seward Park, leaning on his cudgel. Delicatessens and cafeterias brought him tins of noodle soup and bottles of celery tonic. Daughters were a little safer during Ben's patrols.

Sometimes he'd meet Cahan near the chessboards inside the park. Ben could no longer play, having forgotten how to "castle" or move his knight. The baron loved to kibitz. He'd always been an aggressive player, a Cossack on the board. But he grew sad around Ben.

"My broken boy," he'd whimper, "my broken boy."

"Baron, I was . . . born b-b-broken. You unbroke me for a . . . little while."

"I should have left you at the Hawthorne School. You'd be at the *Forward* right now, as one of my printer's devils."

Ben smiled, revealing all the gaps in his mouth. "That's not my idea . . . of heaven."

He went back into the wilderness of the Lower East Side with his cudgel and vanished into the swollen streets so swiftly that the baron had to wonder if he had invented the boy out of some desperate need to have a hero, but Ben was as actual as the ink stains on the baron's cuffs, born in a tenement on Attorney Street, and Cahan could imagine the boy's first screams, blinded by his mother's blood, and the tumult of that cry would roar in the baron's ears for the rest of his life.

Bellevue Literary Press is devoted to publishing literary fiction and nonfiction at the intersection of the arts and sciences because we believe that science and the humanities are natural companions for understanding the human experience. We feature exceptional literature that explores the nature of consciousness, embodiment, and the underpinnings of the social contract. With each book we publish, our goal is to foster a rich, interdisciplinary dialogue that will forge new tools for thinking and engaging with the world.

To support our press and its mission, and for our full catalogue of published titles, please visit us at blpress.org.

BELLEVUE LITERARY PRESS
New York